Lady Sun

Marni MacRae

This is a work of fiction.
Names, characters, businesses, places, events and incidents
are either the products of the author's imagination or used in
a fictitious manner. Any resemblance to actual persons,
living or dead, or actual events is purely coincidental.

For Nehemiah,
may everyday be Sunday-Funday.

Chapter 1

Paradise was within reach. I could see it, right there, off the starboard bow of *The Lady Sun.*

Long white beaches, aqua clear water, leaning palm trees. A postcard perfect island waiting for me to revel in its perfection.

I wondered if I would get there. In my current situation it didn't seem likely, locked in this tiny cabin, staring out the tiny porthole at my intended destination. Right now the question was, whether I would survive this ordeal at all, let alone enjoy a tan on a white sand beach.

I couldn't help thinking about Anna and all her worries and warnings of a woman traveling alone. The likely hood of a plane crash, or contracting a nasty tropical illness.

"Anna would have never predicted this though." I muttered to myself and turned away from the porthole. The yacht was moving again, and I couldn't bear to see my vacation slip away.

"I mean who would ever think I would be trapped on a gorgeous yacht, most likely about to die before I ever step foot on a beach."

That comment shot a bolt of fear through me and I sank down to sit on the opulent bed in my cabin-prison.

Oh my God. I could die here.

The boat began to pick up speed, and I knew I wouldn't reach my island.

Paradise lost.

I could only hope my fears were exaggerated. "Perhaps it's not as bad as you assume Sophie." I spoke aloud just to hear my own voice, hoping it would calm me. But I knew I was fooling myself. It was most likely *much* worse than I assumed.

I could only hope that Lucas would keep his promise.

I wrapped my arms around my waist and lay down, closing my eyes to block out reality.

Why did I ever book this vacation?

I thought back to the cold December winter in Washington, recalling how miserable I had been, and how excited, to plan the trip of a lifetime.

Chapter 2

I've followed most of the classics concerning deserted islands. I had struggled through the long winded prose and painfully detailed descriptions of life alone with raisins, goats, and his boy Friday, of *Robinson Crusoe.* Frankly, when I was finished with the trial of the read I came away with a sense of frustration, no closure, and a craving for shriveled grapes.

I grew up watching *Swiss family Robinson* (no relation to the former *Crusoe*) and as with the rest of my generation, was romanced with the idea of a tree house in the jungle, and witty battles with pirates.

Then came the survivor series, which served to prove there are a good amount of people who could *not* survive, and do it with as little class or effort required to entertain those of us who judged from our couches.

Best of all there was the now classic *Castaway* where only Tom Hanks could make you cry over the loss of a volley ball. And I cried. I wept loudly, trying to hide it as I sat in the theater and Wilson drifted away. Then at home, (once everyone in America had confessed to the tears jerked from them as Tom lay on his raft, wracked with sobs and burnt to a crisp on the open ocean.) I wept openly, no longer afraid of judgment. I loved that ball. All of America loved Wilson. It was pure genius on the part of the writer and mad skill from Tom that caught all of us in a trap where we had to admit, Hollywood had the power to romance anything. Even a Volley ball.

So, with the aid of long dead authors, a family of tenacious Dutch children and the well-loved Tom and Wilson duo, I fell in love with the dream of escaping to a deserted Island, building fire from a couple of sticks and blisters, eating lots of raisins, and fighting off pirates. The Buccaneer type, of course, not the ones with machine guns and really fast speed boats. No romance in those pirates and no sense of fashion either. I was hoping more along the lines of Johnny Depp, with maybe a bath or two under his belt.

No one offers a truly authentic escape to a deserted island and after much Googling it was clear why. No island is truly deserted. First, we can *Google Earth* anything nowadays, so escaping is quite hopeless. I think it might be in the welcome statement at prisons now, just to deter the prisoners from attempting the climb over barbed wire and costing us little taxpayers any medical bills. *Google* <u>will</u> find you. Second, everything is owned. I mean *everything*. Cataloged and named and many a war fought over - or about to. Island or sand bar, somebody has dibs.

During my search, (I know, you ask, how do I expect to find anything lost on the internet. If it is there, then it's not lost, but such reasoning does not apply to my inner logic. So, I *Google* because I believe in my heart that if there *was* an island I could get lost upon, preferably with Sawyer, not Jack and minus the smoke monster, then *Google* would tell me the secret location and I would be able to book a flight, or boat, or ferry, or aborigine canoe, and go there for a weekend.) I found that a man in Mexico built his own Island floating on thousands of collected plastic bottles. Although I was impressed, I wasn't sure if it was an island – more of a really cool raft with Mexican sand on it. Which by the way, Mexico wanted back. There was a lawsuit.

There is the smallest kingdom island comprised of one man who ruled as king over himself. And there were a few brand-new islands that popped up from volcanoes which were yet to be a vacation spot, but as soon as the lava cooled, whoever had dibs was sure to have plans to that end.

No secret island. No Sawyer, or Jack, or Johnny Depp.

I almost gave up. But like I said, *Google* is my friend. (And yours too even if you won't admit it out loud.) A random search about hurricane season (I wanted a vacation not a horror story to survive-- *Katrina* taught us all a very sound lesson.) up popped a little brochure claiming a getaway to a private island boasting sandy beaches, crystal clear water and a private hut a mile from any other hut.

After reading further, I discovered it was much like the *Gilligan* theme song. A three hour boat tour through an island chain in the Maldives comprised of over a thousand uninhabited little pieces of heaven, would bring you to a privately owned island, around eight square miles in size, and had five small huts scattered about it. Each hut was far removed from each other (hence the mile claim) and was stocked with food, sundries and basic living needs for a one week stay. I was sold.

I devoured every page and link inside the website, *Google Earth*ed the island myself, researched the weather for the season in the Maldives, and began arranging my life to get away, if only for one week, and find my castaway island.

*   *   *

The packing was easy. I live in Eastern Washington where we enjoy every single season to its absolute degree. Spring is wet and hopeful, summer is scorching and too short, autumn is wet and beautiful, and winter takes up its own half of the year as wet cold - snowy cold - gloomy cold - then wet and cold again. Thus, the hope in spring that winter may forget to come the next year, and that the scorch of summer will dry our winter chilled bones. So, I had at least a week's worth of summer - scorch clothing. All of them my favorites.

I am not one to bundle up. Well, actually I *do*, I bundle up in layers and waddle around for four to six months, however long winter punishes us with cold or soggy or gloomy, but the minute it's bearable I prefer to strip off the layers and bask. I have been caught many a time sunbathing nude on my lawn in hopes that the tan will last the whole year, and even bigger hopes that for once I won't be caught naked in my own yard. Neither hope ever pans out. But just to be clear, my yard is twenty acres of farmland, which is surrounded by many *more* acres of farmland. I believe my neighbors and family have fine-tuned their nudity radar and find great joy in dashing my hopes, and watching me try to be subtle in covering up my almost perfect tan each time they catch me. My point, you ask? My wardrobe of wraps, and cute sundresses, little shorts and tanks, is well filled out.

A month before I was due to leave I began packing. I spent the next thirty days unpacking and repacking my favorite suitcase as I decided on what to bring, then changed my mind. The struggle was deciding if I should pack more like Bear Grylls survivalist with sturdy shoes and some multi-tools, or fun loving vacationist with little sandals and tiny bikinis. It was a real battle. I tend to be prepared and am known for always having what is needed for almost any situation. I could practically do full surgery with what I carry in my purse if the need arose, and if I had any medical training – which aside from a few biology classes in college, I did not – but I was still prepared.

Since no one makes steel toed sandals, and it sounded painfully uncomfortable even if someone did, I eventually opted for the bulk of my suitcase to be sexy, light, and fun, with the remaining percentage to be functional and useful. For the week planned in paradise I settled on; four sun dresses, three wraps, four shorts, three tanks, two tees, three sandals, two bikinis and a light jacket. I obviously included the necessary bras and panties, and I caved and packed one multi-tool. I figured with my surgery set and the miscellaneous in my purse, I would be able to survive as well, if not better, than Bear Grylls. Maybe not as comfy as the Dutch kids, but way better than Tom Hanks.

*   *   *

The travel arrangements were trickier than I had thought they would be. The Maldives are

situated at the Equator in the Indian Ocean. Getting to paradise was not only going to be costly –
it would take two days. Eighteen and a half hours on a plane, with no direct flight.

Leaving from Spokane my options were to lay over in Abu Dhabi, Qatar, Istanbul,
Singapore, Hong Kong, or Dubai. All of them terrified me. I wasn't sure who was warring with
who at any given moment, or who spoke what language, and even less about the money exchange.

The layover would be overnight and I had a nightmarish vision of arriving and not being
able to read the signs at the airport, not being able to find a room and having to huddle in a corner
of the airport with jet lag and end up missing my connection. I feared I would be sold into slavery
or human trafficked.

I almost gave up the castaway dream entirely at the thought of landing in Korea or Turkey
and never being able to escape or find an American Embassy. I don't even know what an
Embassy looks like or really what it's used for. Other than what Matt Damon taught me in *Jason
Bourne*, I am pretty confused on the whole issue. I may sound ignorant, but really I am quite
brilliant in my own categories. I would just skip the embassy questions if ever I were on
Jeopardy.

I finally discovered that I could take a flight to London, where they speak English (mostly)
and the British pound or European Euro didn't scare me. From there I could take a straight flight
to Malé where my boat would leave taking me to my week of escape. Either way it would take
two days, but at least my layover in London had the potential to be fun and exciting instead of
potentially becoming a blonde country item on the human trafficking market. I watch way too
many bad movies. I vowed, once I booked my safe flight to London, not to bring any murder
mystery or action thriller novels. I love Matt Damon, but I was hoping for less adrenaline, more
endorphins.

All said and done, with every detail addressed and accounting for any minor emergencies,
my week of lost on an island was going to be the most expensive thing I had ever done. My
savings was completely spent. When I returned I would be back to living paycheck to paycheck
until I slowly built up my savings account again, but I was so excited I didn't regret a dime spent.

I had saved for the last five years hoping to do something grand and the money was just numbers on a balance sheet I received from the bank each month. It did me no good unless I spent it, and I was going to spend it in style.

I packed my camera, and extra batteries, as well as extra memory cards. I downloaded new e-books on my tablet for the flight, brought a paperback in case I couldn't charge my tablet, then packed a Sudoku book in case the book sucked, and earplugs in case my neighbor on the plane snored or had a baby. Like I said – I prepare.

I had planned the trip for the last week of December so that the new year would be spent laying on a white sand beach while all the Washingtonian's were struggling to chain up, or scrape ice off their windshield's. January in the Maldives was perfect weather. No monsoons, twelve hours of daylight and bikini sunshine days.

*   *   *

Christmas was a blur. I trudged through the holiday grind, driving the icy streets, chanting in my head, *everyone is an idiot, everyone is an idiot.*

I had taught myself this bit of wisdom at sixteen when my mother had thrust me into the driving world with the keys to our old Chevy truck – standard drive – and a fresh sheet of ice on the roads. She had proclaimed that if I could learn to drive in the dead of winter in a stick shift without killing myself then I deserved a license. I now agree with her, for I do indeed deserve a license, but my idiot chant is a reminder that so many others do not.

I had put the big lumbering truck in many a ditch, but after traipsing home to my mother, she had sent me back to the ditch with the admonishment "*If you got it in the ditch you can very well get it out*". So, with chains and curses, and not a few frostbite scares, I had mastered the ditch-removal maneuvers, and the don't-get-there-in-the-first-place skills.

I was raised a country girl by a tough no-nonsense woman who taught all her children (six of us) that you break what you fix, but your smarter not to break. But if you have to, and you're on ice – do it slowly. Thus, December was spent staying out of ditches, braking slowly, and getting here and there in one piece.

Most of my shopping was done through beloved *Amazon*, so the holiday masses were more quaint, than an annoyance. As for my dose of Christmas spirit, my family obliged by throwing all the usual holiday parties.

My little sister, Lily, held the annual cookie making party, which she traditionally guilted all the women in the family to attending and we in turn, guilted our men to join because, *"It's Christmas"* (code for; *Please don't leave me alone with my family.*) And my cousin, Anna, threw the Christmas eve party, which I had started years ago, before my husband showed his true snake form, and then had passed to my cousin, for although I am the hostess with the most-ess, no one cared to drive to my farm in the winter. (Due to the idiocy of other drivers or a secret fear of their own idiocy)

I find it's better to attend these functions than to host anyway. Fewer questions if you have less responsibility. The most common queries directed my way that never failed to make me flinch were; *"Sophia, I am so sorry to hear about Jon – that snake. What happened?"* Or; *"Sophia, are you dating yet? I know a great guy."* (Code for; *a guy I know can't get a date, will you pity him?*) Or; *"Sophia, why don't you call me anymore, you don't go on* Facebook, *you don't email, you didn't come to the cookie making party."*

Yeah, I had avoided the parties ever since the snake and I finalized the divorce. It's been two years now, but everyone seems to think I need to make cookies. I spent the last two months living on water, coffee and raisins in preparation of the perfect bikini body, no way was I going to screw it up with candy canes and sugary treats. Plus, I'm thirty two, how many cookies does one possibly need that I should attend a party for them?

All said and done, it was the usual Christmas. Which, in the end, I survived. (Despite idiots, guilt about baked goods, and the repeated, *Yes mom, I am still single.* and *No, I am not canceling my 'crazy' trip to a deserted island*).

I couldn't wait. I was ready. Holidays were over, the weather sucked. It was time.

Chapter 3

My cousin Anna drove me to the airport. Of all the people on the planet, I love Anna the most. She is my twin sister born of another mother. We have been inseparable since childhood, only she knows all my secrets and approves of every one of them.

"So there's no chance I can get you to change your mind?"

It was a rhetorical question. Anna had been seesawing between jealousy that I was actually going on my escape-from-the-world-for-a-week trip, and begging me to reconsider. She then took to trying to sway me by pointing out all the facts and odds against me, as she slowly accepted that I was not going to change my mind.

"You know Soso," (a pet name with a long back story I never approved of, but loved Anna too much to forbid her to use it.) "the odds of you dying in a plane crash for a one hour flight is around one in eight hundred thousand. *Your* flight is eighteen hours. That means, your odds are actually one in forty four thousand four hundred and forty four point four, four, four, four, four, four, four, four, four." She deftly went around an idiot driver and changed lanes to head toward the airport exit.

"Really, thirteen fours? Wouldn't that just be forty four thousand four hundred and forty four point four bar?" I was touched she had done the math. She loved me, and I loved facts.

"No, because it's not infinite. Really Sophie, I could ditch the kids and we could drive down the coast, go to San Diego, party at *Sea World*. No fiery crash, no searching for your body in the flotsam or jetsam."

I had to chuckle. Anna would use any excuse to reference *The Little Mermaid* and she knew I was a sucker for *Sea World*. "You would never ditch your kids, I love your kids, *I* wouldn't ditch them. If you weren't so possessive of the little princes I would smuggle them with me. And besides, *Sea World* is cool and all, but they don't have Johnny Depp."

"Neither does this island you're leaving me for, to go be flotsam or jetsam on."

"You never know, but come to think of it, Jon is short for Johnny and I already ditched a Jon. I hope instead, there'll be a Sawyer – way sexier and a total survivor in a plane crash."

"Technically he didn't survive. Why do we refer to Johnny Depp as Johnny Depp instead of Captain Jack Sparrow, but refer to Sawyer as Sawyer instead of his real name?"

"Because we don't know his real name. Don't miss the exit." I saw that she was about to pass it and wondered if she was trying for a run to San Diego after all.

Anna sighed and braked. Slowly. "I realize you won't change your mind. But will you at least toss a bottle in the sea everyday so I can get some news and know you landed safely?"

"I will use my handy cell phone as soon as the plane lands, and if there aren't any 'no littering' signs on my island, I will toss a bottle in the sea. Cross my heart."

Anna deftly pulled into the departure lane and stopped along the curb. Turning to me, I could see her pretty face had turned serious. "I want you to be careful. Have tons of fun, take hundreds of selfie's and beach shots, but be careful. You are my only sister," (which wasn't true, and strictly speaking, we're cousins, but I got the point.) "please come home safe, the princes will be counting the days."

"I will be careful *mom*. And I *will* have fun. I'll see you right here in one week." Hugging her tight, I kissed her cheek twice. "Give those to the princes. Enjoy New Years. I love you Anna." I gave her a big smile and a wink, then got out into the frigid winter air. After dragging my suitcase from the back seat, with my thin jacket doing no good against the icy Washington winter air, I stood frozen, waving to my cousin-sister-best friend as she pulled away from the curb to merge with a line of idiots heading in to town.

It had been a real struggle – my travel day wardrobe decision. I knew, for instance, that the plane would be air conditioned and was a painfully long flight so I didn't want to dress too coolly. I also knew that my arrival and the boat trip would be exceedingly hot and muggy. Then I had to wrestle with the fact that leaving town, it was nine degrees outside and returning would be no different. In the end, I had chosen a pair of white linen slacks, (take that you fashionistas, Labor Day rules or no, there was no such white pant law on the equator.) and a navy blue tank, (as a nod to the boat ride) with a thin white jacket and white *Keds* with navy piping. I thought I looked smashing. Which, in truth, I really did. I was determined to brave the cold for the few minutes between car and airport at both ends of the trip.

So now, with my headlights on, my breath fogging the air and my mind set on much, much warmer climates, I entered the airport at a clip flaunting my smashing summer garb as my *Keds* led me to the baggage check in.

*   *   *

My flight to London was fifteen hours. I had lucked out with a window seat and was gazing out at the tarmac, contemplating whether it was really lucky. One, my window looked at a wing, and two, I hoped I didn't have to get up to pee much. Squirming past my seatmates was always the question of; do they get my breasts in their face, or my butt in their lap.

For all the dozens of flights I have been on, I always, at least once, fall into a strangers lap as I try for the aisle and the much needed tiny, itsy-bitsy closet they called a toilet. I am not a big woman, I fall into the average height/weight category, but those plane bathrooms make me think of a coffin every time. A well-lit, strange smelling coffin with a place to relieve yourself and no silk bunting or wood trim. But coffin. Yep. So maybe I was lucky or maybe I was going to end up in someone's lap, the next fifteen hours would tell. I just prayed it wouldn't be a nun I sat on.

No pun intended at all. A trip to Florida a few years back and I actually *sat on a nun* on my way to pee. Strange things happen to me, it's totally not my fault. I suppose now it's a pretty funny story but at the time I was mortified and had spent the rest of flight praying.

A lovely young British girl turned out to be my traveling companion. I guessed her age to be around twenty five, and she had that quirky exotic look about her that was at once welcoming and intriguing. She introduced herself as Sasha, which I thought was such a fun name and we hit it off right away. We spent the beginning of the flight chatting about what I could do with my four hour layover in London. As it would be between one am, and six am, we concluded napping in the airport as my safest choice. With that settled, we turned to fashion, talk of the royal family, (which she was strangely secretive about – as if we didn't have tabloids in the US and were aware of what the Brits were up to) and the fun differences of speech in the English/American language.

"OK, so I get petrol and even britches, because pants make no sense either, but what's up with loo? Why not bathroom, or restroom, or toilet?"

Sasha laughed. "Oh, you are not the first to ask. We have many serious debates on that question."

"Really?" I had no idea that the word was such a talk of the country.

"No, not really," Sasha smiled lightheartedly "but everyone has a theory. In the end, we just blame it on the French."

With that, I laughed and noted, "Well, they have been a great scapegoat for many a thing. I had no idea the loo traced back to them too!"

Sasha went on to explain that the French had influenced many terms now commonly used in the British (English) language that no one could really explain.

"Same with American!" (Also English) "Of course ménage a trios, c'est la vie, and rendezvous come to mind, and cliché!"

"Oh yes, English or American we speak a mutt language and some people don't even realize we just mashed together a bunch of languages, *stole really*," she whispered conspiratorially, "and then called it our own. Not just French, like omelet, that's French, but

German too, kindergarten and noodle, those are from Germany. And Italy, we use words like bravo and diva that are Italian, but did you know that piano and novel are both Italian words?"

"No!" I was amazed, and thrilled. As I said, I love facts, and this was great info for my future *Jeopardy* appearance. I briefly considered asking Sasha if she knew how to use an embassy, but thought better of looking like a total dolt.

We spent the rest of the flight coming up with words we recognized had originated from other languages. Bess, the older lady in the aisle seat chimed in now and again. Sometimes twenty minutes would pass while I killed time reading a book or picking at the terrible airline food and then someone would say; "*Extravaganza- Italian*!" Or "*Alcatraz- Spanish*!" (I said that one, having been to the prison Island and remembering the drone of the tour guide) and "*Catsup - Chinese*!"

We were completely entertained, and I was having the best flight ever.

The fifteen hours was not as painful as it could have been. I slept, napping with my head on a tiny airplane pillow propped against the window, and Sasha napped with her head on a tiny airplane pillow propped against me. I didn't mind, she was nice enough not to drool, and she reminded me of my little sister Lily. I read my book and chatted with Bess about knitting techniques, she was a Scottish transplant living in England. I didn't pry, not really knowing how the English and Scots had settled their feud or if it was still brewing under the surface. Hundreds of years of battles and strife probably were a sore spot and a confined airplane was no place to awaken those sleeping dogs if in fact Bess and Sasha had any latent grudges. But all told, I was enjoying every moment.

I love to travel. I'm really an odd duck when it comes to it. I love the planning and the packing, the waiting in line and staring at other travelers. I love trying to figure out where they're from, where they're going. Will they have fun or only think of work, or the dog in the kennel, or if they left the stove on? I love the airport seats and the new sights, the lost items and the free hotel shampoo. I'm a born traveler, it really takes a lot to get me into a state to not enjoy every bit of it.

Fighting with a fellow traveler will usually do it. The Snake was the worst traveler ever.

We had fought across America and I had vowed to never travel with him again. Not even in a car to the store, or to dinner. We had actually begun driving separately to any function we attended together a year before the divorce. Now I sighed as the first leg of the journey came to an end. I was discovering again the joy of traveling, now that I no longer had to tolerate a snake as a companion.

As the plane began its circle of the London airport, I felt I had made two new friends and the three of us exchanged emails, vowing to keep in touch. I realized, that now in the twenty-first century, it was a very real possibility we *would* actually keep in contact. With email, *Facebook, Twitter* and *Skype,* there are many quick and easy ways to check in on a person. It wasn't like a decade or two ago where you don't call because of long distance charges, or you don't write, because who sits down to write a letter anymore?

I put my seat in the upright position, checked that my belt was tight and secure, my purse was at my feet with the zipper shut and all my odds and ends safely inside. (The surgery kit was relegated to the suitcase, given the sharp eyes and disapproval of TSA.) I then began the preparation for landing. I checked my ticket for the gate to my next flight, checked my passport, checked the time, checked my makeup, my hair, my breath. Yep, I was ready to land and stretch my legs, brush my teeth, and have a very late breakfast for dinner.

I hugged Sasha goodbye after we exited the gate, and turned to wave to Bess before she strode off down the terminal toward the baggage claim. Then I addressed my first order of business and promptly looked around for a real sized, non-coffin, bathroom, and went to freshen up.

Throughout the bulk of my twenties, I sported a super cute, and easy to tend, pixie cut. But upon leaving the Snake behind I had let my hair grow out. Now, after a few years, it reached down my back, long and blonde and incredibly thick. It's easily either my best feature or my worst, depending on the effort put into it. If I blow dried, moussed, curled and pinned, it was Hollywood lovely. If I left it alone, it was heavy and annoying and I looked like an unkempt llama. Most mornings I tortured my hair into a bun to punish it for not waking up looking fabulous and only ever spent the hour it took for the lovely Hollywood effect if I had to face strangers or needed to feel pretty.

For this occasion I had French braided the stuff into two braids that started at the top of my head and ran all the way to the back to then join into one. I then curled the long plait into a braided bun and pinned it at the nape of my neck. Looking in the mirror in the London airport bathroom, my hair was still perfectly in place. The magic of a French braid is one of the many things I am grateful for, especially since it still looked pretty. Delighted I didn't look like a llama, I brushed my teeth, washed my face and applied mascara, lip gloss and deodorant. With a new spring to my step, I slung my heavy, oversized purse over my shoulder, and went in search of that late night meal.

The London airport is huge. I'm sure the architects had a plan when they built it. There was most likely even some symmetry involved, but unless you are a pilot viewing that symmetry from above you would never know it. I have been in many airports, the Dallas airport had swallowed a few days of my life when I missed a flight, and literally ran for an hour to get to my connection. That's how big Dallas is. You can run, even with the aid of the moving ground strips that always make me feel like *Superman*, (or *Super girl*) and still miss the flight that your stupid travel agent arranged, with no foresight to the length of a Texas hallway. So although London competed with confusion and size to larger airports I've gotten lost in, I was not intimidated at all.

I had four hours to solve the maze, and I was excited that my traveling was going perfectly, so far. This thought had me looking around for anything wooden to knock upon, not one to curse myself with over optimism or gratitude. I found a counter made of wood as I passed heading toward a ring of eateries--only a quarter of a mile away. I gave it three solid taps and continued on, happy I was successful in warding off any curses, or bad luck.

Only one of the eateries had a dining area. I wanted to sit to enjoy my food so I let the hostess seat me and opened the menu. Happily the menu listed only a few odd items I didn't recognize, and more than a few I did, and loved. I ordered crepes with a side of fruit, and a glass of orange juice. I considered coffee, but didn't want jet-lag and the jitters to war with my stomach when I finally arrived, so decided against it. Each bite was eaten with relish. Not diced pickles, but pure joy. I *love* crepes, and apparently, the British have a secret recipe. They were delicious.

As I ate, I began my plan for my stay on a white sand beach. In reality, I knew there would be no men to meet, not Sawyer, or Johnny Depp, or any little Dutch kids. This would be an escape. A recharge. A healing. No men needed. I planned to swim, and tan, and nap, and drink. *Oh crap*! I realized all at once that the brochure hadn't detailed what kind of food or drink they provided. I didn't really care much about the food, I could put up with just about anything, but there was no way I was going to lay on a white sand beach, and not have a Mia Tai or a Peña Colada. A resort with a bar, or a bellhop wasn't necessary, but even with a castaway island as my destination, I would indeed, want a drink. Or two. Maybe three.

I paid the bill, left a generous tip and went in search of my next departure gate, hoping along the way I would find a liquor store where I could buy a few mini bottles, and maybe some juice. Once the plane landed in Malé I would only have two hours to make it to the docks where I boarded the boat for the island. Baggage claim would eat up one of those hours at least, and the other would be taking the ferry from the island that held the airport to Malé proper which was on another island entirely. There would be no time to shop.

I stopped at a gate that just finished boarding and asked the man taking the tickets for directions. He pointed, and gestured, and then finally wrote down on a slip of paper, which rights and lefts to take, and even sketched a tiny little map that he reminded me was not to scale. *Yeah, perfect*. I gave him my best smile and thanks and turned in the direction his first hand gestures had indicated. He'd said there was a little shop, not far from my gate, that sold alcohol and postcards and candy and such. As I made the final corner on the map, a blue sign clearly marking my gate, I sighed with relief and pleasure. I was two hours early, plenty of time to shop for what I would need for my tipsy tanning plans.

The gate guy had been right. There was a little shop just in sight of my gate. I strode inside and began leisurely perusing all the colorful candy, colorful magnets, colorful postcards, and colorful liquor bottles. Everything was so bright and cheery you wouldn't know it was four am on a gloomy, January, London morning. I picked out a magnet with *Big Ben* on it as a souvenir, three postcards, one for Anna, one for my mom, and one for me. Then I went to the candy aisle. I selected a few of my favorites, and a couple new ones to try I'd never heard of, then added two little bags of mixed nuts. I knew my purse would hold a month's supply of candy and drinks, but I didn't want to have to tolerate lugging around the eighty pounds of indulgence. So I grabbed two small bottles of water and headed to pick out my drink of choice.

The store offered premixed selections that made my day. I chose a Mai Tai, a Piña Colada, a Mudslide, and, two of the thickest beers they offered. I believe nothing is worse than a poorly brewed, watered down beer. To top it off, I grabbed a bottle of vodka in the shape of a flask, but made out of clear plastic. I figured if there was juice at my hut, I could mix my own drink, If there wasn't, perhaps there would be mangoes on the island, and I could mix my own drink. Either way, win, win. Finally, I was set -- my purse absolutely bulged.

At the gate, I found the closest seat to the departure entrance and settled in to read. If I fell asleep, the activity of loading would waken me, if not, I could be one of the first to embark and not have to jostle my now-giant-purse around strangers as I found my seat.

I pulled out my dog-eared book on the Maldives and flipped through areas I hadn't read yet. *Barnes and Noble* had offered nothing on the Maldives beyond a small book with lots of pictures, and very little facts. I had gotten that book too, but had special ordered this one. It contained history, and population counts, laws and religions, and maps of the atoll chain. It was a fantastic read if you wanted to study the area and learn of its government or economy, but it tended to bore at four in the morning after a long flight. After half an hour my eyelids began to droop, and I leaned back with my purse in my lap, the strap firmly wrapped over my shoulder to deter any would be thief.

I awoke an hour later with other passengers jostling about the loading area, and the ticket taker planted behind his podium at the gate entrance. I stood up and stretched, groaning at the weight of my purse, but, determined to bear it for the joys of the tipsy tan to come. The other passengers about me were much fewer than had been on my flight out of Washington.

Apparently, this was to be a much smaller plane as well. I wasn't worried. Even if I had a window seat, which I hoped I did, I was sure I could hold my bladder for the flight, and break my streak of lap-sitting. I had only barely sat on Bess on the way here, and she had been sweet about it. She had quickly moved her knitting needles, saving me from an embarrassing impalement, and steered me into the aisle with a smile and a comment about being grateful I was a girl and not a large fat man. *Well me too. Quite grateful indeed.*

I was the third person to board. My seat was at the very back, one row in front of where the stewardess would spend her flight buckled in. (I kept reminding myself to call her the flight attendant, for PC reasons, but, as I never addressed any of them as anything other than 'oh Miss' with a hand raised, I didn't figure I would slip up and hurt anyone's feelings.)

As I settled in and surveyed the rest of the passengers boarding, I realized I was the only westerner on the plane. I racked my brain, trying to remember the ethnicity of the Maldivian islanders, but couldn't recall. I pulled out my book and began the research. By the time our plane was taxiing for takeoff, I learned that I was amongst Dhivehi's. Originating mostly from Southern India or Sri Lanka. At another glance around I saw that there was one other couple not of the assumed Dhivehi's ethnicity. An older couple, obviously British by their accent, most likely in their late fifties, and both a bit portly. *Jolly,* I corrected myself, as they both laughed aloud at a shared joke. *On holiday to a tropical beach.* I smiled as the man reached over to pat his wife's hand and wink at her. I love couples in love. No matter the age, or the race, or the jolly size of them. Love is love, and it's always the best way to make me smile.

My traveling companion turned out to be a woman, about my age, of the Island nation I assumed. Her light brown skin and dark brown eyes along with her long shiny black hair, made her probably quite the catch in the Maldives. She was a striking woman, who ignored me completely, and settled back in her aisle seat to sleep the flight away. I had lucked out again with the window seat and wondered if my travel agent had known he set me up with the view. There was an empty seat between me and pretty Diva (as I decided to call her) and so I plopped my purse into it and buckled it in like it was my own child. I decided Diva had the right Idea, and settled back to sleep the remainder of the flight, intent on storing up all the energy I could for the best vacation ever.

Mentally, I knocked on wood as I fell asleep, and the plane took off.

Chapter 4

So that *is my hut neighbor?*

I sat in the reception area of the travel agency that handled the rental of the huts and arrangements for the boat ride to our destination. Landing in Malé had been magnificent. Circling over the chain of atolls that comprised the Maldives nation was breathtaking. I had never seen such shades of blue or such crisp whites. Apparently every single island boasted paradise. Coconut trees, long beaches, pure and clean, and coral reefs around each atoll that provided a protective barrier from the great big wide ocean.

My blood pressure began to rise, and my stomach tickled with butterflies. I was so excited I tamped down the threat of nausea, inwardly talking myself down at the long wait at the baggage carousel. When my luggage came into view I snatched up the handle and wheeled it outside. The docks floated within eyesight of the airport, and I was incredibly grateful of my choice of outfits. It was muggy beyond belief, the temperature hovered around the nineties. Although I'm accustomed to high temperatures, in the scorch of summer back home, my body now, struggled to adjust to what my mind and spirit were reveling in. In my head a huge party raged, with dancing and drinking and loud singing going on. But outwardly I had stripped off the jacket upon landing and was looking forward to stripping off the linen pants that now clung to my clammy legs.

I need to tan before I show my white legs. No way am I going to bare any more pasty skin than necessary until I'm a golden bronzed goddess. I only hoped that my five days here would be long enough to reach golden bronze. My luck would take me from pasty to beet red and blistering, skipping golden or bronze and nowhere near goddess coloring.

Malé is the size of a small city/large town in America. The capital city took up an entire island of its own and now had nowhere to go or grow beyond its beaches. Every inch of sand had been used to build on. The smaller islands of the tiny nation were the calling card of the Maldives. Private, remote, pieces of paradise.

Now I sat in an open air office at the water's edge with a view of the docks harboring little boats, big boats, and sexy streamlined yachts. And there, across the office from me, leaning against the wall, his gaze surveying the harbor, stood a very handsome, very tall, man.

He's got to be six foot two, maybe six three, I couldn't come up to his chin. But worse than his height, (I do love me a tall man) were his eyes. A striking clear blue to match the ocean beyond, had glanced my way and promptly dismissed me when I entered the office. To top it off, a smile had flashed a hint of dimple when he had spoken to the lady behind the desk a moment before. I can't resist dimples. The smile had shown straight white teeth, but had hinted at a sadness in his blue, blue eyes.

Really? There's no such luck a man like this ends up vacationing in the exact spot I do. My luck ran the lines of nuns, snakes and greasy car salesmen, which was another reason being lost on an island appealed to me. When it came to men, the universe hated me. (To be fair, the nun was female, but still, a good example of my luck.) *This* man, though, still leaning and facing the sea, sported jeans, worn leather boots and a light blue button up linen shirt. He should have been sweltering in that denim and dripping in sweat, but he looked casual and comfortable, if a bit haunted. As if he were a cowboy misplaced in the tropics, mourning a faithful dead horse.

"Johnny Depp Eat your heart out."

Lady Sun

"Excuse me, miss?"

I hadn't realized I had spoken aloud and felt my cheeks flush. I smiled at the travel agent who stepped out from behind the desk with a look of inquiry on her face.

"Sorry, muttering to myself." I smiled at her and hoped she thought my blush was from the sun. *We poor, pale, Americans can't handle the island heat.* Cowboy didn't seem to notice the exchange, but turned as the island native approached him.

"Boarding will begin in twenty minutes. If you take your luggage to the dock, just there, slip Number twelve," she pointed a slim finger toward the water, "Jok will show you where to board. You will pull anchor at noon and should reach your destination around three, enough time to settle in and enjoy the sunset."

She flashed a smile that encompassed us both and handed each of us a sheet of paper I assumed to be a receipt. It had taken a full fifteen minutes to sign and read my way through the paperwork involved at this end of the journey. But with t's crossed, and i's dotted I was now on my way to enjoy my savings spent.

Accepting the sheet of paper, I confirmed it was indeed my signature on a receipt with lots of fine print, and stuffed it in my purse. I was careful not to jostle any bottles, lest there be a clinking of glass, or worse, a breakage. I wanted my beer and liquor intact. Tipsy would begin upon arrival.

Gorgeous cowboy grabbed the handle of his nondescript, small suitcase, and I followed him down the short street toward the water. The view of the harbor was only rivaled by the rear view of the Cowboy, who actually walked like he had recently dismounted. Like a stroll. *His legs are at least as long as my entire body, probably forty inch inseam.* (I ramble inappropriately in my head when I'm nervous). I realized I might be caught looking where I shouldn't so instead, focused on finding slip number twelve.

Jok turned out to be an islander. No surprise there. Probably mid-forties, though difficult to tell. He was a little man and standing next to Cowboy he looked like a child. His accent sounded a bit thicker than the travel agent's at the office, but I still easily understood him. It was a lilting accent similar to an East Indian, his sentences all ending on a higher note which made everything sound like a question.

"Ah, you must be Lucas and Sophia." (*Question*) "You are just in time. I hope that your journey was pleasant." (*Question*) He flashed a smile and gave a slight bow, which I took for a greeting and thought was sweet.

I reached out my hand to shake his small brown one and smiled in return. "Hello Jok, I'm Sophia, I'm so excited to get underway, is this the boat we are supposed to board?" I indicated the impressive looking craft in the slip he was standing in front of.

"Oh yes, this is she." (*Question*) -- *I have to stop doing that!* He beamed proudly at the small ship as if he had birthed it from his own womb. But he was right to beam. The slip moored a small yacht compared to the mightier ones anchored further out in deeper water, but it was beautiful. Clean, sleek lines and high above the water, it was much fancier than what I had expected to be touring the Maldives in.

This just gets better and better. Cowboy and me on an island, cruising the seas in a yacht, Anna will never believe me. --I need to take tons of pictures. I gave myself a mental note to dig out my camera once aboard and start recording proof of this dream world I had stumbled into. *Like Alice in wonderland.*

I kept smiling and glanced at Cowboy. He seemed duly impressed, but not as chatty as me. He nodded to Jok and walked toward the gangplank that led up to the ship, pulling his suitcase rattling along behind. I sighed dreamily, watching him go, then took Jok's arm in mine and followed after.

"So, what's her name?"

He looked proud that I should ask and rattled off a pretty sounding word my tongue would never be able to repeat, then pointed to the bow. There, in a script that also looked East Indian to my untrained eye, was a swirl of letters to confirm that, no, I would never be able to name the boat when I got home.

"It means *Lady Sun*." he explained, seeing my confused expression.

Lady Sun

"Oh, that's perfect!" I exclaimed. Jok took the handle of my suitcase and wheeled it up the gangplank ahead of me. Trailing behind, I was careful not to let him hear any clinking from my over- stuffed purse. "Are we the only passengers aboard for the island retreat?"

"Today, yes." Jok indicated a bench along the back of the boat where we could recline during the voyage out of the harbor. "Tomorrow the remaining visitors will arrive, but if you do not travel to the dock you most likely will never meet. Each visitor is very respectful of the privacy of the others. Exploring is encouraged, but rarely will one hut dweller invade another's piece of the island."

I noticed that he addressed us in a polite way, and realized it was his way of reading the informal rules of our stay without insulting us as if we were children. *How smooth, I should remember that technique for teaching my family and neighbors to respect the boundaries of my tanning spots.*

I smiled at Jok and glanced toward Cowboy who may or may not have been paying attention. "I will certainly respect the others' privacy as I too wish to escape and be left alone."

Jok nodded, gave another slight bow and then trotted off toward the front of the *Lady Sun*.

I was left alone with the tall dark stranger who had yet to utter a single word. My alter ego considered whispering to cowboy that he could visit my side of the island if he wanted, but I realized at once it would make me sound like a floozy. I'm not a floozy. I am a happy lady who wouldn't mind the company of a gorgeous Cowboy to rub suntan oil on my back. *No floozy in that right?* I leaned back and turned my face to the sun. *OK, a little floozy, but he's a cowboy, with dimples, and so cute I could lick him. But not friendly at all.* So I left him alone. *Lucas* -- as appeared to be his name -- *could stay on his lonely side of the island and I would drink my beer alone and rub oil on myself. So there. Oh, petulant floozy.*

My inner conversation entertained me so much that I was smiling when Jok returned to announce refreshments. "We have a light lunch for you and drinks if you wish." He waved his hand to a cart he had wheeled onto the deck and then he disappeared again.

I assumed he was off to inform the captain to weigh anchor, and after a moment was proven right. Deckhands tossed ropes up from the dock and the engines purred to life. Soon we began drifting out of the harbor, into open sea.

Jok popped back onto the deck and stood patiently for us to notice him. I was loading a small paper plate with fruits and cheeses and Cowboy/Lucas was strolling along the deck watching Malé disappear.

"We have a cabin for each of you if you would like to freshen up." Jok gestured to a narrow stairway that led down to below decks. "There is no plumbing on the island, but there will be an outdoor shower that runs from a cistern. Please feel free to nap or change if you like. Our journey will skirt along the Atolls, but we will not enter any or dock until we reach…"

Once again, he rattled off a native word, this one I knew, named our destination Island. I had practiced saying it back in Washington, but had only felt foolish and so had given up and just called it 'castaway', which I was sticking to now. Some of the islands had English sounding names, but some of them might as well of been in Klingon for all the grasp my tongue could make of them.

I followed Jok below deck to a small but opulent cabin where I promptly plopped on the bed, stretching and giggling quietly. *Insane petulant floozy,* I admonished my inner self. Rising, I washed my face and hands in the sink of the tiny bathroom that was not *too* coffin like, then dug my camera from my purse. I would change when we arrived -- where no one could see my pasty white legs.

I went back up on deck, toting my camera and my plate that had only a few bits of cheese left. At the buffet I grabbed a croissant and set about to explore the fabulous ship.

Three selfies and ten ocean shots later I found Lucas skulking about along the starboard railing. I say 'skulking' because he really did not seem to be enjoying himself and he was squatting down, opening a panel along the wall below the railing. I stopped and watched, curious as to what the hell was he doing. *He's on vacation, why can't he just eat some fruit, bask in the sun, and pose for a picture?* OK, that one was my wishful thinking. Again, I needed *proof;* Anna will call me a total liar if I don't get the man on film, -- Or digital card, as the case may be.

Lucas flipped the last latch in a row of three and lowered the door of the hatch. Inside sat a very tidy packed square of rubber. It sported a bright yellow color with black writing that didn't have a lick of English, but I was no dunce. It was an emergency raft. The far end of the compartment held a stack of life vests and the other end a large metal box with its own clasps securely shut. Lucas closed the hatch, secured it, and rose to his feet. As he turned he noticed me standing there. I merely raised an eyebrow in question and he had the decency to look abashed.

"Just curious." He nodded to the compartment. "Always good to know where to run to if we sink."

"Oh, so you're an optimist. Frankly, I am just relieved you speak. The whole tall-dark-and-handsome-silent-type is fun for the first five minutes, but then gets a little unnerving." I grinned to prove I was just teasing, but he gave me a strange look and turned and strode the other way. I rolled my eyes and trotted after him. "Hey, wait, Lucas!"

He paused and turned to face me. *Damn those eyes are piercing*, and I had been right -- Standing next to him I barely met his chin. I took a breath and gave him my very best friendly face. "Look, I wasn't trying to be mean, I just meant, it would be nice to have someone to talk to for the boat trip, and you seem, well, unhappy." He didn't respond, but he didn't walk away either. I held out a hand. "I'm Sophia."

He paused and then seemed to relax minutely. He reached out a hand that swallowed my own. I felt rough, warm, skin with callouses as he firmly shook my hand then released it. *Yep cowboy*. I warded off the tingles his touch had given me and smiled. Genuinely.

"See, now we aren't strangers." I had to crane my neck to look up at his handsome face and tried my best to portray, mature-non-floozy. "I promise not to invade your side of the island, but we have a couple hours. I propose we drink that champagne at the buffet and enjoy the trip." Keeping my smile in place, I shrugged to ease the tension and give him an out if he really did want me to leave him alone.

He was silent long enough, I had to wonder if he was slow, but finally he sighed and smiled back, the dimples melting me immediately. "Yeah, sure. I could use a drink and you're maybe not crazy, just…" he paused. "Exuberant." He turned away again and headed back toward the benches at the rear of the boat.

Exuberant? What the hell was that supposed to mean? Still standing at the railing, I took assessment of myself from Lucas' point of view. I looked like I had money, I know I've been accused of that. Country girl or not I had the bone structure and the posture, and I take pride in my wardrobe so I could pass for money. I *am* chatty, that I will admit to. I like people and I love to learn about them, about everything really. While in college I had made a great student. I wasn't a party animal like my friends, for although I love a good time, learning was the priority. I'm a curious cat and tend to ask a lot of questions. So yeah, I'm chatty. And a little friendlier than the average citizen, and yes, I *am* excited, I am on the best freaking vacation ever! So I realized in that moment, Lucas was right. I am exuberant. But whether he meant it as an insult or not, I would take it for what it was. The truth. Lucas was so very *not* exuberant.

"Too bad for you," I mumbled. "I'm way more fun in happy-land than you are in grumpy-land where tall sexy cowboys live. No wonder I never meet your kind. I don't visit grumpy-land." I knew that crazy-petulant had resurfaced, but I didn't care.

Rounding the corner Lucas had poured two glasses of champagne and was holding one out to me, "Grumpy land?" he asked.

Chapter 5

"Sooo... Lost on a deserted island. Best vacation ever, yes?"

I raised my glass to Lucas who sat a few feet from me along the back of the ship. The view had turned to open ocean and sunshine, with only occasionally spotting the atolls of the Maldives as we cruised passed them.

"Not technically lost, and yet to be seen." He didn't raise his glass, but he did drink, which I took as a positive sign, if not encouragement toward the conversation.

"OK, let's play a game." I proposed.

Lucas looked at me. I wouldn't describe his expression as bland. He was too darn good looking for that, but I could tell he was on the verge of either jumping overboard at the suggestion of playing anything, or simply ignoring me. Which had worked for him so far.

But I am nothing, if not tenacious. Throw in exuberant and I would win this battle of wills. "I will ask you a question. You can either answer, or if you think the question is too personal, none of my business, or you don't *want* to answer, you can reply with 'Pumpkin'."

"Why can't I just not answer, or *say* it's none of your business? For that matter why do I have to play at all?" Lucas took another sip of the bubbly champagne and leaned back.

He appeared to be relaxing a bit. Whether it was due to the alcohol, the warm sun in our faces and the lulling boat ride, or to my exuberance, I didn't care. I had high hopes for Cowboy, and I wouldn't let his grumpy disposition stand in my way of me, forcing him, to have fun.

"Because it would be rude, boring, and because I asked pretty please."

"You didn't ask. Pretty, or please."

I sighed. "Pretty, please?"

"Why does it have to be pumpkin? Why can't I say Porcupine?"

"Because sweet Lucas, I want to hear you call me pumpkin, and because your choice of porcupine revealed more about you than you probably wanted me to know." I winked, smiled, and took a long sip of my champagne. I was feeling relaxed too.

Lucas laughed. It was a beautiful sound. His dimples creased his face, which had a few days growth of beard, and his eyes crinkled at the edges.

My heart stopped, then quickly caught up its beat and I took another sip of champagne. *Need to slow down on the imbibing Sophia, or I'll soon be in his lap chanting "call me pumpkin, call me pumpkin."*

I set down my glass and turned on the bench to face him. "OK, where are you from?" He appeared to be struggling with the answer, and I was betting 'Pumpkin' was his home town but lost the bet when he finally spoke.

"Montana."

"No!" I exclaimed. "Really? We're neighbors!"

I was amazed. Thousands of miles away, on a boat heading to an island few could pronounce the name of and even fewer people knew existed, and I meet Cowboy-Lucas from Montana.

We in the Northwest call Oregon, Idaho and Montana, neighbor – as if they live right next door and we can stop by for a cup of sugar. But even though Montana is separated from Washington by Idaho it's really just a jaunt away. You're likely to find a good percentage of license plates in any given parking lot in Washington, from Montana, Idaho or Oregon. The odds were spooky.

I poked my finger toward my chest in excitement. "I'm from Washington!"

"You're kidding." Lucas studied me for a minute and then shook his head. "I had you pegged as a New York girl, Chicago, or Boston perhaps. He got up to fetch the champagne bottle from the buffet cart and returned with it, filling my glass without asking. "So. Washington. Pretty long odds huh?"

"Oh, yeah! I mean, you and I might have met at a supermarket, or a football game, or you could have hit my truck on an icy road. Those odds are way better than a world away on a deserted island." I shook my head in amazement and took a sip from my glass before I remembered I intended to slow my roll on the drink front.

"Not really." He studied me with a strange expression. *Confusion? Consternation?*

"You think it's more likely for us to run into each other on this yacht, today, rather than any other moment we may have crossed paths?" I wondered if he was being contrary just to be stubborn, or if it's a built in mechanism in all men to disagree at the gate with anything women said or thought.

"No, I meant it's more likely that we cross paths here, on this boat, on this day, than it is that you drive a truck, or that I would hit you on an icy road." Lucas leaned back and propped an ankle on his knee. "I don't hit anyone, ice or no, everyone else drives like idiots. I'm from Montana, my biggest fear on the road is all you yahoos playing at having a license." He gave me a smile so pretty I couldn't take offense.

Throwing caution to the wind I downed the rest of my champagne and set the glass aside.

"OK smug Cowboy. I do in fact drive a truck. A Dodge Ram to be precise. I'll exclude you from my judgment of all the idiot drivers because I happen to agree with you. But I've been chaining up since puberty, and so I'm very protective of my right to carry a license, as well as my life schooling in earning it." I took a breath and settled down before I did any damage and came off as a Harpy Shrew. "Given your Montana heritage you get a free pass this once, as I don't expect you to know the legend of my driving skills."

I crossed my arms defensively and sat back to stare at him. "But you have to admit the odds are crazy. Don't you think?"

Lucas looked me up and down with a hint of a smile. At least he seemed amused and less grumpy than he had been. He finished his perusal and looked me dead in the eye with his pretty blue gaze. "Pumpkin." he said softly, then rose and went below deck.

*   *   *

I sat there for a minute, wondering why this man had me so determined to bring him out of his shell. He was pretty, yes, OK, beyond pretty. He was rugged and tall and beneath his loose shirt I clearly detected a broad back, and strong arms and *what woman* isn't *drawn to tall strong mysterious men*? But his resistance to my friendliness had become a personal challenge. The few smiles he had let escape had hinted at a chance that he might be a *nice* cowboy. Not as grumpy as he was determined to prove.

So I sat, waiting for him to come back, hoping we could continue the game. I had been teasing (kind of) about wanting to hear him call me pumpkin. Until he did. Now my promise to stay on my side of the island would be a struggle to keep.

Twenty minutes went by and I finally had to admit I had lost the war. Lucas proved much stronger in resisting my will than I had given him credit for. Not one to be pushy, (OK, not *too* pushy) or a stalker, I let him have his escape, and went back to enjoying the boat ride alone.

I guessed we were about an hour out from our destination and decided I had time for a quick shower and a change of clothes after all. If nothing else I could take my braids out and find the post cards I had gotten in London. If I asked Jok pretty please, he might mail them for me when he returned to Malé. I didn't figure there would be any other way to get them sent out if I wanted them to arrive before I got home.

I had called Anna when I landed that morning. She had sounded sleepy, and doing the math in my head of the time difference, I realized I must have woken her up. But she sounded happy to hear from me too, and I assured her the first leg of the journey had spared me from any resemblance of flotsam or jetsam. She had signed off with the assurance that my horses were fine. My mother was babysitting the farm and Anna checked in regularly to ease my worries.

Now I wondered as I made my way below deck, how I might sneak a picture of Lucas before I had to return home. I couldn't go back without proof, and no exaggeration would do the Cowboy justice. I had to get at least *one* picture just to put in my own album. Perhaps I would title him 'The sneaky Cowboy who got away.' Chuckling to myself, I wondered if maybe I was a little stalker-ish after all.

"So you amuse yourself as well."

I let out a squeak in startlement as I reached the bottom of the stairs. Miscalculating the last step, I tripped over my own feet and headed quickly into a nosedive. Reflexively I reached out to catch myself but only caught handfuls of shirt, just as strong hands caught a handful of me.

Lucas steadied me back to an upright position and shook his head. "Too much sun, or too much champagne?"

"I. Am. Not. Drunk." I straightened my tank and glared at him. In the small hallway we were practically on top of each other. I never realized how difficult it is to glare at someone when they are a foot above your head. I craned my neck to try and deliver the full force of my glare.

"Excuse me." I stepped to the side to move around him. He may be gorgeous, but he was beginning to border on rude, and I was in much too good of a mood to let even a handsome

Montanan ruin it for me.

"Sophia," Lucas reached out and took my arm lightly as I passed him. I stopped and looked at him, my goal of cheering him up completely gone, but I wasn't mad. Just refocusing. I smiled politely, waiting for him to speak.

He tipped his head at me and released my arm. "It *is* a crazy coincidence, you and I meeting here, being neighbors. And I like your... exuberance. I'm just, well," He seemed at a loss for words for a minute as we stood there packed in the tiny hall. I felt the heat coming off of him, it competed with the muggy heat of the air off the ocean, but he smelled better than saltwater and sunshine. It was distracting, trying to place his scent in my mind... *leather, chocolate? No, it's particular and elusive it's...* "Not OK, but getting there."

I came back to the line of conversation. And realized what he was saying. He wasn't grumpy, he was hurting, and here I was being flippant and forcing him to drink and play games. I'm a jerk.

I nodded and reached out and took his hand. It was warm and dry and the strength in it was clear as I squeezed it lightly.

"I'm sorry. Please just ignore me." I gave him a wry smile and rolled my eyes a bit, "My *exuberance* can get me in trouble, and I tend to drag other people into my circle of reality. I'll give you your space." Releasing his hand I stepped back, smiling. "We paid a handsome price for the privacy of this Island. I won't ruin your trip with my crazy."

He didn't say anything. I turned and went to my cabin, stepped inside, and closed the door softly behind me. I stood there a moment listening to his steps as he went above to the deck. *I suppose my lessons are learned a bit slower than most.* No more stalker or floozy. No more games. I would rely on my own description of haunted Cowboy and not try to get him on film.

*   *   *

I decided to forgo the shower. Instead I lay back on my bed and relaxed for a while. I knew that jet lag was going to catch up to me. Although I had caught some good naps on both flights, my regular sleeping pattern was completely thrown off. Mixed with the excitement and the hot, muggy air, I was betting that tonight I was going to crash hard. But I didn't want to fall asleep now. Only a little longer and I would disembark, get to my hut, unpack, assess my paradise and have a drink on the beach with the sunset. Then I would sleep and wake to start my vacation in a bikini on the sand.

Heaving a big sigh, I drug myself back upright. I grabbed my purse, fetched my suitcase from the corner and decided to wait the remaining fifteen or twenty minutes up in the open air. Vowing to myself I would leave Lucas alone, as I was sure he would have no problem in leaving me alone as well.

I guesstimated it was between three and four local time as I poked my head above deck, dragging my suitcase and pregnant purse up onto the aft deck. Lucas was nowhere in sight, so I parked my load at the end of the bench and went to the buffet to pilfer from the leftover fare. The cheese had begun to harden around the edges, and the croissants were growing slightly stale but I grabbed one anyway. I found a bottled water, and strolled over to the railing to nibble the buttery, flaky, bread as I watched the last atoll of the chain come into sight.

I hadn't seen even a glimpse of Jok since he had wheeled out the buffet and wondered if he was paid to leave the guests alone. It seemed pretty unprofessional, considering we were out at sea and one of us may fall overboard. A fleeting question of whether sharks lived at the Equator entered my mind and then was replaced with a bigger question of; *where was everyone?*

The string of islands that consisted of the edge of the Maldives nation began slipping past and the captain had not changed course to enter the protective barrier, inside which, our castaway island resided.

I began walking along the starboard side of the ship, thinking I would most likely find the Captain, or Jok, up front, in the wheel house. I intended to ask them why we weren't turning, or veering or whatever ships do when they aim sideways. Just as I was about to open the little door I assumed led to steering, Lucas jumped down onto the deck beside me from the low roof above.

I would have shrieked in surprise, or maybe toppled backward over the railing, into the water. (Which again brought to mind the question of sharks) But Lucas grabbed me, full body, and wrapped his arms around me. I was so stunned at the contact, and the overwhelming delicious sent of him, that I swallowed the shriek and stood stiff in his arms, wondering what the hell was wrong with the man.

Talk about running hot and cold. Lucas' entire body was tense. He had me pressed along the entire length of him, the muscles in his arms tight against my shoulders. His long legs ran up the front of mine and his hands pressed in the middle of my back. Then, Cowboy dropped his head to align his mouth to my ear and spoke very calmly. His intense tone immediately terrified me and had me panicking even before I made sense of what he was saying.

"Sophia. A boat is approaching,"

I was registering the sound of an engine even as he said it, far out, and to the port side of the ship.

"It's clear they're pirates. They *will* board us. Don't do anything to give them a reason to hurt you. If you can manage it, stay close to me, I'll do everything I can to protect you." Lucas paused and his grip on me loosened. "I don't know if they only want the ship, which is the custom of pirates, or if this ship is smuggling something they want." He spoke fast now, trying to cram as much information into the short time we had before the Lady Sun was boarded. "If we're separated, I'll try to get to you if I can."

"But…" I started to argue, pulling away from him, *what the hell? Pirates? This couldn't be happening and what was he talking about; get to me? This cowboy wasn't going to stand up against gunned men for the sake of a crazy exuberant tourist that annoyed him.*

Lucas pulled me closer and his grip moved to my arms. It hurt, I was sure he was bruising me, but I felt myself growing numb, serious panic threatening below the surface, I talked myself down in my head, soothing the panic away through denial. *No pirates, just another boat. Cowboy is crazy, a nice smelling tall crazy Montana man…*

"Please, just don't do anything stupid." He hissed in my ear. He released me suddenly and my knees began to buckle.

I caught myself against the railing and just stared at him, slack jawed and speechless. I could come up with no witty retort, no sarcastic or fun comment. I simply stood there until he took my arm and guided me toward the back of the boat where my purse and suitcase sat happily waiting for me to take them to an island and unpack them, wear my bikini, drink a Mai tai.

Lucas deposited me on the bench just as I heard the droning engine cut out and a bump against the side of the ship.

Holly crap.

We were being boarded.

Chapter 6

I took a deep breath and looked into Lucas' eyes. He stared at me. Waiting, for my meltdown, or crazy to surface. He looked wary, but concerned, and very, very, tense.

"Did you see them?" I asked, hoping I could find a flaw in his claim.

He reached behind him and pulled a small pair of binoculars off of his belt. "I wondered why we were passing the atoll. I climbed up top." He jerked his head toward where he had jumped down, almost sending me over the side. "The boat was coming fast. I made out three men, all have guns. Pirates are not uncommon out here, but Jok or the Captain must have known to expect them, we never changed course." Lucas shrugged his shoulders in a tense acceptance of what he could not change. "I'm pretty sure they didn't radio in for help either."

Lucas sat beside me abruptly and clasped my hand. The lady sun came to a full stop. Willingly. I heard boots on the deck. This was real. Stupid, crazy, awful real. Lucas' grip hurt, but I didn't want him to let go. I sat, saying nothing, and waited for our fate.

*   *   *

The sun prepared to set in about an hour.

I refused to believe my first sunset in the Maldives would be spent locked in a cabin on a yacht while pirates planned my death. I punched a pillow and then threw it across the small cabin where it hit the wall with little force and slid soundlessly to the floor. It didn't make me feel any better. The panic I had been systematically forcing down into my inner denial land threatened to surface and explode out of me in tears, shrieking, and a chanting of '*Why me? Why me?*'

The pirates had boarded about an hour ago. They were small men, with skin so dark they looked like shiny shadows with guns.

There had immediately been some kind of argument between Jok and two of the pirates that I struggled to make out. I soon gave up, gleaning only that it was loud, and in a language that may have been a mix of Klingon and Russian. It wasn't a pretty sound at all. I figured though, if they had been arguing in French I would have found it romantic, or funny. That would not have served the pirates well for their purposes of instilling fear and taking your stuff, – your yacht, your wallet, your passport, your freedom.

I listened to the fight as one dark shiny shadow stood over Lucas and me with a very scary looking gun and a scowl. He said only one English word, but it was all we needed to hear. "Stay." We stayed. After twenty minutes – that drug on like years – Jok and the others had come to some resolution. I figured that they had to of agreed on something, as the engines fired up again and we changed course. We now headed in the direction I thought may be south but couldn't be sure.

A taller shiny shadow with a machete in his worn leather belt, yes an actual machete – that I was thankful wasn't covered in blood stains – came to give orders to our personal guard.

Lucas and I had been sitting, as commanded, saying nothing, clasping hands. I had long ago lost feeling in my fingers, but refused to give up my lifeline to Lucas. During the twenty minutes/years that the pirates and Jok argued over whatever pirates get mad about, Lucas was calmly studying the man who held the gun. Who was, in turn, – studying me.

I felt naked and terrified and refused to look at the man. I stared at my feet, my shoelaces, Lucas' feet, he had no shoelaces, but his worn leather boots told their own story. Focusing on them, I tried to imagine where they had been. – Montana fields. Stirrups. Pedals of a farm truck. Anything to not see the scenarios the pirate planned for me, clearly written on his face.

Lucas saw the plans too. He tensed with every leer the shiny shadow gave me. He had scooted closer to me, and I leaned into him. Any closer and I would be in his lap, but I didn't care about propriety, or whether I would look like a crazy chick. I wanted to curl up into Lucas' arms and wait for the nightmare to be over.

The taller Pirate said something in their angry language to our guard, and gestured toward the entrance to below decks. We were then marched, at gunpoint, to our cabins below.

Once inside with the door closed, I immediately turned the lock on the handle. They couldn't lock the door from the outside, even though I knew they didn't need to. The pirate and his gun were more than enough to keep the door firmly shut. I also knew the flimsy lock, and even flimsier door, would not keep them out, but I wasn't going to leave it *unlocked.* It seemed almost an invitation.

Now, it had been another thirty minutes or so. The boredom and not knowing what was happening, what was *going* to happen, wore away at the small bit of control I had left. Shock, had kept me from blubbering, or freaking out, or passing out. But that was wearing off and nerves threatened to take over, promising nausea, jitters, and a need for oxygen.

I vowed I would not throw up. It would make me weak and sluggish. I hate throwing up, I would make a terrible bulimic. I sat down on the small, cramped floor of the cabin and did stretches. Breathe slowly. Stretch. Breathe in. Stretch. Breathe out. After five minutes I had the jitters under control, and the tightness in my chest loosened. As long as I didn't think about my future, I could get through. Minute to minute.

I lay on the bed. I got up and paced. There was no room to pace properly – it made me dizzy. I lay on the bed again. The ship was moving faster than we had been going before. At first, I had caught the sound of another engine, to the port side of the Lady Sun, but that soon faded. I wondered briefly if the Pirates had gotten off and left, but conceded that was wishful thinking. These men were probably just the small boarding crew, and now we speedily headed to the pirate nest, where very bad things would happen. I stopped that train of thought and got up to splash water on my face. I was in total mental lock-down. I refused to think of Anna or the princes. Of my horses or my mom. They all made my barrier crack, and I felt the panic rise – so I forced blankness. Nothing.

One minute. Two minutes. Ten minutes. Fifteen. It sounded quiet in the hall. I began to wonder if the guard really was a shadow. With a spurt of bravery – or stupidity – I quietly turned the lock on the handle of the door and opened it slowly. So slowly. Reveal just a hair of a crack, a slim view into the hall. He was there. Dark and shiny and armed – and looking the other way. I almost slammed the door as my bravery/stupidity turned to fear and nausea again, but I forced myself, panting now, to slowly, slowly, close the crack. Turn the lock.

Back on the floor. Stretch. Breathe in. Stretch. Breathe out. One minute. Four minutes. Ten. The tiny porthole in my cabin showed the sunset. I refused to look. It made me tear up again. But the walls of the cabin glowed rosy in the reflected light. I closed my eyes. Conjuring numbers, I counted in twos to a hundred, then threes to a hundred, then fours. After I finished the nines I wished I had my purse with my Sudoku book. It always calmed me and passed time. I went on. Tens to a hundred. Elevens to ninety nine.

I heard something. Someone in the hallway. The machete pirate? A changing of the guard? I stood frozen in the middle of the small room, wanting to rush over to the door, take another peek. Wanting to bar the door, crawl under the blankets. Then a tap, like a knock, and the handle tried to turn. Suddenly my entire world was that handle. It was shiny, and gold, and smooth. And the one thing, with its flimsy lock, that kept me *this* girl. Before the door opened and bad things happened and I became another girl. Not a better Sophia, but a broken Sophia, and I couldn't handle the thought of that.

"Two," I whispered. "Four, six, eight, ten, twelve," A tap again – and my name.

"Sophia!"

I barely made it out, but I knew. It was Lucas. Crazy, gorgeous, stubborn, grumpy, sad, Lucas. Not machete-pirate, or shiny-shadow-gun-pirate. I flew to the door – almost fell in the few steps it took. I couldn't get the lock to turn, I was yanking on the handle and the door *wouldn't open.*

He came for me! He said he would, the stupid, brave, man – and he did, and I CAN'T OPEN THIS STUPID DAMN DOOR! I was screaming in my head now and then stopped. Stood still and counted. *Three, six, nine, twelve, fifteen.* I turned the lock. The door opened easily, quietly, and he was there. I threw myself at him – almost a body slam. I hugged him, and he hugged me back. It seemed like we stood there for long minutes, just taking stock we were both fine, but only seconds had passed.

In a low and clipped voice Lucas whispered in my ear. "We have to go. Get to the raft." He pulled me away from him and stooped so my face was right in front of his. "Listen, Sophia."

I nodded. Mute. Listening. He was so beautiful – my savior. Just for being there when he said he would – he was perfect.

"It's dark now, they won't see us go. I hope it's loud enough they won't hear us. We will have to be fast. Once the raft is over we *have* to be in the water. The ship is moving too fast. If we wait even a moment, we will have to swim to find it. It's dark, we may not – If we lose the raft…" He stopped, and I understood what he was trying to tell me. *We would drown.*

I nodded. Fast. Got it. "Tell me what to do."

Lucas smiled, huge and brilliant in the dim light, and I saw his relief. He must have been worried I would be a blubbering mess, and he would have to drag me, weeping, and toss me over. I felt ashamed for a brief second. While I was counting, and stretching, and not freaking out – he had been planning, and waiting for dark. *To rescue us.* I would not freak out. I owed him at least whatever mettle I had in me to get through this and help him.

"Good." He nodded. "Just get to the railing where the raft is. Stay next to me. Don't make a sound. Don't get seen. Be slow and careful. We have one shot." He looked at me as if asking if I understood him. I did. Perfectly.

"Got it."

He said nothing more, but reached out and squeezed my hand, then turned and stepped into the hallway. As I left the cabin and followed him I had a moment of surprise – I almost shrieked, but choked it down and went on as if nothing were amiss. There, lying on the floor outside the door of Lucas' cabin, lay shiny-shadow-pirate. Minus his gun, which I now noticed was slung over Lucas' shoulder, hanging at his back.

That's fine. I'm glad he has the gun. I almost stepped on the pirate on purpose out of spite, but thought better of it. Due to the dark hallway I couldn't be sure if he was dead or unconscious. There appeared to be no blood that I could see, and Lucas didn't seem like the kind of man who would kill, but then – I didn't know Lucas at all. I realized that fully in that moment. The teasing, the flirting, the drinks. All I knew was his name, and the state he lived in. *And that this man may or may not be dead at his hands.* I stepped over shiny-shadow-pirate and followed Lucas.

Whether I knew him or not, he was still perfect to me.

We snuck up the stairs. Quiet. Slow. At the aft deck we crept to the starboard side. I caught a glimpse of something in the pale light of the runner strips along the back of the ship. *My suitcase. My purse.* Both still sat right where I had left them. I noticed too that Lucas' suitcase lay on its side at the other end of the bench. He'd never taken it to his cabin. *We have to get them.* I reached out and touched Lucas' back. Lightly trying not to startle him. He stopped and leaned in close, making it easy to whisper in his ear.

"Our bags! We need them!" I pointed to where they sat and he shook his head no, turning to continue on. Grabbing his arm this time I pulled him down so my mouth was on top of his ear. "I have food, water, and meds!"

He looked at me and I saw in his eyes he was almost amused at the stash I announced, but too caught up in escape to indulge. He nodded once and quickly and quietly went to his bag. I took the steps over to my end of the bench and expertly slung my purse over my shoulder, putting the strap over my head so that the bag sat on the back of my hip like a messenger satchel. I picked up my suitcase to keep it from rolling and making noise and was back to the railing the same time as Lucas. He said nothing, just carried his suitcase in his arms and went directly to the hatch.

It took Lucas less than three seconds to unlatch the three clasps and open the compartment. I reached into the end where all the life vests sat stacked in the corner and pulled one on. My fingers proved surprisingly steady, and I was able to snap it up quickly. Three clasps. One. Two. Three. Now that I had a goal, something to do, to focus on, I felt settled. Sane. I hoped it lasted, but shoved the thought away and reached and pulled out the rest of the stack.

Lucas focused on dragging out the square of rubber that comprised the life raft, turning it, and looking for the emergency handle. I set aside a life vest for him and tied two vests to the handle of my suitcase, then grabbed his luggage and did the same. In seconds we were ready. We were moving quickly, efficiently, like a team that had practiced this a hundred times. It's funny what one can do with the threat of a gory, machete death, we had been at the railing for less than two minutes.

Lucas drug out the metal box that had been stored at the far end of the compartment and flipped the latches, lifting the lid. Inside was a small motor. *It must go to the life raft! We won't be adrift – we'll actually be able to choose a direction*! I was so excited I almost bounced up and down. I handed him the remaining vests and he tied one through each handle of the box.

Finally, I stood holding my suitcase handle in one hand and his in the other. The wind on my face was warm, the night sky had stars sprinkled across it. *I'm on a boat with pirates and a Cowboy.* I felt like I was in a movie, waiting for my cue, for the director to yell *"Cut."* It seemed all just too surreal.

Lucas looked me up and down as he slipped his arms through his orange vest and fastened the clasps. "We must jump together." He said in a whisper. "Are you ready?"

I nodded. I was ready. I couldn't be *more* ready. Anywhere was better than here. Better than what would happen if we *didn't* jump. Lucas lifted the life raft to the railing. It stood only waist high on me and there were about ten inches of ledge on the other side. I lifted our bags over one at a time and set them on the ledge. Next, I climbed up and sat with my feet over the outside, my hands gripping the rail and the handles at the same time. I didn't feel secure at all and hoped that I didn't plunge into the water before we said 'go'. I pushed that thought aside as well.

We can do this. We will do this. A soft internal chant as I watched Lucas step easily over the rail, the raft balancing on the silver bar on one side, the motor, in its box, on the other.

Lucas looked at me and said in a regular voice to be sure I heard him. "On three. One. Two…"

I stared at his mouth. Perfectly shaped. Soft.

"Three."

Chapter 7

The drop was further than I expected it to be. But the water was warmer.

The splash of two bodies, a couple of suitcases, a raft that inflated almost as it hit, (Lucas

had yanked the handle as he jumped) and a large metal can, crashed loud in my ears. I almost expected the *Lady Sun* to turn around and come after us like a large, sleek-lined whale intent on machete-ing us into tiny pieces and storing our remains in her hull/stomach. But the lights of the Yacht slid away from us, quickly motoring off to the pirate nest – minus two hostages and a yellow raft.

I had only submerged beneath the water a foot or two, then my vest defied gravity and I bobbed to the surface, still holding on to my suitcase. Splashing around me I turned in a slow circle until my hand met the vest that was tied to Lucas' bag. I grabbed it and pulled them both close as I frantically began looking for Lucas and the raft. Yellow was easy to see against the black of the water and the lighter color of star studded sky. Pushing the luggage in front of me, I kicked through the dark water toward the raft.

It was only twenty feet away, I don't know how many nautical miles, or yards, or whatever sailors use to judge distances that is, but I'm an excellent swimmer. The added incentive of getting out of the deep dark ocean – where anything could grab, chomp, lick, or nibble at my legs – was enough to close the distance fast.

I heaved my suitcase over, and then heaved again with Lucas' smaller one and I suddenly felt lighter, even happier, to have achieved a goal. I reached up and grabbed the large rounded sides of the raft. My fingers felt a rope that ran alone the top rim but I ignored it not knowing how securely anchored it was to the rubber. With much kicking and splashing, I was soon plopping into the rubber boat with a splatting sound that on any other day, moment, or time, would have been funny. Now though, I hurried to the other side, crawling on hands and knees to where I could hear Lucas splashing around, still not aboard our tiny, little, plastic, island.

I looked over the side. His dark form was there, he had the metal box, barely afloat, even with the assistance of life vests, pushed up against the side of the raft. It was difficult to make out the shapes and forms of him and his burden, but I understood that he was having trouble pushing it up over the edge inside with me. I reached over and got a handful of vest and yanked. Between the two of us we had the box in the raft in seconds. I managed to lay it on its side, on top of one of its orange vests, where it posed no danger of tearing our island with its sharp corners.

Lucas wrapped his long arms over the edge and hauled himself inside the raft. I scuttled back to the opposite side to keep it from tipping, or the side from dipping too low and letting in anymore salt water. Our load seemed to me, to already be at max for the weight limit. I figured the raft measured barely longer than I am tall, and maybe that wide. *For a sexy, expensive, yacht, they sure skimped on the emergency vessel.*

But I loved the little thing. It was my new best friend. The raft, - that I promptly named Ducky- and Lucas, were my saviors from Pirates and unspeakable things. So I hugged my side of Ducky while Lucas dripped on his side catching his breath.

"We're alive. We made it." I was excited inside, but the words came out a whisper. I was quickly running out of steam. The adrenaline, having run its course, had stripped away with it, strength, and even joy.

"Thank you." I said to Lucas whose dark form seemed like a dripping shadow. I was sure I appeared as a dripping shadow to him too. "For saving me, saving us."

Lucas remained quiet for a minute. Then said "You're welcome."

We both took a moment. The entire escape plan had gone off without a hitch. I counted us lucky beyond belief and then checked that thought. I began to tally all the luck I had been thanking the universe for over the last several days. Lucky window seats - twice. Not missing my connection. Not sitting on passengers. Finding alcohol. Meeting nice people on the plane instead of fat rude men, or screaming children. The weather. The island, - which technically I never reached. The shiny yacht. Cowboy. Weigh all that, and a perfect escape against pirates that would have done things no luck would heal, and I was certain the universe still owed me.

We had escaped yes, but surviving promised to be the next challenge, and we would need lots, and lots of luck to come.

Lucas stirred first. I wondered if he put any stock in luck, or just his mad escape skills. He didn't seem to be inclined to discuss either. "Do you have a light?" He crawled to the metal box and carefully untied its buoys and laid them on the floor of Ducky then set the box on top of them.

"Do I have a light? I promise, Marry Poppins would be jealous of what this bag holds." I pulled my purse strap over my shoulder and unzipped the main pouch. I was shocked the interior proved to be nearly bone dry. Water had soaked into the outside leather of the bag, but inside only a little sea had made its way through the zipper. My purse was added to my list of new best friends.

I began rummaging, watching Lucas open the metal box as my fingers deftly searched for the penlight I knew was in my bag somewhere. I know I sound like a hoarder with the things that I carry in my bag, but I will defend the usefulness of each and every item. The penlight in question, I've used over the years for finding stray chickens that got out at night, to chaining up in the winter to get down my long country road, to finding things inside said purse when my fingers failed me. I mentally identified and cataloged the things I grabbed, but were *not* the pen light. Bottled water, candy bar, wallet, hair clip, rubber band, ball of string one of the princes had tied me up with last week. Pen-light.

"Ah ha!" I brandished my treasure and clicked it on. The light shone bright and steady. I had ordered this specific light off of *Amazon* for its brilliant LED and its sturdiness. I've gone through at least a dozen over the years, as flashlights are a lifeline in the country – especially in winter when the power company is iffy about repairing downed frozen lines. So my light shot across the raft and out to sea for a good many feet before it faded. Lucas knelt, dripping wet, across from me. He had the motor out of the box – and blood was streaming down his arm.

"Oh my god! Lucas, you're bleeding!" Of course he was bleeding. At this part in the film the actress stitches up and bandages the hero and they have a 'moment'. It makes the viewer's respect the damsel, who had been in distress, and humanizes the hero. Always one of my favorite scenes in any Matt Damon movie, and most romances. I crawled carefully over to Lucas and he looked down at his arm. His blue shirt was torn, and then his skin right down along his bicep.

"The box caught me on the way down in the water."

"Does it hurt? Looks like it stings like fire, I'm sure the salt water didn't help."

"Yeah, it made me take a lungful of ocean at the time." He grimaced as he glanced at the blood. "I'll live."

"I can bandage it." Of course I can, the viewers expect it. I shook my head and sat back with a little sigh. This was not a movie and romancing it wouldn't help. I knew we were still in serious trouble, but my mind has its own avenues it travels under stress, so I let the self-admonishment go and looked at dripping Cowboy with pity and real concern. "You really don't want it to get infected, it could make you very sick."

"Ah yes, you have the valued meds. Seriously?"

"Yes, seriously. I can stitch you, or staple you. I can wrap it, disinfect it, and kiss the boo boo to make it all better." I smiled and reached out to pull aside the torn sleeve.

"I thought you were just trying to convince me to save your clothes." He said wryly.

"Really?" I wasn't mad, it's something a woman would do, and a man would *expect* a woman to do. "Well, good thing I like my clothes – and my meds."

Lucas pulled away. "You can treat it, we just need to get this hooked up and running," he nodded to the motor. "Once we're moving you can staple and stitch to your heart's content. I don't think the blood is coming from anything major."

I shrugged, "That's fine, it will help wash out any ocean water that got in the cut anyways. What do we need to do?"

"This anchors there," He indicated two heavy duty plastic rungs at the far end (two feet away) of the raft. "It should simply start up and we can go."

"Really? That sounds almost too easy."

Lucas ignored the comment and lifted the motor into his lap. "Help me hold it onto the rungs while I fasten the bolts. If it goes overboard we'll be paddling."

I pushed the luggage to Ducky's nose end for ballast and shoved the metal box on its orange coasters there as well for good measure. Then I sat at the end of the raft and steadied the motor on its anchors. Lucas slid a long bolt through each anchor loop and secured each bolt end with a clamp that clicked over from the body of the motor. It fit perfectly.

"OK. Head to the nose, we have a lot of weight back here." Lucas wasn't being rude. I could tell he was distracted and concentrating and I obeyed at once. I scrunched myself up to the opposite end of the raft and watched as he found the pull chord and yanked. And yanked. And yanked. I heard him curse but couldn't make out his word of choice. Then he turned to me and held out his hand.

"Light."

I handed him the light. Like a nurse slapping a scalpel into a doctor's hand. He, in turn, shone the light on the motor and turned a cap on top. Once it was removed, it hung, connected by a plastic leash. Lucas shone the light inside.

I saw his chin drop to his chest and then the word of choice again. He clicked off the penlight and sat, his back to the motor, his legs stretched out, our feet meeting in the middle of yellow Ducky's floor.

"No gas."

"No gas?" I wasn't sure if this was an even bigger joke from the universe. *OK, here's the perfect guy, but he's grumpy and not interested. Here's the perfect vacation, but there are pirates. Here's an escape, but you have to paddle.*

"Where the hell is the gas?" A stupid question I knew, but I no longer cared if Lucas or the universe thought I was stupid. Mad was replacing the adrenaline, followed up right behind with frustration.

Lucas closed his eyes and laid his head back against the raft. "On the yacht." He said in a very resigned tone that made me worry – which replaced mad and frustrated. I scooted across the raft toward him.

"I won't even go into my opinion of the yacht owners and their stupid emergency planning abilities. Hand me the light." I held out my hand. Lucas handed me the light. I began searching through my purse again. This time for my little first aid kit, which wouldn't help much for his wound, but I knew it held a small packet of gauze. Further down in my bottomless purse, I found my little bottle of hand sanitizer. I zipped up my best friend and scooted back to Ducky's nose. There I untangled the life vests from my suitcase and unzipped it. Opening the top flap I saw that it was not as lucky as my purse had been. The outer layers were soaking wet, with only a few items in the interior having been spared a salt water bath.

"No wonder the damn thing was so heavy to heave over the side of Ducky." I rummaged through the wet clothes till my hands found a plastic box. It was the size of a lunch box and is waterproof. I never travel without a med kit. I have one for my truck, my home and even one in my barn. I'm always having to band aid, or stitch someone, or something. (The *thing* being my stubborn horses that like the neighbor's stallion enough to bang themselves through gates to get to his sexy self.)

The kit I had brought with me had sutures, and a small stapler that could be used on animals or humans. I had only ever stapled animal skin with it. It also held a scalpel, a couple pill bottles for pain or allergy, along with miscellaneous med stuff I had gathered over the years and stuffed in there. I took out a strip of heavy duty butterfly tape that would act as stitching, and some antibiotic ointment. That and a roll of bandage tape would have to do.

I took my hoard of supplies back to Lucas who now sat watching me with a strange expression. I paused and caught his eye. He didn't look away, and I didn't know what to say. I assumed he was tired or defeated. He looked tired, but as I looked closer only a little defeated. He kept staring.

"You're not what I thought." He said quietly.

"This is the moment" I smiled and scooted to sit beside him, returning to the movie again and the 'bonding moment' the viewers expected. I pulled his torn sleeve back and rolled the material out of my way to reveal the long slash down his arm.

"What moment?"

I shook my head and sighed. "Never mind, ignore me, just saltwater on the brain. Does it hurt?" I pressed my fingers alongside the cut. The bleeding had stopped. A good sign at least. He was quiet a moment longer, but didn't answer my question when he spoke again.

"I thought you were a socialite. A silly rich girl with too much money and time on her hands. I'm sorry I judged you."

"Well, we all judge." I squeezed some antibacterial onto my fingers. "Don't scream, this will sting." I lightly ran the clear gooey stuff down the line of the cut. He cringed and hissed out his breath, but there were no screams. So far, so good.

"Can you hold the light? I'll need both hands for the bandage." Lucas took the light in his other hand and held it pointing toward the cut, careful not to shine the beam in my eyes. "I don't mind that you judged me." I glanced at him. His blue eyes seemed to glow in the LED. It briefly crossed my mind if my blue eyes were the same shade as his. One tends not to stare at their own eyes so I couldn't remember off hand if they were as pretty, but I didn't think so. I shrugged and looked back at his cut.

"I can come off as a socialite *and* silly, but rich? No. Time? Only because I paid every penny I had to get here, and now, with our given situation, I'm positive we both *way* overpaid for the experience."

He chuckled softly. It was a nice sound, and I relaxed as I wiped away blood with a piece of clean gauze. I began applying the butterflies, pinching the skin together as I went, hoping they held because it took eight of them to finish the entire cut and that was all I had. If they came off it would be staple, or needle.

"Why did you come on this trip?" His voice was low and close to my ear. It held sincerity.

I looked up at his face. He leaned so near me, our brows almost touched and I could feel his breath on my cheek. A shiver ran through me in reminder that this man had a very physical effect on me.

"Truth?" I asked.

"Truth."

"Escape." I didn't embellish. I knew I was just escaping life and the everyday reminder of my failed marriage. My lonely farm was the only thing to occupy my days. The need to escape what everyone else thought I should do, be, say, had been the impetus behind the decision. "Why did you come?"

Lucas looked away for a moment and then turned back again. I finished fixing the last piece of tape and sat back. Looking him squarely in the eyes. *Tit for tat.* He had evaded every personal question I had asked him up until this moment and I wondered if he would be honest now. He surprised me when he answered with no evasion, and with perfect frankness.

"Today is my tenth anniversary. This was supposed to be the honeymoon we never had." He shrugged his shoulder and grimaced at the pain the movement caused. "It's actually fitting though," He said, and I thought I detected a touch of humor in his voice. "The vacation is as much of a disaster as our marriage ended up being."

I mulled over his words for a moment before I replied. I didn't want his honesty to be dismissed, he was clearly going through something in his life I'm familiar with. Divorce. The sense of failure, all the questions of why didn't it work? Were all the years wasted? Why couldn't love be enough? It's a tough road. One half of American couples walk it if you can trust the statistics. But statistics aside, for each person it's different, but it always hurts.

"I'm sorry Lucas." I knew better than to pry. I had hated the prying people when I left Jon. There were always questions I didn't want to answer, and really, I couldn't. To this day, I *had* no answers. Sometimes shit happens and we just have to survive. But as appropriate as that little nugget of wisdom was to our current situation, I didn't think it would be something Lucas would want to hear.

We still sat close to each other, and I reached out and laid my hand on his knee. "Ten years is a long time. Mine lasted six." I squeezed his knee lightly and let go. "It does get better. Easier."

"How long has it been for you?" Lucas looked at me with real interest. It was almost unnerving after our day of cat and mouse play, with my pursuit of a picture and some friendly banter. *My god, it's only been a day.* Half *a day.* It seemed like a week had already gone by and I realized I had grown very, very tired. Jet lag, and sun, and panic. Adrenaline and jumping off a ship. Etc. etc. etc. I wanted to just curl up, go to sleep and wake up in my own bed. I leaned back against the raft and closed my eyes.

"It has been two years. His name is Jon. I call him Snake." I opened an eye and saw he too had leaned back, his face pointed up toward the stars.

We were quiet for a while. The raft floated along with a slight lulling motion that was soothing, barely perceptible on the calm black sea. My body began to relax and the siren call of sleep teased my eyes closed. I could hear Lucas' breathing and feel the warm, gentle breeze on my face. The night air caressed my skin, but my clothing and hair were still wet. My braids remained magically intact so the wet hair wouldn't bother me much, but my pants clung to my legs and my tank was chilling even with the light breeze. Now with no adrenaline or movement, with a moment to be still, I realized how uncomfortable I was – and how exhausted.

"Lucas" I rolled my head to face him, still lying back against the side of Ducky. "Do you think they will come back?"

"No. I don't expect so."

His eyes were still closed and he hadn't moved. I wondered what he was thinking. Had his mind turned to his wife and the failure he'd flown thousands of miles to escape, or forget. We never forget. We can ignore, and deny, but memory has a way of keeping us in the trap of life. It happened. Jon happened. I wondered what his wife's name was. *Is* I corrected. She hadn't died; she was just out there – somewhere. Living her life.

"We're of no value to them. They wanted the yacht." Lucas continued with the line of conversation, reasoning away any attempt the pirates may make toward our demise. "Maybe something that was aboard. It would be costly for them to turn around and search for us. I think they won't."

"What about shiny shadow pirate?" I saw the dark skinned man in my mind, lying still and quiet like a puddled shadow on the hall floor. I wanted to ask Lucas if he had killed him. If he had it in him to kill. I didn't know how that would make me feel.

Lucas had opened his eyes and was looking at me now. He knew what I was thinking, I saw it in his eyes. I just looked back and waited for him to answer.

"The death of one pirate wouldn't be enough to risk their catch. They were after a prize, I can't imagine revenge will sway them from keeping with their plan." He didn't look away. I wondered how much of my face he could see, we were still close, only a foot apart, had he seen me flinch at the word 'death'?

"*So he was dead.*" I whispered it. A statement not a question. An acceptance of what I already guessed to be true.

Lucas turned slightly to face me. He sat up straight and reached out and took my hand. It was warm, and as dry as before we made our plunge. I briefly wondered how he managed to shed the ocean and become this warm when *I* had goose bumps rising on my skin in the breeze. I realized that the goose bumps had popped up with his touch. When he ran his thumb along the back of my hand a chill went up my spine. I sat still, looking at him.

"He would have raped you Sophia. He most likely would have killed you. Or he would have handed you to the other men who would have done worse things and you would have wished he *had* killed you."

I realized it was true. I kill spiders and snakes on my farm. Lots of them. Not because I hate spiders and snakes, even though I really don't like them much, especially the spiders. But because I balanced out a long time ago, that I could let them live, and hope to live in peace with nature, but nature does what it's made to do. Snakes and spiders will bite and their bites can kill. I love my horses, my dogs, and myself. The fear of having to rush one of the princes, or my little niece, to the hospital for a snakebite that I might have been able to prevent, is all the justification I need. I don't kill them because I am a killer. I do it to survive. Just as Lucas had done what he needed to, to help us both survive. I didn't feel mad or shocked or horrified, I understood and in that understanding I was grateful.

I reached out and held his hand in both of mine. Giving a light squeeze I smiled, not knowing if he could see or not. "I know." I assured him. "Thank you."

We sat like that for a while. The breeze picked up with the drop in temperature and I shivered. Lucas ran his warm hands up my arms and back down again.

"You're cold." He leaned forward, reaching toward the suitcase nearest his feet. "Do you have a jacket in your bag?"

"It's no use Lucas," I waved at the bags, "they're soaked through. Nothing is dry inside." I suspected that by now, the wet clothes on the outside layers had surely seeped to the inner layers that had only been damp.

He turned back toward me and his shape blocked out the sprinkle of stars behind him. *Such a large man,* I mused. *Built like he can carry the weight of the world with shoulders that reach across the sky.* I shook my head and wrapped my arms around myself. I was tired and my mind was rambling again.

"Should we try to sleep? I don't think we will get much done in the dark."

Lucas sighed and slid closer. "Yes, we should sleep." He pulled me against him, his light shirt still damp, but warm from his body. I curled into him with my arms still wrapped around myself, and his arms wrapped around me, and closed my eyes.

I felt strangely safe suddenly. I was adrift at sea with a stranger. There was no telling if the sunrise would bring hope, and I had no idea if we would stay on this raft named Ducky until we perished at sea, or, if by some miracle, we would be rescued. But as sleep began taking hold, I relaxed my body against this stranger who had saved me and breathed in the scent of him I was finally able to name. Beneath the salt water and scent of the sea, Lucas smelled like fields, and sunshine, and leather, and comfort. Home.

Chapter 8

Lady Sun

I awoke before the dawn with a cramped neck and one foot completely asleep. The sky had lightened to a gray-blue, hinting at yellow directly in front of me, beyond the nose of the raft.

I didn't move. Not wanting to wake Lucas, who lay with his arms still wrapped over my shoulders, and his hands clasped under my right elbow. I flexed the muscles in my leg trying to wake up my foot, wincing at the rush of pins and needles the movement brought. But I kept at it, flexing and releasing, adjusting slightly and relaxing against Lucas' chest as the sun began to lighten the horizon with a brilliant orange gold. The yellow slowly washed away all the gray, until finally, the sky was crisp, and blue, and the giant star was blinding me, tearing up my eyes and immediately warming my skin. It would be another hot day on the equator.

The rising sun and new day infused me with hope. In the dark, the night before, I hadn't been able to see, or think, or plan. But now, I felt a surge of need. Need to plan, organize, figure out and achieve a goal. Overcome the challenge. *I will not perish at sea.* This would be my new mantra.

Slowly, I untangled my arms from myself, and began pulling away from Lucas, careful not to rock Ducky. We sat high enough above the water that the ocean wouldn't slosh in with a little rocking, but I wanted to assess myself and center my intentions, before Lucas woke up. No more panicking, no more chasing of the gorgeous cowboy. He was unobtainable, and I was more concerned with survival than romance. I may be a woman, and do silly female things from time to time, but I was far from stupid. I needed to prioritize the day and hope to find a way to get the hell off of Ducky. "Sorry Ducky" I gave the yellow raft a pat as I scooted away from Lucas, who had stirred with my leaving, but still seemed to be sleeping.

I maneuvered myself around until I had my back tucked into the nose of the raft and the sun behind me. I then carefully tugged the two suitcases within reach, pushing the metal box that had held the motor still on its coasters, to the middle of the raft and along the side. As far out of the way as could be managed. There wasn't much room to assign spots for everything but I always function better when items have their place to be, and they stay there until needed. As I unzipped my suitcase I saw that Lucas was watching me. I wondered how long he had been awake. I had only been fiddling about for less than ten minutes, but the movement must have been enough to wake him up.

I smiled and gave a little wave. "Good morning!" I said cheerily. "Coffee?"

He laughed. An actual real laugh, and I stared at him in surprise. I hoped he hadn't gotten feverish and sick with his cut. The offer of coffee wasn't really *that* funny. For me, it was heartbreaking torture, but I went with it and smiled again. "How's your arm?"

Lucas pulled himself to a sitting position and looked down at the bandage that was still securely adhered to his bicep. He flexed it carefully and turned to look at me. "Good job doctor. No need to amputate."

"Oh my god, you do have a sense of humor!" I gave him a thumbs up and went back to unzipping my suitcase. "I was concerned you may have lost it in the war or something."

Lucas stretched and rolled his head from side to side, working out cramps. "Well, there's nothing funnier than an offer of coffee while lost at sea with a pretty woman and no hope of rescue." He scrubbed his hands over his face and took a deep breath, blowing it out as he closed his eyes and let the sun warm his face.

I paused in my sorting and stared at him "You think I'm pretty? Wait, you think there's no hope?" My heart had skipped at his offhand pretty comment, but then sank with the *no hope of rescue.* I was praying he was being flippant, we needed hope, hopeless was next to giving up and dying, and there was no way I was allowing that. *Lucas can sit in his corner of futility, but I am going to hope and pray and paddle if that's what it takes.*

"Yes." He said. His voice was soothing, and I looked up from my pile of wet clothes to see he was looking at me kindly. "You are pretty. Beautiful really, whether I say it or not, you're just made that way. And no," He shook his head, still speaking gently, "I don't really think there's no hope. We can't be far from an island chain or at least a shipping lane. We just have to be patient and careful and we will be fine."

I wondered if he was being nice all of a sudden because he didn't want me to flip out and have to deal with a crazy lady on a raft. But as I studied him, his face glowing in the sun, his expression easy and calm, I realized he meant what he said and he was genuinely being kind.

"Wow." I let the handful of wet clothes drop back into the suitcase. "Thanks." I gave him a big genuine smile. "I'm relieved we are on the same page. Both counts too, your pretty stunning yourself, especially with that bandage, it makes you look tough. And yes, we *will* get rescued, or find a ship. I can be as patient as it takes, even without my morning coffee."

"So we're agreed." He leaned forward to peer in the suitcase I had been pulling clothes out of.

I held out my hand to shake. "Agreed."

His hand clasped mine, and he gave it a shake, then chuckled lightly as he asked, "So really, no coffee?"

Something he had just said registered in my mind suddenly. He had mentioned shipping lanes. My hand squeezed his tightly. "Oh my god! Ships!"

"Yes ships." Lucas peered at me, curious, "What about ships?"

"What you said, about shipping lanes, I read there are only two of them in this area, through the Indian Ocean, along the equator."

I was still squeezing his hand, and I saw he looked concerned, "Uh, yeah Sophia, ships. OK."

"No, pretty Lucas, you don't understand." I let go of his hand and scrambled toward him -- toward my purse that sat on his end of the raft. "I have a book, it tells about the ships, the book has maps! We can figure out where we are!"

Lucas grabbed me around the waist and plopped me back down on my side of the raft. "Easy, let's not get too excited and capsize before you reach said rescue." He grabbed my purse and heaved it into my lap. "Holy cow Sophia, do you always travel with cannonballs?"

"Oh, you may laugh now Cowboy," I said excitedly as I unzipped my purse, "but this baby holds many a treasure you'll be happy I lugged onto this little plastic island."

Lucas leaned forward to peer inside while I dug around in the depths, finding and pulling out my book on the Maldives. "No coffee in there, huh?"

"No, but I will buy you the biggest latte ever when we get home, here!" I thrust the book in front of his face almost hitting him in the nose. "Find Us!"

"Find us?" He took the book and flipped through the pages. He appeared as interested as I was to have anything to reference our current situation, but not nearly as excited.

"Yes, find us!" I jabbed my finger at a page that had opened to a map of the Indian Ocean and the Maldives atoll chain.

"Sophia there isn't a red dot that says 'you are here.' Look around, what reference am I supposed to use?" He looked at the map and then out to the open sea.

I could tell he was indulging me now. That he was trying to explain that the map meant nothing, but I didn't believe him, I knew there had to be a way that this book could help us. He just had to figure it out.

"Use the sun, see, that's east." I pointed to the big ball of burning heat in the sky. I was completely dry now, the morning was hot already and promised to creep to scorch levels by mid-day.

"Yes, I know, that's the sun, and hence east, but still, Sophia," He took my arm and settled me back to sitting. I had risen to my knees in my frustration to get him to see hope my way. "I will check out the map, I know where we were when the pirates boarded, and the direction we took after that. I 'm pretty sure we traveled for about an hour, hour and a half and we drifted for about eight hours overnight. So with all that information I will try for you, but frankly, when I booked this vacation, I was told there would be no math."

I was stunned into silence for a brief second, and then I laughed. I plopped back against Ducky's nose and laughed until it turned into a giggle. "OK." I gasped, finally settling down. I lay there looking at him, shining in the hot sun, holding the book with the useless map, and a small smile on his face. "I see that what you are trying to explain to me, in your funny cowboy way, is that my book is not, in fact, a ticket off this raft."

Lady Sun

He nodded. "Not a ticket."

I put my hands over my face and lay there, my elbows propped on the sides of the raft, the back of my head growing warm in the beating sun. Then I sighed. And sat back up. "All right, you win. There will be no math."

"I'm not saying I's not useful Sophie."

He called me '*Sophie.*' Like we were friends, and this was just another chat we would have over coffee, or sitting at a bar with friends. It made me feel happy, so I didn't say anything, I just looked at him as he went on.

"Let's continue with what you were doing," he indicated the suitcase with the pile of half damp clothes. "Let's take stock and make a plan, figure out what we have, what we can do."

"And keep hope." I said simply.

"Yes. Keep hope. I will look at the map, we can study it and figure out if it has any ticket potential."

I gave him a light punch on his good shoulder. "OK. Lucas. Good plan"

We began pulling out our treasured belongings. I lay my wet items of clothing carefully along the side of the raft to dry and then turned to emptying out my purse. As I pulled out the bottles of beer Lucas let out a low whistle.

"Of all the women in the entire world to get trapped on a raft with, I get the one who brings beer." He knelt in front of his suitcase, his hands full of wet clothing staring at the pile of stash I had been stacking in my lap. He looked at me, his blue eyes sparkling, "I think I love you Sophia... what's your last name?"

I grinned proudly hugging the beer to my chest. "Canon."

"Sophia Canon. So is that an everyday item, along with, what is that a frog?" He pointed to the plastic frog that sat on my knee.

"I got the beer to celebrate on the beach once we got to our castaway island. The frog is my friend." I carry toys with me because the princes and my sisters little girl were always treasure hunting in my purse when I went to visit. It gave them something safe to play with if they were fussy in a restaurant. It's not like I could give them my car keys.

"I'll be your friend if you share your beer with me." Lucas winked and went back to sorting his wet clothes, laying them alongside the sundresses and shorts I had lined around the edge of Ducky.

"Let's save the alcohol for a celebration when we get rescued. It will dehydrate us and we don't want that. Friend."

"You have alcohol?"

I laughed and looked at him, "OK, let's tally up our stuff so we both know, what we both have."

He laid his last item of wet clothing over the motor and sat down with his back against it.

"OK. I'll go first since my list is clearly, shorter than yours. I have no frogs, but I do have…" he leaned forward and drug the gun that had been tucked safely behind the metal box along the edge of the raft overnight. "An AK-47 with," he paused as he took out the clip of the angry looking rifle and counted the bullets out into his hand, pushing them from the spring loaded clip with his thumb. "twelve rounds."

"Well, it's nice to know we can defend ourselves from pirates and sharks. Maybe we could shoot a fish or a bird. Are you a good shot?"

He looked at me quizzically. "I am better than decent. How about you?"

"I'm just decent." I smiled. "What else you got?"

He reached into his suitcase that was now empty of clothing, and pulled out a medium sized knife in a leather sheath. Next he retrieved a leather satchel that he unsnapped and dumped into the bottom of the suitcase. "So." he summarized. "I have a gun, twelve rounds, and a knife. Some fishing line and a hook, although the line is only about twenty feet and not a very strong test, so no big fish would be hauled in on it. A magnifying glass, a small pair of binoculars," he continued, "a coffee cup," he held up a small insulated metal cup, "a multi-tool, a knife sharpener, a little tablet and pen, and a pack of gum. Plus there's my shaving kit with my toothbrush and razor and such. Oh, and this." He held up a large thermos water bottle. "I've had this for years. I don't know why I put it in my suitcase, just habit I guess."

At least we have a little more water than I thought. I began a mental list of positives, attributing nothing to luck. Luck was a bitch, I refused to acknowledge her anymore. "So, two questions; why do you carry a magnifying glass, aren't you a little old to be setting ants on fire, and why are bullets called rounds? I never understood that."

He shrugged, "Well the magnifying glass was given to me by my uncle when I was ten, it ended up in the bag and I never took it out. As for the rounds, there are a couple of answers for that. The nickname *round* started when they were. Round I mean. They were lead balls, even stone, sometimes, and so they were called rounds, or balls. Also a bullet has many parts, the lead that is fired is at the head of the casing, which is packed with powder and has a firing cap inside to ignite the explosive when the firing pin in the gun strikes it. So I don't know really, because technically if we call it a round, we are only referring to one part of the bullet. Makes no sense. I just do what the other guys tell me to do." He shrugged and pointed at my pile. "Your turn."

I looked down at my lap and realized it was going to be a long list with quite a few useless items but forged ahead anyway. "I have two bottles of water, two beers, a bottle of vodvka, a Mai tai, a Mudslide and a Pina Colada."

"Jesus, seriously Sophie. How about we celebrate now that we escaped the pirates, why wait?"

I shooed his hands away as he reached for the Pina Colada. "No. Bad Lucas. I have five candy bars, two bags of nuts and a package of peanut butter crackers that may have been smooshed." I held up the cracker package. The contents were mostly crumbs, but I set it in the food pile. We would relish those crumbs, I was sure.

"I have a ball of string," I felt myself getting choked up, recalling Prince Anthony tying my hands to a chair, what was it, five, no, six days ago. I moved on quickly, "a hair clip, a rubber band, a wallet, a flashlight, dental floss, tooth brush and tooth paste. My makeup bag, and a brush, two pens, one broken pencil, a small notepad, and car keys" I took a deep breath and forged on with the rest, even I was astonished at how much stuff I had crammed into my bag. "I have sunglasses, chap-stick, a bottle of sunscreen, fingernail clippers, a multi-tool, a lighter and a half

empty pack of *tic tacs*." Which I set in the stack of food items. Between the two of us we boasted

two phone charger chords and the chord to my tablet, but I didn't bother counting those aloud. "I

think that's it. Other than my tablet which has been dead since my flight out of London and my

phone. Also dead." I looked around to be sure I hadn't dropped or missed anything, "Oh! And

our mascot the frog, whom we will call Freddie and will bring us luck." I gently laid Freddie on

Lucas' knee and gave the green head a friendly pat.

Lucas took Freddie and put him in his shirt pocket. The little green nose poked out and

made the pocket bulge, but I thought it was nice Lucas hadn't dismissed our good luck charm.

"My phone has no service," Lucas pulled an old style flip phone from his jeans pocket. "I

checked on the boat last night after we were marched to our cabins, even if it did, it succumbed to

a saltwater death last night." He tucked the phone into his damp suitcase and turned back to stare

at our hoard. "We'll have to be stingy with the water and the food." Lucas seemed impressed at

the stack our combined items made. "But our first order of business should be getting all this

packed up and secured so if there is an emergency or a storm we don't lose any of it."

"Agreed." I said. I began pulling my now dry clothing, off the edges of the raft. A few

pieces were still damp and I shook them out, letting the sun do its work, before folding it and

putting into the suitcase. After twenty minutes the raft was back in order and I sported a sundress

wrapped around my head to ward off the heat that had caused a headache to creep into the front of

my skull. I insisted that Lucas do the same with a white t-shirt out of his bag. I passed the bottle

of sunscreen to him after rubbing some on all the exposed area I found on myself. After he

obeyed, and put the white lotion on his face, arms and neck, proclaiming all the while that only

women used sunscreen, I then took out a bottle of water. We each took a mouthful, wishing we

could guzzle it down, but knowing we needed to ration. I gauged how many mouthfuls a bottle

would render before returning the warm liquid to my purse. Not many.

Lucas fetched the book that was, so far, not our ticket off the raft, and began flipping

through each page. He scanned the pages as he went. I assumed he hoped he would stumble upon answers, or hope, or guidance. While he read, I carefully pulled back the corner of the bandage on his arm and checked his wound. It didn't seem swollen or infected and the butterflies had all held through the night. By the time I sat back down in the nose of the raft to stare at Lucas while he read, it was late morning and the sun burned high in the sky.

It beat down on us relentlessly. No shelter and no breeze, no relief, just heat and a view of either miles and miles of deep blue water, or Lucas, who sat engrossed in my book. I chose the latter and sat studying him, trying to sum him up in my mind.

Yesterday at the travel agents office, he had seemed withdrawn and aloof, and later, on the *Lady Sun*, Lucas had been determined to rebuff my friendship. *Even if I had been a rich silly socialite, there's a modicum of politeness that all humans afford each other.* He had been set on keeping me beyond arm's length. I figured at the time, he must be one of those grumpy travelers, or moody men, who won't admit that they're moody, but when things don't go their way, they throw quiet tantrums and make everyone else miserable. *Of course he hadn't been* that *bad*, I admonished myself. I *was* being a little pushy, and kind of stalkerish. I decided, that Lucas must have been strung out from two days of flying. It couldn't have been comfortable for him to fold his long form into a small airline seat, and endure sixteen - plus hours, of the cramped position. *And no telling who he was seated beside. Maybe he hadn't been lucky enough to encounter a male version of Sasha like I had, or even a female version.* Most flights I've taken over the years inevitably placed me next to some real crackpots, and none too-few smelly, and annoying passengers. Without my cheery travel attitude, I would have been grumpy too at the end of one of those flights. *Not to mention being twice my size and not being able to find a comfortable position.*

Today, and last night in the raft, Lucas had been kind, even funny, and handled me well with my exuberance, and my insistence of finding us on the map. He had to be worried too, and hurting, and hungry, and neither of us had coffee, but he was behaving as a really nice guy. I studied him closer as he flipped through the pages, holding up the book on the page with the map and glancing around us, perhaps looking for a compass in the sky or any sign at all that might give him a reference to where our little raft drifted.

He had dark hair, a dark brown that curled naturally and flipped out a bit at his neckline. His eyes were that crisp, clear blue that made me think he could see what I was thinking when he looked at me. He was tall, that I had noted before, but not skinny. I wouldn't call him wiry either, his long arms and legs were well wrapped in muscle and from what I had felt beneath his shirt as I lay against him last night, his chest was well wrapped as well. *A tall, strong, pretty man.* The stubble on his face would turn to a beard in another day or two, it had red streaks in it, a throwback from some Irish heritage I guessed, but my eyes kept wandering to his mouth. His smile flashed straight white teeth each time he let one slip, but his lips looked soft, inviting, and I began fantasizing about how he would taste. I had already become addicted to his scent, the comfort and warmth of it. I wondered if his taste would compare. Looking up from his mouth, I saw he had caught me looking, and was staring at me in much the same way. I shrugged and grinned.

"You're the best view I have."

He didn't move, or respond. He just kept looking. I wondered what was going through his mind. If he still thought I was silly. If he wondered what *I* tasted like. *Stop it Sophia, no romance. Just survival.* But it was hard to not look, not to wonder. Our eyes locked and a slow smile began to warm his face. It reached all the way up to his eyes where the creases there crinkled in slight crow's feet and his dimples flashed making me smile in return.

"What?"

"You're the only woman I've met, who manages to look sexy without having showered in three days and with a dress wrapped around her head."

I grinned and reached up to touch my turban. "Wow, that's a really nice thing to say." I almost blushed when he said *sexy*, but clamped down on the flush and tilted my head, still staring at him. "How long has it been for you Lucas? Since your Divorce."

His smile faded and I almost regretted asking, but he had asked me, and I wanted to know how far along he was in his healing.

"Six months." He set the book aside and turned his full attention to me. "It's been six months. And I know you are right. It does get easier, has *been* getting easier." He looked out to sea. "When I got here, to the Maldives," he waved his hand toward the north, "I was hurting. We planned this trip for over a year, every detail and penny. We had saved up and looked forward to it. Then sometime last year she started to grow distant, and, well," He paused, took a breath and turned to face me again." She met someone else, got pregnant with his child, and left me."

"Oh!" I clapped a hand over my mouth. I'm sure my expression showed pity and shock, but that was just awful. He loved her. She hurt him.

"God, that is really terrible." I finally said. "Why did you come on this trip? You had to know it would hurt."

"Yes, I knew. But I wanted it to." He shrugged, "I wanted all the hurts to be done and over with, get them out of the way. The trip was non-refundable. I took a loss on her ticket, but didn't care. Mostly, I didn't want to be in the same town when her baby was born."

"My god." I whispered. "No wonder you were having a bad day yesterday. And here I was, some silly socialite, not letting you brood. Sorry about that."

"I'm not. Don't apologize." He shook his head and leaned toward me slightly. I couldn't read his expression, but I thought he looked... happy. "You're the first thing to make me smile in a really long time Sophie. Even in this raft, even if we get out of this and go home and we never see each other again, I'm grateful I got stuck here with you. It put things in perspective." He reached out and touched the turban on my head. "I'm glad the pirates didn't take your exuberance."

Leaning back again, he picked up the book and beckoned for me to join him on his side of the raft. "I think I may have found something in here."

"Really! You found us?" I had been distracted by his comment that we would never see each other again if we got rescued. *When* we got rescued, I quickly corrected. The thought depressed me, but his announcement of having found a clue pushed that thought aside.

"Maybe, look." He pointed a finger to the bottom of the map. "We started up here, and took the Lady Sun to here." He indicated the last atoll in the chain. "Then the pirates boarded and we came down this way." He ran his finger into open water. "I have no idea how fast we're drifting or where the currents run to, but it's a good bet we're somewhere in this area." He drew a small circle with the tip of his finger, "Which, according to page thirty two, is one of the two shipping lanes in this area."

"You did it!" I hugged him, wrapping both arms around his neck, then leaned back, still hugging him, and kissed him soundly on his cheek. "And no math, so your brain should be just fine." I felt his chuckle in my own chest, pressed up against him as I was, and the vibration set off a chain reaction in me. I loosened my grip and began to pull away just as his hands came up behind my back. We were staring at each other again and I felt an overwhelming urge to put my mouth on his, to taste how warm it must be. To press against his body, feel the strength in him, borrow his heat, and sweet scent, and be home for a moment. But I didn't move. I didn't know what to do. We might ruin everything, the companionship we found, the partnership, by attempting something that was surely doomed. He was a wounded man and I wasn't going to be the one to put us in an awkward place when we had no way to escape each other.

I drew back from him, all my senses screaming at me to go the other way. *Kiss him, taste him, grab him.* My chest was growing tight with the sudden draw and desire I had for this moment to become something else entirely.

Lucas didn't let go. His eyes were on my mouth and he ran a hand up the small up my back, pressing me closer till I was back where I had been, my chest pressed against his and my arms wrapped around his neck. He didn't move further. I dropped my head toward him and laid my brow against his.

We sat there, less than an inch between our mouths and neither one of us moved. I was suddenly too warm. I could hear my heartbeat, I felt his through my breasts, and the flood of desire and need that hit me, made me gasp. I let go of his neck and ran my hands down to the front of his chest, then slowly up to his shoulders.

"Lucas," I whispered. "We…" I didn't know what I was going to say. I just couldn't stay like that a moment longer. My insides were roiling, and reason was quickly escaping the decision making realm of my brain.

"Shouldn't." He finished for me. But he didn't move.

His breath was warm against my mouth and his skin was like touching the sun. I took a breath, and then slowly, I sat back. My hands ran down his arms, over the bandage on one side till they ended in his grasp. I was practically panting. I hadn't been with a man in two years, but in this moment, I was more aroused with Lucas than through my whole marriage to the Snake. I didn't want to let go, so I sat holding his hands, and he sat calmly looking at me. I could see the pulse in his neck, it was keeping time with my own, and so he too must be affected. That comforted me. I didn't want to feel like the floozy again. *At least the attraction is mutual.* But I still didn't know what to do, or want to let go.

The weather decided for us. In a split second, water was pouring from the sky.

Chapter 9

I was so startled I let out a little scream, and we both looked up to see big thick clouds sweeping in from the west. The sun still shone from the east, and the air weighed as hot as ever. It was such a strange sensation to be drenched by warm rain while the sun still lit up the day.

Lucas was laughing and still looking at me. He pulled me forward by my hands that were still clasped in his and said in a seductive voice, "Our first shower together. Got any soap?"

I pushed back and threw him an exasperated look. The rain had put a halt to whatever had been brewing between us, but had in no way doused the fire.

"No soap, but I'll definitely enjoy the shower."

We laughed like kids as we moved around the raft that was now slick, and shiny with rain. I had never experienced such a torrential downpour before. It brought weight to the term 'raining buckets'. Within minutes, the raft began to hold water, and we both realized that the storm represented both a curse, and a boon.

As quickly as possible, I piled all of the life vests on top of the luggage, to attempt to keep it dry. Lucas pulled the metal can to the middle of the raft and opened the lid, letting it capture as much rain as possible to save for drinking water. I noticed that Ducky had begun holding water. I was sure it would take forever to dry out, and the extra weight would threaten the raft's ability to carry our load. I stripped off my tank and quickly began sopping up the water on the bottom of the raft and wringing it out over the side. I hesitated briefly, thinking perhaps I should wring it out in the metal can, but the water it was not very clean. With the salt in my tank, and mine and Lucas' dirty shoes, the rain water would probably make us sick and defeat the purpose in the end if we threw it all up. So I went back to sopping and wringing. My tank was so small it didn't

seem to be doing much good so I stripped the dress off my head and began using it. The cotton of

the dress held much more water, and soon I appeared to be making some progress.

Lucas had joined me in my attempt to bail. He had both the shirt off his back, and the one

off his head, sopping up the large puddle in Ducky's bottom. Glancing up briefly, I caught sight

of him. Stripped to the waist with the bandage on his arm flashing white against tan skin. He was

a true sight to behold. I had been right. His body boasted well wrapped muscle all over. It was

distracting and beautiful, like watching a work of art, or an opening scene to porn, I couldn't

decide. I came to my senses and realized I had been sitting, staring, when he stopped and stared

back at me. I gave him a sheepish grin, and ducking my head, I went back to sopping up water

with my dress and wringing. Sopping and wringing.

The storm moved quickly. As suddenly as the sky had opened up and dumped, it just as

suddenly turned off the faucet.

I finished wringing out the dress and took a break for a moment. The sun was still shining

strong. The storm moved northeast, and not one cloud blocked the rays of the hot ball of fire that

now turned the air into a warm wet mass, making it hard to breath.

Lucas was grinning, kneeling in the middle of what was left of the puddle, shining with his

wet skin, and those damn distracting muscles. I threw my dress at him and it landed with a splat

against his chest.

"Well, now I've had the shower you said I needed." I fished around for my tank, found it

beneath my legs where I was kneeling and rolled to the side to pull it loose. The raft was slippery,

now that it was wet, and I went sprawling, sliding straight into Lucas' knees.

Laughing, and moving very carefully, Lucas closed the lid on the metal box and slid it

toward the back of the raft on its life vest water sled. Then, still kneeling, towering above me, he

leaned down and placed and hand on either side of my waist.

"You look cleaner." His hair was dripping, the drops were landing on my face. I lay

smiling and half laughing, on my back in a puddle, in a raft, half-dressed, beneath a half-dressed man. It was actually fun for that brief second, no worries of death and doom, no thoughts of starvation, or thirst, or rescue. Just this view of Lucas and the warm bath I lay in.

A drop landed on my mouth, sliding down my lower lip, I licked it off and Lucas tensed. The fun suddenly turned back into the moment just before the rain had started. We were trapped again, where I couldn't move toward him, and he wouldn't move away.

Lucas' arms straddled my sides, his body leaning over me, blocking the sun. His eyes were roaming, taking in my wet form, and I suddenly realized I was wearing all white. White bra, white pants, white panties. I may as well have been nude for all the coverage my wet clothing provided, and he saw that. It was clear by the change in his expression and the sudden stillness in him. His eyes traveled back to mine.

Another drop fell, it landed on my top lip this time and as I parted my lips to let it slide in my mouth, Lucas lowered his head and caught it. His mouth closed over my upper lip, warm and soft and tasting of salt and rain. I had nowhere to go, I couldn't back away. I didn't want to tell him this was a bad idea because this was all my body was screaming to do. My hands reached up to his chest, damp and warm, firm and wide. He pulled his head back far enough to see my eyes clearly, and I knew he was offering me a way out. To say no. To answer the question his mouth had posed without words, but with the sharing of that raindrop.

I was powerless to do anything but what my body commanded, and then I stopped attempting reason altogether. The scent of him surrounded me, and I reached my hands into his hair, pulling his mouth back down to mine. He came willingly, and then we were both lying in the puddle. Our legs tangled together, his hands on my waist, his mouth as warm and sweet as I thought it would be. I couldn't taste him enough. I arched toward him, my mouth begging his to give, and we opened up to each other, our tongues dancing, teasing. The wet skin between us was slick and warm. His long, strong, arms wrapped around my whole body and pulled me close. We were almost sewn together, the entire front of me was in contact with him. His legs wrapped with mine, my breasts pressed to his chest, and our mouths catching and tasting and reaching. It felt as if my ears were ringing and I would vibrate apart with need. I wanted more of him. I heard him make a small noise in the back of his throat, like a growl, and he moved his mouth down my neck, biting and kissing as I pressed into him. Our centers were lined up perfectly and I was unable to stop myself from thrusting my hips toward him. His arousal was apparent and as strong as mine. He pressed back and then his lips took mine again.

"Oh god." I whispered, against his mouth. "How can this be happening?" My hands were on his hips, pulling him closer, trying to get every piece me in contact with him. The need had become so large it hurt, the craving in me for him. I had never experienced such a rush of passion. Such a clawing for release. It was like a drug and I didn't recognize me. I just wanted. *Needed.* Only need. My hands ran up his back. That huge, strong, back that blocks out the stars, that carries all that weight. "Lucas..." His name came out of me in a half moan.

"Sophia" He bit my neck.

Another moan, "Oh God, *Lucas*,"

Need.

I bit him back and then found his mouth again. We were grabbing, and touching, and tasting each other in such an explosion of intensity, that when he stopped and pulled away, I thought I would die. I had just lost myself. When his body left mine, I lost all feeling, thought, warmth.

I looked up at him in confusion, and he, looked up at the sky.

"Sophia," His face was alive and smiling when he looked back down at me. "A plane!"

*   *   *

I hadn't heard it. The blood rushing in my ears, and my focus being consumed by the taste and enjoyment of Lucas, had completely blocked out the far off droning sound of the plane.

I struggled to my knees, using Lucas' body to climb to an upright position, and looked to the sky, in the direction he was now pointing.

We yelled. Together we yelled, and screamed, and waved our arms. Ducky sloshed around on the water as we clamored for balance, trying to make as much movement as possible, throwing our arms out wide and calling out.

"Hey, over here! Over here!"

We both knew no one could hear us. Logic was inconsequential though, and we screamed anyways.

"Help! Hey! Help us!"

The small plane was flying lower than a large airliner would, but it was too far away. I could make out its wings, nose, and tail, but no detail. I wondered if we looked like a shadow on the big open ocean to them -- the pilot, or the passengers. If we looked like seaweed, or flotsam, or jetsam, or if they noticed us at all. We waved and yelled and the plane slowly crossed the blue, blue, sky. Heading north. Not turning. Not slowing. Not rescuing us.

In the space of a few minutes it was gone, and the silence was deafening. Lucas and I knelt in the center of Ducky, our arms hanging limply at our sides, our faces turned north to where the plane had disappeared.

We didn't say anything. I slowly sat down. I looked at my hands, already turning brown from one day in the sun. They were tinged with red and I knew I should hunt down the sunscreen and reapply. But I sat there, my mind blank, and my nerves numb.

Lucas was there suddenly. His hands took mine, and he knelt in front of me. I lifted my face to look at him and saw he had a strange expression on his face. Not defeat, or disappointment, not resignation or anger. I couldn't place it at first, but then he spoke quietly, and calmly, and I figured it out.

"No rain Sophia. No excuses. No plane." He reached out and lightly ran his fingers down my cheek. "No reason at all not to."

What I saw in his eyes was desire. And peace. A strange combination, but I saw clearly, that he was actually fine with no rescue. That the interruption of the rain, the bailing of the raft, the plane that couldn't possibly see us, they were only pauses to what we both knew would happen. What we *wanted* to happen. And it all rushed back. Just like that. A flood of heat and desire, the painfully sweet need. And we agreed. Without words or explanation. Having each other, and this new thing we had found, this joy in each other, rivaled rescue. I knew somewhere in the back of my mind that maybe I would regret it. Maybe I wouldn't, but there was nothing to stop us. No reason to not revel in this passion and thrill of attraction. Being happy in the raft, would not rescue us sooner or later, we were here, and I wanted him. Between a choice of drifting for God knew how long, trying to *not* touch him, to *not* enjoy him, or giving in to what we both wanted, and seeing if we might comfort each other until rescue came, seemed an obvious choice. I would be a fool, we both would, if we pretended anything else.

A huge smile spread across my face and I simply said "Yes."

He didn't smile back, he just took me. Took what I offered. My mouth, my body. He pulled me into him, and we lost everything. Time, sound, I was no longer thirsty, except for the taste of him. The hunger that had been rumbling in me all morning, turned into a burning desire to consume him. The heat of the sun couldn't rival, with the heat off of his skin, his mouth.

We took each other.

We were lying in the bottom of the raft again, the puddle almost gone, but the wet still seeping through my already soaked pants. I kicked my shoes off and struggled with the buckle on his belt. Lucas' fingers deftly untied the knot at my waist that held up my linen pants and stripped the wet material down my legs. It felt wonderful to have them off of me, the uncomfortable clinging fabric now gone, my legs felt free.

Lucas quickly shed his boots, and equally soaked jeans, and returned to me before I had a chance to miss him. Our skin pressed close, the room in the raft completely taken up with the length of both of our bodies. Our mouths found each other again, tasting the salt off our skin from the ocean, the sweetness of lips and tongue. We were grabbing, pulling close, touching and claiming. I had never wanted anything so much, had never had every piece of me yearn together toward something.

Lucas pressed a knee between my legs and I spread my thighs, wrapping my legs around the outside of his and he settled between them pressing his desire and need against the flames of mine. I grabbed his mouth with mine again, pressed my hands against his back and thrust up to him, bringing him into me.

It was an explosion of sensations. I gasped and let out a moan and clung tighter, *how had this never felt this good before?* How had I gone my whole life without knowing completion? He was my home. We fit tightly, but perfectly, and he thrust again. Fire and lighting crawled through me, tightening my breasts, and blurring my vision. I clung to him as we found a rhythm and pushed each other into the storm we had brewed together.

His filling me was heaven. The length and broadness of his body blocked out the sun and made me feel consumed, even as I consumed him. I fought to keep his mouth on mine as we rocked and swayed the raft. I couldn't imagine not having him to taste, my need wasn't lessening at all, only growing larger, until I thought I may die, here, on our raft, the first day afloat. It wouldn't be thirst, or hunger, or lack of rescue that would kill me. It was this wonderful all-consuming need. And then Lucas bit down, his mouth on my neck, lowering his head to take my breast and torture me even as he thrust deeper, and I sensed the edge of the cliff. The peak of the storm. I flung myself into it, meeting his efforts with my hips, pulling him to me with my hands at his waist, and we both jumped together. Into release. Into the need. I came with my mouth on his, our breath one.

Chapter 10

The sun was hanging in the west, promising the end of our first day aboard the little raft. My hand ran up the side of Lucas' arm and I wondered if the dampness that clung to him was from the muggy air, or if it was sweat. We lay wrapped in each other, our heads pointing to the east at the nose of the raft, our legs still tangled, pointing toward the setting sun. I was thirsty, but didn't want to move.

Although we were both naked, I felt warm. The air was muggy, and the sun shone on our skin, setting fire to the exposed areas that weren't covered by each other's limbs.

Lucas turned his face toward me and buried his mouth at the base of my throat. His tongue flicked there, and I moaned lazily. My fingers wound into the thick curls at the back of his head, and I pulled him closer, arching my neck, pressing my hips tighter to him. I felt a stir there and chuckled.

"Ah, you plan to kill me." We had made love through the afternoon and his stamina and passion had me sore, sated, and wondering if I had bitten off more than I could chew.

He brought his mouth up to mine and the moment I tasted him, I wanted him again. Maybe not more than I could handle, but I knew we needed to pause. Reluctantly, I pulled back, just far enough to see his sleepy eyes and gorgeous mouth. *I may have to close my eyes to have a conversation with him.* The draw I felt to dive back in and reignite the fire was like a drug and I, a weak junkie. I laughed again and kept my eyes open.

"We need to get dressed Lucas. We're burning and we should drink and have a bite of something."

My hunger had come back. Lucas had been terrific in distracting me from all my bodily needs but one. The need for him, but the logical Sophia was fighting to take control. I needed to pee. I was thirsty, and the sunburn we would suffer if we didn't put our clothes on would be painful, and our own faults.

"Really?" His eyes crinkled with the smile and his dimples lured me back to kissing him.

After a moment though, my urge to pee began sapping away at my arousal. "Mmm" I said. I slowly unwound my body from his. "Yes. Really."

Lucas rolled to his back and put his arms under his head. He looked relaxed, and gorgeous. As if he were sunbathing on a beach, not roasting in a rubber raft with the chance of no rescue, and the threat of no food, or water in our near future. He didn't seem to care at all that his skin was covered in the red stripes of a sunburn that had already begun.

"I think we have the right idea right here. Clothes are wet and uncomfortable." He reached out and ran his fingers down my rib cage. "And you look better like this. Your clothes cover up all your tasty bits."

"You know, yesterday you wouldn't even talk to me." I smiled at him and shivered a bit at his touch. "Seems you changed your mind about me. Maybe you'll let me take your picture." I grinned and raised an eyebrow. He looked like a male model, stretched out and glistening in the sun. I still planned to prove to Anna that I had met and tasted the most gorgeous cowboy alive.

He ran his traveling fingers down my thigh. "What are you talking about? I called you Pumpkin didn't I?" He flashed his perfect white teeth, and I laughed. "We went for a late night swim, I took you out for a boat ride to explore the ocean. And I…" He rolled over and trapped me beneath him, "…did this to you." His mouth was on mine again and he entered me with one thrust, pulling a moan out of me, and awakening the fire that seemed it only needed him for fuel.

I met his thrusts and my fingers clawed down his back lightly. My legs wrapped themselves around his waist without my permission and my body took over, shutting down my boring logical mind. I let him fan my flames until the fire consumed me and I was left just ashes, drifting at sea.

*　　*　　*

Now the sun was setting. The orange streaks stretched overhead, painting the sky into a Phoenix wing, and I watched as the colors deepened, then slowly, so slowly, faded away. Grey with deep blue, a few straggling yellows, and then dusk was upon us and I sat up.

"OK, now we can treat our wounds." I ran a hand over Lucas' hair and bent to kiss his forehead. "I'm going for a swim."

At this he sat up quickly and grabbed at my waist. "Swim? Sophia, this isn't a pleasure cruise, you can't just jump in the water. What if there are sharks?"

I sighed and looked out at the darkening ocean. "I know, I don't really want to, but, well, nature calls." I looked at him a little sheepishly and shrugged. "So I will be in and out. Promise. You watch for sharks."

He sat for a minute looking concerned, and a little scared. I realized that his fear was real, and I wasn't sure how to process it. *Was he afraid of sharks? That I'll get eaten and leave him alone on the raft?* I knew he could swim since he had jumped off the *Lady Sun* alongside me, and he knew that I was a decent swimmer for the same reason. I wondered how *I* would feel if *he* had to jump over the side and my heart clenched at the thought. I *am* afraid of sharks and I certainly didn't want to float alone out here, but I admitted the fear was based in losing him. The realization startled me. I knew his effect on me was extreme, and new to me, that my body responded to him in a way I had never experienced before. But the idea of him being gone, by the jaws of a shark or even through rescue, and a flight back to Montana; It hurt, and I forced the thought aside. Wondering as I did, if that was what he felt too.

"I'll be quick." I repeated and rose to go to Ducky's edge.

"Wait." Lucas was rising and moving to the end of the raft. His tone was firm and commanding, I was sorry now that our mood had been ruined. I saw that he was dragging the gun out from behind the metal box. He quickly and efficiently loaded the clip, and pulled back on the slide, chambering a round. "Quickly." He said, nodding to the water.

I slipped over the side, keeping one hand on the raft, and thought what a funny scene this must make; me relieving myself in the ocean while being guarded from sharks by a naked man with an angry looking gun. *Maybe they won't make a movie out of this after all. Or they'll cut out the nudity and edit this scene altogether.* I giggled to myself and pulled myself back into the raft.

Lucas held the gun out to me, the barrel pointing toward the first star that had appeared in the blue-black sky. "Now me."

I took the rifle and waited for him to slip over the side of the raft, keeping my eye on the surrounding water for any tell-tale fins or dark shadows that may be sneaking about, waiting to strike. The thought unnerved me, and my grip on the rifle tightened. It only took a moment and Lucas was pulling himself back in the raft. I let out a breath I didn't know I had been holding and grinned in relief. "Feel better?"

He nodded and grinned back. "Yeah, actually, I do." He leaned forward and kissed me softly on the mouth and took the gun from my hands. "This looks sexy on you." I watched as he took the clip out and shot the round out of the chamber. He pressed it back into the clip and stored them both behind the box again.

I picked our damp clothing up from the bottom of the raft, and lay them over the back end of Ducky, near the motor. Then I pulled four of the life vests off of the pile over the luggage, and shoved them to the nose of the raft, creating a make shift bed -- or at least pillows. I fetched my purse and pulled out a water bottle, and a candy bar. A Twix. I took the treasure to the pillows and leaned back, my body propped up enough to be almost sitting. Lucas joined me and we curled up together, our body heat and the warm air, better than a blanket.

"Are you cold?" He asked.

"No." I took a mouthful of water and passed the bottle to him.

"Good. I like you this way." He took his ration of water and capped the bottle handing it back to me.

"Naked?"

"Available." He corrected.

I opened the Twix and handed him one of the bars. "To a starry night tour, and your attempt to make this go by so much faster." I touched my Twix against his and took a bite.

He held the candy in front of him, looking at me as I enjoyed the warm chocolate and caramel cookie. "Thank you." He said. I saw he was smiling, "Pumpkin."

*   *   *

The stars spread in scattered diamonds across the night sky. Laying side by side, our fingers entwined and my head on Lucas' shoulder, I watched as a tiny shooting star made its way across the black velvet. I didn't recognize any of the constellations. It made me feel even further from home, despite the beauty of the sparkling lights.

"Lucas?"

"Hmm." He sounded as if he were drifting near sleep. And no wonder, the last two days had been more full of adrenaline and endorphins than any other time combined through my thirty two years.

"What's your last name?"

His arm came up over my shoulder behind me and his fingers lightly stroked my arm, soothing me, arousing me. God I was hopeless, this man had complete control over my libido.

"Lael. My name is Lucas Josiah Lael" His voice was low. I could feel his breath on the top of my head as we drifted and rocked on the water.

"That's very pretty. I mean, handsome. It's nice to meet you." His chuckle shook me a little, and I wrapped my free arm across his rib cage. "Tell me about Montana." I felt a need to know him. Not just to experience his body, or to take pleasure in his physical beauty. The earlier thought of losing him had seeped its way past the barriers I had shoved it behind. Now I wanted to learn about him, this lost, and comforting man whom I owed my life to.

His fingers kept their pace, running up and down my arm slowly, and I forced my body not to respond as I waited to hear his answer. "It's big." He said quietly. "With a sky like this one, so that on a night out in the fields you can look up forever, and ever, but not see all of it at once. Different stars though."

He kissed the top of my head and I felt tears come to my eyes. *Home. Open fields, and different stars.*

"I have a ranch there." He continued. "Horses and cows, room to run, to stretch." He turned toward me and his other arm wrapped over me, encasing me in a warm blanket of heat from his skin.

"I'll show it to you." His voice was still low. "If you want, when we get home. We can go for a ride, take the horses up to the creek that runs down from the mountains. Make love in the grass."

And then I did cry. Silent tears crept down my cheek, and I wasn't sure if it was the thought of home, or the relief and joy that spread through me, that he wanted to show me his. *So this wasn't just convenient sex. It mattered.* I knew it mattered to me, but I cried, lying there in his embrace, grateful that it mattered to him too.

"I would like that." I whispered. And the rocking raft lulled us to sleep.

*   *   *

I awoke in the night, chilled and cramped. Dragging myself out of sleep, I sensed that something was different but couldn't place it. I snuggled closer to Lucas, contemplating fetching my clothes and getting dressed for the warmth they would provide, but I was still so sleepy. Instead I burrowed deeper into Lucas' arms and started to drift off again. The rocking of the raft, rising and falling, like an unsettled waterbed. *The rocking. That's what's different.* And the wind, I was cold because a wind had picked up and we were bouncing on the water in the little raft more than usual. I pulled away from my warm, safe, haven, and shook Lucas.

"Wake up Lucas." I sat up fully and my eyes began to adjust to the dim light. There were no more stars in the sky.

Lucas came awake and sat up beside me. He must have registered the change quicker than I had because he said, "A storm is coming in."

I reached for my purse, a dark bulge at the end of the raft and dragged it toward me. I fished around inside until my fingers found the flashlight and I clicked it on. The beam shot out, brilliant and blinding and I closed my eyes briefly, trying not to lose my balance in the rocking raft.

Lucas took the flashlight and held it over his head, shining it all around us like a lighthouse, out to sea. The waves were picking up. It wasn't storm level yet, but with the dark sky above and the wind, we could assume it was coming. I looked at Lucas and he reached out for my hand.

"Get dressed Sophia, put on a life vest."

I crawled to the motor where our rumpled cloths lay, dry now from baking in the sun. I pulled on my bra and panties, pants and tank and put the sundress where I could grab it easily. We would need to bail again if it rained. The pressure in the air promised it. I handed Lucas his pants and shirt. We both ignored our shoes but pulled on life vests and sat in the middle of the raft, one hand on the side for balance, the other clasped tightly to each other.

"We should tie down whatever may go over." He said.

I could hear in his voice that he was thinking, planning, and I was grateful he had a take-care-of-business attitude. It would help my jitters to have something to focus on.

I attached the life vests to the luggage again, tying two to each, and two to the metal can. I lay the rifle along top of the can and wrapped the straps over it, snapping them securely and tightening the slack. "Is there anything we can use to fasten them to the raft?" I had to raise my voice some as the wind picked up and Ducky rose and fell in the dark swells the storm was kicking up.

Lucas joined me at the suitcases and unzipped his. He reached in with one hand, searching in the dark for the knife at the bottom of the case. He came up with it and re-zipped the case. Carefully, he turned to the side of the raft, and sawed at the rope that ran along the length of the rim. It only took a few strokes, and the rope separated.

I crawled to the nose of the raft, dragging my purse and our precious supply of food. Unclasping my vest I put the long strap over my shoulder, over my head and back into the messenger position. Once I had I refastened the vest, I watched Lucas' dark shadow thread the rope through the handles of the suitcases, the metal box, through the plastic loops along the edge of Ducky's port side, and tied it all securely together. The whole pile was now buoyant if it went over, and, attached to the raft. We were as prepared as we were going to be. Lucas held out his hand and I joined him, sitting low in the center of the raft, holding the sides, holding each other.

The storm hit as it had earlier. It just opened up above us and began dumping water. But this time the rain came from all sides as well, whipped by the wind that had picked up. We rode the waves and swells, up, and down, up and down, slightly sideways, then up and down again. The swells were nauseating, but not enough to capsize us. If we were careful, and a little lucky, we could ride it out.

Water in the raft began rising, and Lucas started sopping and wringing with the extra shirt he had stuck in his belt. I scrambled to my sundress, and together we tried to stay in balance as we rose, and fell, and sopped, and wrung out, over the side -- into the ocean.

We were so wet, it was hard to tell if the ocean was above us or below. There was no light, no lightning, or thunder, just black sea, and dark sky, and water everywhere. I let the rain run into my mouth, let it moisten me. It was perfect for hydration, for washing away the saltwater from my clothes, and skin, and hair, but perfect too, for sinking us. Drowning us. I kept sopping, and wringing, my arms beginning to burn, my hands raw from the twisting of the material, over, and over, and over. It seemed like hours passed.

We didn't talk, we just methodically did what we could. I endured the rocking and swaying, as I fought to keep down my Twix. *I will not puke,* I commanded myself. *I absolutely will not puke.* My stomach muscles could feel the strain of keeping my balance in the rocking raft, of the leaning and holding myself out over the side to wring, to not slip in the wet, not fall down, not fall overboard. I stopped thinking and worrying, I even stopped my mantra of not puking. I just bent and sopped, and bent and wrung, and then did it again, then again, then again.

And like before, the rain stopped. Suddenly. I kept at the bailing, knowing if I stopped I would collapse. The raft had more water in it than it ever had with the first storm, so I kept working, and Lucas, on his side, kept sopping and wringing as well.

The gray sky began to lighten. I noticed it when I finally paused and stretched my back muscles. The clouds and wind were passing. The waves were just choppy now, no more swells. And I turned to Lucas, who nodded, and bent to sop some more. We worked at it until the raft was almost bone dry.

The dawn was hinting at an appearance in the east by the time Lucas took the dress from my hands and pulled me to lay down and rest. We didn't say anything. I was just glad to have made it through, nothing lost, only sore muscles. *It could have been worse.* And sleep took me.

Chapter 11

My face and left arm burned. I opened my eyes and winced. I was sore everywhere. My back and arms and stomach, even my leg muscles were mad at me. I reached up a hand and touched my face, wincing at the stinging pain. The sun shone high in the sky already and looked particularly angry today.

Slowly sitting up, I began assessing myself. I was thirsty and needed to brush my teeth badly. I was hungry, and sore, and desperately craved a cup of coffee. Thick, rich, coffee. To top off the morning, I sported a wicked sunburn down the left side of me.

Every bit of skin that had been exposed was now pink, and very angry. Even my left foot sported a sunburn. I groaned. This sucked. I wanted to go back to yesterday when I was only slightly hungry, not ravenous as I felt now. We could spend the day making love, and reading the Maldives book, or sharing stories with each other. But today, I sensed, was not going to be fun.

I looked down at Lucas. He was burnt on his right side, having fallen asleep facing me. I sighed and began the tedious details to begin the day. I crawled to my suitcase and rummaged for the sunscreen. It felt delicious to rub the white creamy stuff on my burn. I then fished out my light jacket and pulled it on. I would be hot, and clammy, and uncomfortable, but it was the only thing I had to cover my arms with. With that done, I found my toothbrush and toothpaste, then dug around in Lucas' bag for his metal cup. I put a tiny amount of paste on the brush and began scrubbing my teeth.

I was so happy to have any semblance of normalcy, I didn't notice when Lucas woke up and propped himself on an arm to watch me brush. When I finally deemed I had scrubbed away the last two days, I spit over the side of the raft, rinsed my brush in the ocean and dipped the cup over the side. I swished a small amount of salt water around in my mouth and spit that out as well. My mouth tasted like salty mint, and my teeth felt smooth and clean.

"Better?"

I jumped and glared at Lucas. "You aren't supposed to watch me brush my teeth, it's gross."

Lucas shook his head as he sat up. "Sophia, I watched you pee in the ocean yesterday, and I'm pretty sure my mouth tastes like yours did before you began that chore. I was thinking what a brilliant idea that is." He reached out for the cup and I handed it to him.

I wrapped the dress turban around my head as he brushed, then fished the *tic tacs* out my purse and shook out six. He returned his brush and cup to his suitcase and I placed three *tic tacs* in his hand.

"Breakfast. Pretend its bacon and eggs." I popped my three mints in my mouth and he leaned down and kissed me. Reaching up I touched his face, his whiskers were coming in more, but his short beard was unable to hide his dimples. "You're the best breakfast." I said, and I meant it. His kiss reminded me that yes, I was sore, and sunburned, and still lost as sea, but I had Lucas. Somehow that made it not only easier, but sweeter.

He kissed me again, tasting of salty *tic tacs*, and I set him down to take his medicine. I checked his bandage. The tape lost its ability to stick with all the rain and moving about, but the cut beneath still showed eight butterflies in a row, and seemed to be healing well. I took off the bandage, the wound would do better with some air now that it was beginning to heal. Once I applied a layer of sunscreen to his burned and exposed areas, I handed him his shirt and he obediently turbaned up. Finally, I opened my purse, took out the half empty bottle of water and we each took a mouthful. It wasn't refreshing, the liquid was warmer than my mouth, but I was grateful for it.

Morning ablutions taken care of, I stuck myself in the nose of the raft and prepared to avoid the sun as much as possible.

Lucas rummaged around in his suitcase and dug out his little binoculars. He perched himself near the useless motor and sat staring out to sea in every direction. From time to time he would rise up on his knees and look around, but never announced "Land ho!" or "Ship ahoy!" So I just sat and let my mind wander.

If we were rescued today (fingers crossed) what would happen? It was still a few days until my flight back to the states and home. Would I stay in the Maldives, try to visit the castaway island? Would I book a flight straight home, hoping the airline would change my ticket. Would I ever see Lucas again, he would return to Montana and I would fly to Washington. We had separate lives, priorities. It might be, the time on this raft was the only time we would be together. I hated thinking about that, so I went back to wondering if I would stay the rest of the vacation, or would we be caught up in red tape. The Maldivian police would want us to identify the pirates and help with hunting down Jok, and the *Lady Sun*. That made me realize, that as we floated at sea, hoping for rescue, there was no one who *knew* to rescue us.

"Lucas," I said suddenly, "do you think anyone knows we're missing?" I hoped he would assure me that yes, they would be here any minute, and I could go back to fantasizing over a big cup of coffee and a giant cheeseburger. They were the first two items I planned to buy, the first chance I got.

Putting the binoculars aside Lucas crawled over toward me. He aligned himself beside me and took one of my hands in his.

"I mean if no one knows we're missing, then no one is looking for us are they?" My optimist had lost the battle with my realist.

"No. I don't think they are." He said it matter of factly and I sensed he knew something I didn't.

I squeezed his fingers, "Why not?"

"I've been wrestling with some things." he said slowly. "Things that don't make sense."

"Like what?" I asked, my focus solely on him. What did he know that made him so certain rescue wasn't coming? The panic I commanded myself not to indulge, tickled at my heart, causing my blood pressure to rise. *No rescue.* So our only hope would be to drift into an Island, or a ship. The chances of either of those things happening seemed as likely as the pirates coming back and apologizing.

Lucas pulled my hand to his mouth and kissed my knuckles. He was watching me as my panic began to rise and I took a breath and blew it out.

"OK, spill. I want to know."

"Well, Ducky is a big question." He nodded to the motor on the back. Sitting useless and flaunting itself with its empty gas tank and brand-new, shiny, parts. "This raft is out dated. By a lot. Emergency vessels are much larger, have emergency supplies stored in them like flares and such, and if they come equipped with a motor they're battery powered. Some of the pricier ones have solar charging cells on them. This raft should have never been on the *Lady sun.*"

I mulled this over for a minute. "What if Ducky was a ship to shore vessel, like when they needed to weigh anchor beyond a reef, and take a smaller boat to shore. Maybe you just found the wrong panel."

Lucas looked impressed and kissed my knuckles again. "The yacht *had* a ship to shore boat. It hung below the deck we were sitting on. I noticed it when we boarded in Malé. But that's good thinking, the only reason I'm sure this was intended as the emergency raft is because the hatch I opened when you caught me snooping, had *emergency* written on it."

"I never saw that," I mused aloud, "but I wasn't looking for it either."

"Even if you had been you may not have known what it said," Lucas explained. "It was written in Thaana."

"You read Thaana?"

"About five words; Emergency, bathroom, seat belt, no, and please." He shrugged when I stared at him, my expression portraying my amusement. "It was a long flight." He defended himself.

"Anyway, the question is, why would a multimillion dollar Yacht equip its self with an inappropriate and out dated emergency raft? I have a sneaking suspicion Ducky is a fishing vessel."

"What? Why would anyone put a fishing boat on a yacht as an emergency raft?"

"That's the question. Or one of them"

I went back to the problem and tried to analyze the clues. After a few minutes of no answers forthcoming I nudged him in the ribs. "OK, tell me the rest, maybe it will piece together."

"Well, Jok is the other question. His behavior was strange. We were on the *Lady Sun* for hours, and other than a greeting, we were left completely alone. It seemed like he didn't know how to do his job as a host, or he was occupied elsewhere. It was supposed to be a tour of the islands remember?" He looked over at me. "Were you told that too?"

I nodded, "I thought it strange that we never went sightseeing, as that was part of the brochure, but I was distracted, and jet lagged, and then of course there was you." I nudged him again.

"What about me?"

"Um, you're very distracting."

"Oh." He smiled then and leaned in to kiss me. "You're sweet." Lucas continued on with his point. "So, when the pirates boarded, it appeared like they knew we would be there. I can't figure out why Jok even picked us up if he never intended to deliver us to the island, and he only wanted the yacht. Also, why was he working with the pirates at all? What could he possibly gain? He would lose his job, be banished from the Maldives, or worse, imprisoned, even executed. The risks were high. So the whole thing is a mystery."

"But why wouldn't they be looking for us?"

"Because Jok is the only one who knows we're missing." He said simply. "Our families won't be alerted to us not arriving on our planes for another five days, then they may wait a day in case we just missed our connections. After that they would contact the authorities and start a search. We have a week or so before we could ever expect them to begin."

A week. Anything could happen in a week.

I refused to panic. I refused to cry. I sat there holding Lucas' hand and tried with all my might not to let futility catch me. Beat me. *I'm Sophia, frickin, Canon, I do not give in, or give up.* There had to be an answer, a way out of this. I closed my eyes tight and began counting in my head. *Two, four, six, eight, ten, twelve…* I got to thirty-four and felt calmer. I opened my eyes and released Lucas' hand. I had been gripping it too hard and my fingers hurt.

I was disappointed in myself that I hadn't put it all together. Connected the dots, noticed the strangeness. But in my defense, the last forty eight hours had been pretty full. A lot had happened, and I comforted my ego with the explanation of all the distractions. A shiny yacht I had chalked up to good luck, a pleasure cruise with a handsome man who wouldn't talk to me, the anticipation of reaching the castaway island. The champagne, the pirates, I mean who can think when there are pirates holding you at gunpoint? Then the escape, the jump overboard, the raft, the storm, the sex. Yeah, I had a lot on my mind. It was easy to miss, to not see the red flags.

But Lucas had seen them. He *had* been thinking. It came to me all in a rush that he must have noticed something was amiss from the start. Why else would he have been messing around with the panel, and he kept his head when he spotted the pirates, had warned me, kept me close. He'd risked himself to rescue me, *killed* a man, god knows how, perhaps with his bare hands. I looked at his hands now, strong and rough and capable of killing, of caressing. They were hands that held me and made me feel safe.

Through everything that distracted me, Lucas had been puzzling out the pieces and knew we wouldn't be rescued, not anytime soon. And he hadn't freaked out. No cursing or throwing the stupid motor overboard. He had instead, been calm, and caring. He had made love to me as if we lay in our own bed, safe on land, not a worry or a care. I couldn't figure him out. What kind of man lets things roll off of him like that?

I drew in a deep breath and let it out, slowly blowing out the fear and the tenseness in my shoulders. *Well if he can roll, so can I.* What we needed was a plan.

I looked around, out at the sea, hoping the plan would present its self. The breeze that had picked up cooled my skin as it blew across my damp neck. I was clammy with sweat, wearing the jacket had kept the sun off my skin, but it made me warm and muggy. I unzipped it and held it open for the wind to get inside, cool my chest and dry the sweat that trickled down my cleavage to end in my bra, which was already damp with it. The breeze fluttered the back of the light material and I felt like a limp kite, unable to take off, but dreaming of the sky.

My eyes flew open wide, and I turned, letting my jacket cling back to my skin as I grasped Lucas' shoulders.

"A sail! We can make a sail!" I was so excited with the idea I hugged him hard, and kissed him loudly on his mouth, which I noticed was dry, and starting to chap.

Lucas hugged me back and looked to our suitcases thoughtfully, "Yeah," he said slowly, "that may work." I saw he was thinking it through, he turned his face to the breeze for a minute, then reached over and grabbed my face and kissed me. "We'll make a sail," he said softly, "and we will get home."

I took his meaning of home to be America, not an invitation to his house, but it warmed me and excited me that we had a direction. A plan.

First things first, I dug through my purse and found my chap-stick. I applied some liberally to my lips, which were also quite dry, then handed the tube to Lucas who did the same. Then I pulled out the bottle of water and took a mouthful.

The sweating and heat were sapping away all my moisture, and I contemplated stripping off the jacket. On second thought though, I knew the sunburn would do more damage to me, so I left it on and resigned myself to being clammy and uncomfortable. *Because we will make a sail, move across this ocean and go home.*

Lucas finished the bottle of water and I replaced it in my purse. I made a mental note to refill it from the metal can later. By my estimation, with Lucas' water bottle, the one left in my purse, and the water stored in the can, we had about three days of water between us. We would have to ration more than we'd been drinking, with the heat of the sun and the inevitable sweating. We would need our wits and every bit of focus if we were to get off of this raft. I hoped that three days of sailing would be enough to land us somewhere. Anywhere that had a phone would do. *Or cell service.*

Lucas and I rummaged through our bags and decided that my wraps would be the best choice for a sail. I had brought three. A white one, a black one with white turtles running up the hem, and an orange one that was the color of a sunset, and displayed blue dolphins dancing diagonally across the brilliant material.

I love wraps. I have stacks of them. In the summer they're light, and sexy. I wear one almost every day, matched up with a cute pair of sandals and a bikini, they're the perfect summer garb. Now my three favorite wraps would be a perfect sail.

As I removed the small sewing kit from Lucas' shaving bag he said behind me, "Sophia, there's a small problem with the plan."

I turned to him, sewing kit in hand. "There always is isn't there?" I refused to let the comment ruin my optimism.

He smiled but I could see it was just to make me feel better. "We don't have a mast."

I sat there, clutching a handful of brightly colored wrap, and the small plastic box that held needles and an array of tiny cardboard spools of thread. I looked away from him, not wanting to see his face that only showed indulgence. Not wanting him to see my face, that I was sure was close to cracking and letting out the panic, or worse, tears.

I took a second and concentrated on the feel of the sweat that was slowly dripping down my back, then, I steeled my spine and set my shoulders and turned back to him.

"Then find one." I gestured out to the water around us. "Find some driftwood, the ocean is filled with it. We haven't been looking for anything, but we could have passed by dozens of masts since yesterday and not even known it. So," I said in my best schoolteacher voice. "I will sew the sail. You look for the mast. We will figure it out as we go."

I knew I was in denial, but once I said it aloud, my idea actually sounded logical. There's always stuff washing up on the shore of every beach I have ever been to. Washington gets the debris from Japan and China all the time. Tons of it. So asking for a stick wasn't outside the realm of expectations.

I set to my task.

*   *   *

The sewing kit was really quite pathetic. It had little spools of thread that would do for sewing a button or repairing a tear but to actually *make* something it would be nearly impossible.

I decided I would make individual stitches every two inches, I would make them strong and tie them off, then make the next one. It wouldn't be a seamless stitch job, but it would hold the wind, and maybe with luck, and a mast, and the rope we had tied everything down with, it would turn into a sail that would carry us home.

I began sewing.

The sun beat down on my turban and the back of my neck. I had reapplied sunscreen on both of us and hoped it did its job, the tube was already half empty.

Lucas picked up his binoculars and sat, turning slowly, looking out to sea, scanning the calm water for any anomalies, a bump, a shadow, anything. We discovered almost right away, I had been right. The ocean was filled with debris. Every time Lucas said, "I got something!" I would put down the sail, secure the needle, and we would paddle, me on the port side, Lucas on starboard, toward whatever treasure, or trash, he had spotted.

In the first two hours we found and old Styrofoam buoy that was crumbling apart, a huge beam, that at first we had thought was a stick, but found once we were upon it, that it was like an iceberg. It was so waterlogged that only the tip showed above water, the giant length of it floated below. We found a ragged fishing net that held the decomposing remains of a bird tangled in its knots, and a couple dozen tiny little sticks that had been trapped in the mass of rotting rope. We found a tree, impossible to tell what species it had been. Its trunk was smooth and spongy from the amount of saltwater it held and its branches were short and stubby, all the limbs having broken off close to the trunk long ago. But we found nothing that would serve as a mast. Yet.

I was still optimistic, so after each discovery and each disappointment, I went back to my stitching, and Lucas went back to scanning the great wide ocean.

The day went by slowly. I finished the sail and held it up to the sun, letting the sunlight beam through the orange, and light up the white turtles in the black. The slight breeze ruffled it and I felt certain it would do well, once we found our mast and rigged up a line.

Lucas and I traded off searching the waters, I sat roasting, eyes straining through the magnification, looking at small swells, floating masses of seaweed and lots, and lots, of nothingness.

We talked about Jok and the *Lady Sun*, trying to come up with theories as to why we had ended up here. Why Jok had been willing to give the pirates the yacht. We tossed around ideas of drug running, or an inept yacht builder who ran out of the appropriate emergency rafts and stored Ducky to pass inspection. We thought maybe the pirates had someone Jok loved, and so he was willing to scout out booty for them. Lots of colorful explanations, but as we talked, we both knew that it didn't matter. It didn't change our situation, and knowing, having answers, wouldn't save us. So we kept looking for our mast and Ducky kept floating. Keeping us alive, for now.

By the time the sun began coloring the western sky, my arms and eyes were tired, I had a headache in the front of my skull again, and I was pretty sure the back of my neck was beet red.

Lucas took the binoculars from me and pulled me into the bottom of the raft. We shared a bag of mixed nuts and half a bottle of water. The nuts were salty and I knew they made me thirstier but they were delicious and I ate each one slowly, letting my stomach enjoy them as I swallowed, and sipped warm water to wash them down.

"If I had known I would be stranded on a raft I would have brought some fruit, or a cheeseburger." I popped the last nut into my mouth and settled back against Lucas.

"I would have brought a mast." Lucas leaned over and began pulling off my jacket. "You don't need this anymore." He said softly, his breath tickling my ear. "In fact I'm pretty sure you would do better without any of it." He kissed my neck, and nibbled at my ear, and I felt the rush of heat between my legs that his touch always brought on.

I stripped off the jacket, and then we both pulled the rest of our clammy, uncomfortable, clothing off. We let the breeze dry our skin, as the sky turned to a dusky blue-gray and slowly faded into black.

We made love against the pillow of life vests, and I sank into him. Lucas' strong arms and sweet mouth wiping away the soreness of the day. I forgot my sunburn and my hunger, I forgot about the sail and the mast. There was only him, the taste, and feel, and sweetness of him. We fell asleep with our arms wrapped around each other, the gentle, lulling, ocean rocking us, like children in a bassinet.

Chapter 12

We slept till dawn. I opened my eyes to see that the sun was beginning to peek out of its blanket of water, and the sky had put away all the stars.

I lay still, enjoying the rocking of the raft, the temperature before it turned to blistering levels, and the feel of the man beside me. His gentle breathing told me he was still asleep, and I was grateful. He needed to rest; we had both needed the full night's sleep. Doing the math quickly, given when we drifted off soon after sunset, to now, Lucas and I had gotten ten hours of uninterrupted sleep. No storms, no rain. *But without rain we can't catch water.* I sighed, hoping that maybe we would be gifted with a light deluge, not a full force hurricane. I wished for rain with the warning of *be careful what you wish for,* tempering my prayer.

I closed my eyes again, in no hurry to rise and begin the day. I could sense my natural optimism fading. This was day three. Three and a half if you counted our first night aboard Ducky. I tried to do nautical math in my head. How far had we drifted so far, with the storm and the hour or so on *Lady Sun.* How fast had we been going then, how fast were we going now? I couldn't put numbers to speeds or even miles to ocean, so I gave up and turned into Lucas who was better than math. *Better than anything, except rescue. Even a cheeseburger.* I smiled at that thought. Choosing a man over a burger, but Lucas was a no-brainier. What would I do when we got home?

I would have to go back to the farm, spring was coming and my mare had a foal due in April. The sheep would be popping out little lambs around the same time, and I would have to schedule the shearer to come, the farrier and the vet. Spring is always the busiest time. I don't make much money on my little farm. Enough to get by, save some, buy hay, firewood, pay for repairs for the truck, but I loved my life. I work for no one, I was surrounded by animals, ate from my garden, canned in the fall, knitted in the winter and rode my horse through every season.

I had the perfect life and I missed it terribly. But the thought of returning home, to the cold of January, then the mud of February and no Lucas, well it almost seemed better to stay in the raft. Silly and very female of me, but aside from the life and death stuff, I was actually very happy, right now, in this moment.

Lucas was someone I could see growing old with. He's easygoing and capable, kind and funny, terrific in bed. OK, mind blowing in bed, (even though we hadn't encountered a bed yet) and he farmed like me. Or ranched. You couldn't find a man anymore who wasn't concerned with being 'metro' or the competition with the Jones', the ladder climbing, the cars, and suits, and hair products. The Snake used more hair product than I did, and had more shoes. What kind of man has more shoes than a woman? 'Metro' men. Lucas was a salt of the earth kind of guy, and I wanted to learn about him, not lose him as soon as we found land.

I wrapped my arm over his waist and he stirred. He put his arm around me and nuzzled into the top of my head, his beard catching in my braided hair. The Snake never cuddled. No man I ever dated had cuddled. As if touching me was too annoying, or inconvenient after the deed was done and they had gotten what they wanted.

No, I resolved, I was not going to lose this man. When we got home I would drive to Montana, we would ride to that creek and I would profess my love for him there as we made love in the grass.

Love? I felt my heart clench and my blood pressure begin to rise. *Really? OK Sophia, no worries, I'm sure he has no idea, just calm down.*

I got a hold of myself and sorted through my feelings. Yes, I loved him. He had saved me and he treated me with care. It may have been only three days, but I hadn't experienced this level of emotion or attraction in the six *years* I had been with Jon. So yes, I fully admitted to myself. I loved Lucas.

I felt a stirring between us and pushed away all thought. I opened up to him and Lucas took what I offered, we came together as the first rays of light crept over the edge of the raft to warm our already heated skin.

*   *   *

The day drug by. The heat had brought back my headache, and I wondered how it didn't affect Lucas. He seemed to be comfortable and relaxed, scanning the water with the binoculars, paddling to spotted debris. Usually the discovery consisted of sticks that were too small and rotting, or trash that was broken bits of things that held no use to us. By mid-day my head was throbbing and Lucas urged me to lie down. He draped the sail over the edges of the raft to keep the sun from beating on me, and insisted that I take two of our precious supply of Tylenol and an extra mouthful of water. I dozed on and off until I sensed dusk was coming. The light beating through the orange material, lighting up the dolphins in a bright blue, had faded, and I climbed out of my cave, folded up the sail and stretched.

"How are you feeling?"

"Better, thank you," I gave him an apologetic smile. "How are you? I left you to do all the work, you must be roasting."

I began gathering our daily meal and ration of water just as the last light slipped below the horizon. Now was my favorite time of day. The sky was streaked in color, the sun no longer torturing us, and the wind always picked up some with the change of temperature.

"I'm just fine." He said. He joined me against the life vests at Ducky's nose and we shared a snickers bar. The chocolate had melted completely and the entire candy bar had turned into a mushy pile but we wiped the wrapper with our fingers and licked the chocolate off like little kids. The bottle of water was finished, and we opened up Lucas' thermos that he pulled out of his suitcase. Surprisingly the water was cooler than the air and I held my ration in my mouth, savoring the refreshing liquid before I swallowed.

"No luck with the mast?"

"No, but I found this," He reached into his pocket and pulled out a bobber, bright orange and smelling of fish. It had a long string of fishing line attached to it that Lucas had wound into a tidy coil and a rusty hook on the end. "I'll rig up a fishing pole tomorrow and see if we can catch something."

"Sushi" I grinned. I love sushi, but even though my choice ran the way of tempura, deep fried, I would happily eat whatever Lucas could catch, and I wouldn't complain.

"Yeah" He reached up to touch my face and then ran his fingers down to my jaw. God I loved his touch.

"You don't look as red. More tan now" His eyes held worry, and it touched me to see that he cared.

"Well let me look at your arm, I didn't check it this morning," I sat forward and turned, sitting Indian style with his bicep at eye level.

"It doesn't hurt, I think your doctoring did the trick."

He was right, the wound had scabbed over nicely and the redness had receded, the skin was healing and there appeared to be no infection.

"Good, you're a tough nut." I leaned forward and kissed his arm just beside the butterflies. "All Better."

He chuckled and pulled me back toward him. "You would make a good mother." He turned his head suddenly to look in my eyes, "*Are* you a mother?"

He must have realized he didn't know that much about me, we hadn't exchanged stories other than our divorces, where we lived and random bits that came up in conversation.

I smiled reassuringly, "No. But I would love to be." I took his hand and leaned into him, deciding now was as good a time as any to share, and began to tell him about the princes, Anthony and Evan, about my niece, Audrey and my family. The farm. He listened and asked questions now and again, and I found that as I told him about all the animals and my home, I was crying. Not sobbing or wailing, just a few tears jerked free from the tightness in my chest, the overwhelming homesickness, and the hope that dwindled each day, that I would get there again.

I wanted to change the subject. Stop crying, be happy again, so I wiped at my face, not ashamed that I missed home and wanted off this cursed raft, and asked him to tell me his story.

"Tell me about your ranch, your horses. Do you have any brothers or sisters?"

"My parents live in town, Billings, the closest town to my land." He sounded reminiscent, as if he too wanted to remember home, but knew it would hurt, not knowing if either of us would get there. "And yeah, I have a sister and two brothers. They're scattered around, but all within a day's drive. We don't talk as much as we used to. Now we just see each other on holidays, that kind of thing, you know how it is, you grow up, start your own life, your own family. Cassie, my ex-wife," He paused, and I knew that sounded new to him, the 'ex' part. I was familiar with that feeling. "she didn't like my family." he continued, "So it got easier and easier to find reasons not to be there for birthday parties, or barbecues. Now I'm out on my ranch and it feels too secluded. Lonely." He stopped talking for a while and I turned and kissed his neck.

After a minute or two he went on. "I have five horses. A stallion, two brood mares, my gelding and a young filly. Boomer, my gelding, I trained him from a young colt. He was the first foal out of my mare Happy Life." I smiled at the name, it made me think of Lucas as a young man, starting his ranch, starting his dream, and it made me love him more.

"Boomer saved me during the divorce." His tone was quiet, it seemed he was realizing the fact as he told me. "I rode every day. Sometimes we would go out and not come back for days. Sleep under the stars, explore just how big Montana is. He was good therapy. He let me talk to him and he never had a mean thing to say."

I chuckled and looked up at the blanket of stars above us. "Like here, but different stars." I whispered.

"Yes." He said, and then we were quiet.

We made love again that night, but it was different. Less need, and more sweetness. He was slow and tender and my heart reached out to him, embraced him. I think he was healing, and I hoped I was helping.

Our fourth night floating at sea I fell asleep in the arms of the man, I knew for certain now, I loved

Chapter 13

In the gloom before the dawn, something bumped the raft. It must have bumped it before, because I was already coming out of sleep, thinking Lucas was moving, maybe waking up. I looked around, processing the darkness in the sky. The stars were still out, speckling the deep gray, but dawn would come in an hour or so. I rubbed my face, stretching, and yawning, trying to remember what had woke me. *Oh! It was a... **Bump**...* the raft moved again, and I sat up, fully awake, reaching for the side of the raft with one hand and shaking Lucas with the other.

"Lucas, I think something is..." and suddenly the world turned upside down.

I was in the water, I gasped reflexively as my body was thrown out of the safety of Ducky's small space, and into the great wide not-safe-at-all ocean. I inhaled water. Forcing my head up, my arms reaching, I broke the surface and coughed. Sputtering and choking I gasped again, the air burning its way down my salt lined throat. Something crashed, and I felt my leg being grabbed, bitten, pulled, and I was under the water again. I started to scream but the water that rushed in my mouth made me clamp down. Whatever had grabbed me had let go, but my leg was on fire, the pain screaming through me, sharpening everything with the flood of fear it brought.

Again I scrambled toward the surface, got my head above the dark water and coughed out the lungful of ocean. For a brief second I was able to tread on the surface, frantically looking for the raft, for Lucas, but I saw nothing, just a wall of dark water rising, cresting, crashing, and I went under again. Again my body was grabbed, drug along by something with sharp scraping teeth, and again I was let go, the buoyancy of my lungs bringing me up to the surface to gasp and scream. The scream came out choking, and I tried desperately to get my bearings, *where is the damn raft?*

"Lucas!" I did mange that scream, choking out water and twisting in circles, my side and leg were growing numb with pain, the fire burning to a white hot that I blocked out, didn't care, just the raft. I only wanted the raft.

Find it, find it, where… oh Jesus, another wave. I held my breath this time, tucked my legs up and let the wave crash me under, then stroke, push up to the surface again. Breathe.

The next wave began rising, I saw it, creeping higher, eating the stars, eating me, I took in another breath, held it. Still hoping the raft was near, I kept my eyes open until the last second, and then, just as I went under, the wave tossed me to my side and I saw it. Not the raft.

Land.

*   *   *

I knew instantly I hadn't been attacked by sharks, it wasn't something grabbing me, dragging me. I was being crashed into a reef by the waves. Real fear and panic flooded through me and I tried to stay calm. My head popped back up in the air, I spun till I saw the dark shadow against the sky and struck out toward it, keeping my body and my legs as high on top of the water as I could. When the next swell began to rise behind me I rode it, surfing with its force and pull, but not letting it take me under. The wave crashed, and I relaxed rolling in the water with the force, not fighting it, then I struck out again.

I was born in California, before my family had moved to the north to 'live off the land' as my dad had said, and I had body surfed along with the best of them. My brothers and cousins and sisters and I would spend an entire day letting the waves roll us along toward the sand. The trick is, not to fight a rip tide, swim with it, it always has an end, to not fight the waves; waves will always win. To not ever, ever be crashed on a reef. There are not a lot of reefs in California but there are rocks. A trip to Hawaii with the Snake had ended when he had fought the waves and landed on a reef. He had been lucky to survive it. Many don't.

Another wave, I knew now I didn't have time to find the raft, or to hunt for Lucas, I had to survive this, and hope he was a good swimmer. I had to focus. I went under, relaxed, rolled, kept my legs up, let the water carry me forward, do the work for me. Push up, into the air, breathe, stroke. I was getting closer. Another wave and this one took me down. It crashed heavily with such force I couldn't stay near the top and I was drug along the bottom of the seabed. I realized my feet were in sand and I pushed myself up with them, up, and forward, toward the shore, still riding the force of the wave, *take me in you bitch.* I broke the surface.

Breathe.

The next wave let me ride it. I wasn't enjoying my surf, I was angry with the ocean, wanted to beat it, wail at it, *where the hell is the raft? Oh god, Lucas*! The wave crashed, and I screamed at it in my head as I went down, rolled, came up. Breathe. *Give me Lucas you stupid, stupid ocean! Let me go!* But the lesson of not fighting the waves was deeply instilled, I pushed forward, almost there. Another wave, ride it, own it, be its friend. And my feet hit bottom.

I could stand, but I let the wave carry me a little further. At last I was up, pushing through the water, struggling toward the shore ahead of me. My feet dug into the wet sand below and the adrenaline in my veins gave me a rush of strength, a ringing in my ears. The next wave knocked me down, but I landed on hands and knees, it was shallow here, and then finally, finally. I stood on Land.

The sky was lighter, a dull gray now, but overcast. I briefly registered the clouds that now layered the heavy sky in a pearly blanket as my eyes strained to look back out to sea. I peered into the crashing waves and great dark blue beyond searching for yellow, for Ducky and Lucas.

"God please let him be there, please." I whispered the prayer aloud scanning the water in the dim light, blinking the salt and sand out of my eyes.

I stood naked on the shore, my right side and leg screaming in pain, my heart still pumping adrenaline, the fear feeding me, sharpening my sight, flushing me with warmth and an inner stillness.

The pain didn't matter, I would deal with it. Clothing didn't matter. I didn't even care in that moment if there stood a resort behind me, just up the beach. I needed to find Lucas. I *had* too. Everything else was inconsequential to this singular goal.

I began striding down the beach, searching the waves, every swell and crash blocked my view to the ocean beyond. I half jogged two hundred feet down the beach, seeing nothing, not on shore, or in the waves. I jogged back to where I had crawled on shore and continued, two hundred feet the other way. I could feel myself flagging. The adrenaline and shock were wearing off, but not the panic. *It* was growing, like a banshee, screaming in my head. I turned back, running now, needing to move, to do something, and I set the banshee free.

"*Lucas!*" I screamed his name. "*Lucas!*" I called out over and over, running the football field length up and down the shore.

My leg was red and sticky with blood. My waist and hip were covered in scrapes and scratches that the reef had scored into my skin, but I knew my leg was worse. I had glanced down at one point, and seeing the flesh torn, the deep red of muscle below the skin, I knew I was in trouble. That I would begin to feel it, that panic and shock would only keep me going so long and then my leg would own me. Maybe kill me.

I let the blood stream. The running was helping it to wash freely from my body, wash away the saltwater, clean it, I hoped. Then I prayed. Hoping and praying were now all I had. No clothes, no meds, no water or food. No Lucas. A sob broke free from me, my eyes were streaming tears, and I was gasping now, in pain, and anguish, and absolute fear.

"Lucas!" Had I been unhurt, or even a little bit calmer I would have known he would never hear me calling. My screams were eaten by the waves. The ocean was a loud, roaring, monster that swallowed my voice, crushing my eardrums with its incessant crashing. After days of calm, stillness and quiet, now this *noise*. It was too much to take in.

My leg was burning now, insisting I notice. I stopped close to where I had crawled up to shore, my footprints and hand prints were there to mark it. It should have been triumphant, landing here, having found land, and hopefully, a way home, but there wasn't a speck of triumph in me. I would rather be at sea, safe in ducky with Lucas, making love, than right here, right now.

I caught a flash of yellow. Then a wave broke, and all I saw was white and gray and an array of blues. Turquoise, navy, aquamarine. Again, yes, yellow, just there! A swell began rising, and I saw that Ducky was carried on its back. The swell started to crest, then break, and then the grays and blues again.

I surged forward, running and splashing frantically into the water toward the raft, though it floated still some distance out, and suddenly my leg screamed. I heard it. No, that was me, screaming high, and piercing, and white stars appeared across my vision. Then Black.

*   *   *

I went under. I had only been thigh deep. The mistake I recognized instantly; saltwater in a wound. The water washed away the black, and I came up coughing and choking and then screaming again.

The fire in my thigh was now lightning, the pain so acute all reason was null and void. My body took over, ignoring my heart and love for Lucas, to save him, find him, ignoring the feeling of sand that my hands clawed at to get out of the water. Ignoring too, the rain that began falling as I pulled myself up on the beach. Every detail of the world was gone, only pain now. Then my mind was kind. It shut down, saving me from knowing this, from suffering this. And the blackness came again.

*   *   *

Warm rain pelted me. I awoke thinking I was in the shower. Had I slipped and fallen in the tub? The trivia that most household accidents happened in the bathroom ran through my mind before the pain brought me back to reality. I remembered the beach, the rain, my leg and… *Lucas.*

I opened my eyes and rose slowly. I had collapsed on my left side, my wound on my waist and hip and thigh faced the sky and the rain was doing a decent job of washing away the salt and gritty sand and blood.

The pain had turned from lightning and fire to hot coals. *I can endure,* I told myself, *just find Lucas. Make sure he made it. Then I can sleep. Then I can figure this all out. Find that resort, call a doctor.*

I sat up slowly. The blinding flash of light across my vision made me dizzy, and I gasped as tendrils of lightning flickered along my thigh. Looking at the wound I saw it was still bleeding. The rain wet my skin as it poured down steadily, promising the day to be a long and wet one. Less of a storm, like the one we bailed out ducky in during our time afloat at sea. More of a drenching, gray skied, I'm-gonna-do-this-for-a-while, kind of rain. But it was warm, so I was grateful for that.

Between the constant seeping of blood and the water from the sky, the gash would have a decent chance of washing out anything bad that may have gotten into it. I knew nothing major was torn in the vein or artery department, so blood loss wasn't my greatest concern. Infection would kill me. It would take me slowly and painfully. So I went back to hoping and praying as I slowly, so slowly, got to my feet.

There she was, my little Ducky. The raft had washed ashore only fifty feet away. On impulse I began to run to her, my eyes searching the beach for any Sign of Lucas. My leg shrieked and the lightening almost brought me down. I slowed to a gimp like stroll, my left leg bearing the bulk of my weight as I stuttered down the beach, limping to the yellow raft, now clearly, almost completely deflated.

Ducky lay with her nose on shore, and her featherless butt still dipped in the water. The useless motor rose and fell as each lap of wave came up the sand. Dragging there, in the water, were mine and Lucas' two suitcases, and the metal box, along with the angry gun. All still tied together, and secured to the raft. They had gone overboard, and the rope had allowed enough slack that they drug only a foot or so behind the motor. No wonder it took Ducky longer to get to shore. She was basically dragging an anchor, trolling behind her a weight of water logged suitcases and a metal box. My purse was nowhere in sight but I only noticed this as a side note of a female missing a part of her. For there, on the starboard side, draped half in the raft, half dragging the sand with the rise and fall of each wave, was Lucas.

I forced myself to be slow. I didn't want to risk passing out again. I might not wake up. I limped around Ducky's nose, toward Lucas' form. He lay face down, his arms and torso wrapped over the side, his left hand tangled in the rope that held the luggage, near the motor. I could see the binding was cutting off circulation. He must have been hanging as dead weight for some time because the hand was swollen and purple. I immediately went to the back end of the raft, stepping into the water gingerly, being extra cautious not to fall, not to pass out. I had been clenching my jaw in pain through the long stroll to the raft and now my jaw hurt, but it was nothing compared to my leg, so I kept clenching, grinding my teeth. A whimper escaped every now and then, as I worked on the wet rope, unwinding it from Lucas' wrist. It was twisted and tangled and I had to admire his quick thinking in tying himself as well as he could, to the only thing afloat, as he had been tossed from sleep, into the ocean.

I finally got his wrist free, and began massaging his hand, working the skin and rubbing down his forearm to his wrist to encourage blood flow. *Please don't lose your hand. You would have to get a hook and everyone would call you a pirate, and we hate pirates.*

"Please, please, please." I whispered it while I stood, clenching my jaw, massaging his arm, grateful that his skin was warm, he was alive.

The purple began lightening to a pinkish blue and then a somewhat normal color of skin tone began to show its self, and I whimpered again. But it was a grateful whimper.

I moved over to Lucas' body. He lay face down, and I knew I would have to turn him over. I steadied myself on my left leg, standing like a stork, or a flamingo, with my bloody right leg holding none of my weight. I leaned over, concentrating on my center of balance, *don't fall,* I commanded myself, *don't you fall Sophia. You're a ballerina. You can stand on one leg for Christ's sake.* I am not, in fact, a ballerina, but every girl pretends to be, so I forced myself to stand, and lean, and balance, on one leg. *Grab his shoulder. Oh god, that big, strong, world bearing, shoulder.* I lifted, my flamingo leg bearing my weight and his briefly, as I lifted, and shoved, and flopped Lucas unceremoniously onto his back.

"Aha!" I whimpered it out, my jaw still clenched, and my waist reminding me that it and its friend the hip, were also not happy with me, but I ignored them. *Now, check for a pulse.* I hopped closer to Lucas' broad chest like an ungraceful flamingo/stork/ballerina and leaned again, my fingers reaching for his neck. *Find a pulse.* And saw the blood.

His face was turned away, and my hand swerved from its goal to grab his chin and turn his head. His entire face was covered in blood.

"Oh!" It was a moan/wail. My voice a whimper, and a sob.

I almost fell but as my stork leg began to give, my right leg screamed, the foot jolting against the ground. I sobbed again, catching myself before I did any damage or passed out. Choking and crying once more, the tears blurring my vision, I reached for his face. There was nowhere to touch that wasn't covered in blood. I pulled my hand back refusing to look at the morbid scene, Lucas' eyes were closed and coated in red, his beard soaked and still dripping, small drops landing on the yellow of the raft. A few dropping onto his tan shoulder to run in a lazy line down to join the bloody pool now forming on Ducky. I reached again for his neck. I pressed my fingers up under his jaw, and there I felt it. A pulse, clear and strong.

I was still crying. I needed to find a way to wash away the blood, find the wound. Stop the bleeding.

"Oh god Lucas, you damn cowboy," I cursed and looked up at the sky. The rain fell steadily, and I saw no edge to the pearly gray clouds. They didn't seem threatening, just big, and full of water. *Keep coming.* I encouraged the rain. *Wash us clean.* Already the blood on Lucas' face had begun streaking and running. It was matting into his hair and streaming rivulets into his ears, but it would wash, and wash until I could see clearer, find his wound.

I hopped back, ungracefully, to the suitcases. Splashing into the water, careful to make the splashes delicate, keep the lightning from attacking again. My leg was growing numb, and I knew that soon I would need to bandage it. Tourniquet or wrap it, help the torn edges together. But right now, I needed Lucas. If I fixed him, then *he* could fix *me*, because although I knew my first aid kit was in my suitcase, I also knew there was no way in heaven or hell, I was going to be able to sew me up.

I lifted, and grunted, tossing my suitcase up on to the edge of the raft. Ducky was now almost completely flat, the air in her having escaped through an unseen wound of her own.

"We're all messes, aren't we Ducky." I shook my head as I unzipped my bag. I had found my own version of Wilson and understood in that instant, why we all connected to the volleyball, to Tom Hanks and his island friend. We all need someone, even if it's our own imagination imbued into an inanimate object. I actually felt bad, knowing Ducky was wounded too. She had kept me safe. She had done her job. She had held Lucas and me upon the big scary ocean, and she brought us here, maybe to save us. The actual answer was ocean current, but I gave Ducky the credit, and thought it was sad she had lost her life in the process.

I pulled a shirt out of my bag and dug around until my hands found the first aid kit. Then I hopped back with clumsy ballerina style, to Lucas, whose bloody face was already looking less bloody.

Leaning over him, I began to wipe away the red. The rain helping as I wiped his eyes gently, and then his nose and mouth and chin. I cleaned off his brow, running the shirt up into his hair line, and there, I found the wound. A long gash that already had a good mound of a goose bump rising around it. It ran from the center of his forehead into his hair. The entire cut was about two inches, but upon close inspection, with the help of the shirt, and the rain cleaning away the site, it didn't look too deep. No skull showing. No brains. *Ugh*. The thought was awful, and I kicked myself for even going there.

"You'll be OK babe. I'll fix you."

I opened the lid of the first aid kit that I had propped on Lucas' shoulder, careful not to let any rain into the precious dry interior. *Thank God for water proof boxes*. I found a small tube of iodine, and a bottle of super glue. Then I pulled out a square of gauze from a zip-lock baggy, and a roll of ace bandage. The med kit was looking weak. I should have restocked before the trip, but honestly, I had never imagined I would need *all* the meds. I closed up the medical kit and set it inside the raft. Holding the shirt draped over my head and Lucas', I leaned into his shoulder. Letting his body bear most of my weight, I made a roof over us with one arm, then with the other I parted his hair along the gash, and tore open the iodine pack with my teeth.

The bleeding had almost stopped with the pressure I had applied while cleaning the cut and sopping up the blood. I knew that head wounds always bled a lot, but until today hadn't seen the full force of that adage, and hoped never to again.

Carefully, I aimed the torn edge of the package over the wound, and squeezed the ugly yellow iodine into it, being sure to get a liberal amount around the wound. I didn't want any sneaky germs trying to crawl in later. I waited a few minutes. Breathing slowly, clenching my jaw. While the iodine did its trick and began to dry I attempted to stay focused.

I was getting dizzier and started to think maybe I should have bandaged myself first. Maybe I was losing more blood than I had thought. The hot coals were still smoldering in my leg and my lips had begun to tingle, but I couldn't think of what that might mean.

Back to Lucas' wound, I twisted open the superglue, again with the assistance of my teeth, and drew a line in his scalp where the skin had torn, careful not to touch the glue with my fingers. I pressed the edges of the wound together, holding it while the glue proved its super, and set. *Better than stitches*. Within a few minutes I was able to put the gauze over the site without worry the glue would make it a permanent fixture to his scalp. Then I wrapped the ace bandage around his head to hold on the gauze, not having any other way to attach it without shaving the site and using tape.

With no energy left, and the numbness in my lips slowly spreading to my nose and face, I leaned over and kissed the crown of Lucas' head and whispered, "*All better*." Then I felt myself falling, very slowly, and a tunnel of darkness met me at the bottom.

Chapter 14

Someone was holding something to my mouth. It tasted sweet and refreshing so I drank. I felt groggy and hot all over. My eyes burned and felt like they had been sealed shut. My entire right side from the waist down, burned in a throbbing pulse that kept time with the pounding in my head.

I concluded I had been hit by a truck and decided to go back to sleep, let the doctors do their thing, patch me up. Give me some aspirin, *man, I would kill for some Morphine*. But something in my mind -- I concluded it was a nasty little voice that had moved in without permission -- whispered that there were no trucks on the island.

The island. Land! I woke up with visions of waves and blood, and a deflated raft. I tried to sit up. A strong hand pushed me back down gently, and I turned my head to see Lucas hovering over me.

"Lucas!" He was alive, and whole and gorgeous, *and dressed*. I registered that fact just as I registered that I too had something covering me, a blanket. I glanced down. No, my dresses. They were damp and a little crusty with salt but it was a nice feeling. As if I were tucked into a bed. Albeit a wet bed, made of leaves and palm fronds. On the ground. But I didn't care. Lucas was there, and the sight of him lifted the worry, and made the pain just bearable.

"Hey." His voice was low, and full of concern. I saw that he had stripped off the ace bandage but the gauze I had applied was still in place on his brow, probably glued there with blood. "How are you feeling?"

I almost laughed. What kind of question was that? I felt too much to name them all, but decided to try, if nothing else, to see if I could figure them out. Attempt therapy via acknowledgment.

"Lousy, and thirsty." My voice sounded raspy in my ears, and my throat burned, probably from saltwater, and screaming. "I'm hungry," I forged on, identifying my state of being, "tired, I have a headache, my leg was hit by a truck or eaten by a shark, except I know it's there because it's screaming at me. I'm relieved, and so happy to see you. Curious -- where the hell are we? And really sad that I didn't wake up in a hotel where I can order room service. Morphine with coffee, and a cheeseburger."

Lucas laughed. It was a sound full of relief and exhaustion. I saw in his eyes that he was stressed and worried. I wished I could make him feel better.

"How are you?"

He leaned down and kissed my forehead. "I'm well, thanks to you. I woke up in the rain, naked, with a bandage on my head and a nude woman in my lap. It was weirdly arousing. Until I saw your leg." The worried look came back. I could tell he was at a loss as to what to do. "You were bleeding all over me, and so pale." His voice grew soft, almost a whisper. "I've never been so scared in my life Sophia." He reached out and took my hand. "I thought you were dead. You had bandaged me and then died on top of me. I almost lost it." He closed his eyes and then took a second before continuing.

"I took you into the trees, I found this clump here where the rain barely gets through. I drug our bags up and wrapped the ace bandage around your leg. It helped, the bleeding has stopped now, but Sophie, I don't know what to *do*. Should I sew you up? Should I boil water?" He had my hand in a death grip and I could see he wasn't kidding, he was really very scared.

Of what, I wondered? I mentally kicked myself, *of having to bury me, of being alone. Just because he's afraid of losing me doesn't mean he's in love with me.* I suddenly wanted that so badly. For him to tell me that he did. And I wanted to tell him, I wanted to be with someone that I loved and was loved by, if I had to endure, survive.

These last few days had stripped away all the frivolous things. All the tedium of normal life, and broke it down to the base; to feel, to survive and to be grateful. I was grateful, and I didn't care about embarrassment. I let it go and chose honesty.

"I love you Lucas." I said it softly and plainly. Not expecting a reply, but I took his other hand and brought it to my mouth, kissing his knuckles and gripping his fingers tightly.

Lucas brought his mouth down to mine and kissed me. I could almost taste his pain, the fear that vibrated through him.   "God I love you Sophia. Ever since you asked me to call you pumpkin you've had me running around in my head trying to figure this out." He took my face in his hands and looked me in the eye. "I thought you were dead. The most perfect, brightest, thing I've ever encountered in my life, and I couldn't handle the thought that I only had you for a few days." He kissed me again, sweeter and slower this time, but with an underlying urgency. He pulled away and brushed a stray strand of hair back into my matted braid, "I do love you, please promise me you can get through this. Tell me how to fix your leg."

I was crying. All the rest was small because my heart was so full. Love is an amazing medicine. It heals so much. I would get through this, because I'm a tough lady, and because there was a reason to, a really good one. *Lucas loves me.*

"Help me sit up."

I put my arms around his neck and Lucas propped me up, scooting me sideways a bit to lean back against a tree. I took stock, noting the cove of trees we sat under was almost completely dry. The spot was damp and muggy, but we weren't getting soaked in the rain. I was grateful Lucas had used the ace bandage to bind the wound. It was more sterile than anything in our suitcases, and they would have been soaked in sea water.

I had to believe that with all the rain and the bleeding, the wound had been washed out. I didn't have a choice. I had to hope for the best and maybe pray some more. I knew that Lucas would have to close it. Use the stapler, it would be the smartest choice. He couldn't disinfect his hands to sew me up and the stapler was sealed and sterile. I had concerns the scratches along my waist might get infected, they hadn't bled as much, but I had to deal with one thing at a time.

"I'm guessing you didn't find a resort or a hospital"

Lucas shook his head. "Not so much as a Tiki hut. We're definitely on an island, not a continent, and so far, I haven't found any structures. I didn't explored very far, but I'm afraid no room service. No doctor"

I sighed, resigned to what I had already guessed was true. We were on our own. "Where's the med kit?"

Lucas took it from one of the suitcases and handed it to me. Opening it up, I quickly cataloged the contents. One iodine left, we would have to use it, as well as the two alcohol swab tissues. I added the stapler, gauze, and superglue, to my pile, as well as the box of band aids. That was all I would be able to use. Everything else wouldn't help, it was just miscellaneous. I would need clean bandages. Lucas would have to wrap the leg, and my waist, for the first day to help the wounds close and start stitching themselves. After that I could let them air out, form hard scabs and do all the fixing behind closed doors, or skin as the case would be.

"We'll need a few things."

"Name it." Lucas' expression changed from anxiety to concentration, laced with a bit of hope.

"I need water, do you have something to catch it in?"

Lucas held up his metal cup, and I realized that was what I had awoken to. I reached out and drained the rest of the rain water he had caught in it and asked for more. Lucas grinned and then disappeared into the trees. A minute or two later he came back, the cup full again, and I was thrilled I could finally drink to my heart's content.

"Where did you get it?" I hoped that there was more because we would need it for the surgery.

"You were out for a while, more than two hours. I saw that ducky was holding water, so I dumped it all out, let the rain wash it, and dumped it again. She's almost completely deflated, but she has quite a few gallons of water in her now." He grinned, flashing his white teeth and dimples beneath the scruff on his face. "I've had five cups already." He nodded to his coffee cup. "Glad we had that in the bag."

"Mm hm… me too." I put the cup down and continued on with what we would need. "Lucas, I need you to take the largest item of clothing you can find in our bags. You'll have to wash it really well in fresh water, and then tear it into strips about two, to three inches wide. If you do that now we can hang the strips to dry while you do the rest."

Lucas smiled again and shook his head. "I tell you I love you and you set me to doing laundry."

I gave him a big grin in return. "Yep, next you'll be grocery shopping, so let me know when you're ready for the list."

My headache had receded some, and I sipped at the cup of water while Lucas went off to the laundry mat with one of my favorite sundresses in hand. I wished I had repacked the wraps I had sewn into a sail. They would have worked better as bandages. *Sunk to Davey Jones' locker by now.*

Sighing, I looked around at my surroundings. Lucas was right, barely any rain got through here under the trees. The ground below me was sandy with some ferns scattered about, and old fronds padding the floor. It seemed almost like a little hut. I closed my eyes, trying not to think about the pain, replaying Lucas' words in my mind. *The most perfect, brightest, thing I have ever encountered in my life.* I felt a thrill in my heart, and settled in, listening to all the new sounds around me.

The rain dripped and dropped, the plopping noises making a soothing lullaby. I figured we must still be close to shore as I heard the waves persistently crashing themselves against the beach. In the trees, birds chirped, and squawked, calling out to each other, enjoying their baths and not caring a whit about the new featherless visitors

Looking up into the branches I saw that we would have plenty of coconuts to eat, the heavy fruit hung in clusters in all the trees nearby. I wondered how we would get them open without an ice skate handy, but had faith that Lucas would figure something out.

I was about to nod off again, figuring sleep would keep me from feeling anything consciously, when Lucas came back holding my dress, wet and limp in his hands.

"OK, if you tear it up, just be sure to try to keep it as sterile as possible." I pushed the call of sleep away and gritted my teeth as he made the first tear.

Lucas stood, to avoid letting the material touch the ground, and tore my pretty dress into strips. To ease the pain of watching my expensive article of clothing die, I imagined he was tearing it off of me. That made me feel much better, I was smiling by the time he had all the strips hanging from the loop of one sleeve. He then stuck a stick through the sleeve loop and wedged it in the crook of one of the trees of our shelter.

"I don't know if they will dry completely, the air is pretty muggy, but…" Lucas shrugged, indicating he had no power over the weather, but hoped for the best. "OK, ready for the grocery list dear."

I laughed, and the movement sent shooting pain through my waist, then down my hip and for good measure my leg screamed at me too. My laughter ended in a cringing gasp and Lucas was kneeling in front of me, hands on my shoulders, worry in his eyes again.

"Easy Sophie. Just be still, take it easy."

Like he's calming one of his mares, I thought. But I loved him for his gentle concern, and his help.

"I'm alright." I took a breath in slowly, and let it out, boxing the pain away in one corner of my mind. I needed to focus.

"I need you to find an Aloe Vera plant. Do you know what one looks like?"

Lucas nodded and looked around us. "How do you know they grow here?"

"They do," I assured him. "It's tropical, and south of the equator, they grow in this region all the way to Australia."

He stared at me like I was a curious animal he wanted to pet, but wasn't sure if I would bite.

"Don't look at me like that, I'm not weird, I'm curious. I read. I remember stuff, and I happen to own three Aloes." I stated it as if that were reason enough for me to contain encyclopedic information on a plant.

"OK, Sophie." He kissed me quickly and rose to head into the jungle. "But you would make a great teacher, or librarian." he said, "Sexy little glasses, a bun, short skirt..." He disappeared into the trees.

"Librarians don't wear short skirts." I called after him. "And neither do teachers." I mumbled. But if I were a librarian I would. Just for fun.

I started to organize in my head what Lucas would need to fix me. But the thought of my leg being stapled made my blood pressure rise, and I felt the tell- tale panic threatening to make an appearance. So instead I closed my eyes and thought of home.

 I had been gone now for seven days. My flight left today, I realized. I was supposed to board at the Malé airport at three this afternoon. "Looks like I'm gonna miss my plane." I said to the birds. They kept up their chatter and didn't appear to care at all. Probably wondered why I didn't just fly home, use my wings. *Oh I would if I could.*

It was probably snowing at home, January snow, which meant cold and bitter. December snow is light and fluffy and fun for sledding, or snowmen. But in January, the ground is frozen solid and icy, and the snow is usually more tiny ice particle, than actual flakes. The hot, humid, air didn't match up to the vision of snow, so I let it go and wondered why it was raining at all. I had been told that January in the Maldives was perfect weather. The wet season was in summer, or fall, I couldn't remember now. Being so close to the equator made seasons confusing, but I did remember clearly, the travel agent who handled the scheduling, had promised no rain, or very little at most.

Of course I had no Idea where I was now. Maybe the distance we had traveled, had changed the seasons, now we were in rain-every-day-month. But I didn't resent it really. If the island had no fresh water source on it, the rain would keep us alive.

I worried that the muggy air would hinder healing though. Bacteria thrives in warm, moist environments. I sighed and changed the topic again. I needed something cheery, something the opposite of the burning coals eating my leg, or the feverish flush I felt throughout my body that might be sickness, or possibly, the tropics. *Go to your happy place Sophie.*

My happy place. *I'm on my horse on a late spring day. Everything is green, and alive, and full of promise.* Gypsy, a little mustang mare I trained from scratch, is fast, and she loves a good run. With my eyes closed, I leaned against the tree and took Gypsy in my mind, over the hills, up into the trees, and explored the high plateaus. *The wheat farmers are out on their tractors. Plowing and planting or spraying. There we take an old, overgrown, road into the neighboring canyon, finding deer trails and spotting wild rabbits...*

Lucas brought me out of my happy place with a light caress.

The pain was still there, and it felt like it was growing. I needed to get this done.

"Hey." I knew I looked tired and probably like a ragged bum. I had sand in my hair that was now a matted mess, no longer the pretty braids. The bun had come out in the water and now the one braid hung tangled and limp, over my shoulder. I'm sure there was blood matted in there, and I was probably pale and sickly looking. I felt pale and sickly.

"Hey back." Lucas held up a handful of large Aloe Vera leaves. They were bigger than any Aloe plant I had seen in the states, and I was relieved he had found some, let alone such a great many.

"Oh good" My voice sounded weak in my ears and I steeled myself to get out the entire plan in case I passed out.

"The plant has antibiotic properties. It will help heal the flesh and keep bacteria out as well. It may even help the pain. If I pass out, when you're done, mash some up and mix it with water and make me drink it that will help too. This," I held up the iodine. "Is for my leg. Wash the wound with water. Let it dry on its own don't touch it with anything. Then pour this in it, around it too if there's enough."

I noticed Lucas was growing a bit green, but ignored it, I couldn't do this to myself, he would have to. I knew he would. I had faith he would do anything it took.

"After the iodine dries, use this." I held up the super glue. "We can't get in to stitch up the muscle, but it's torn, it needs to be held together, not just the skin above."

At this I thought he might actually puke on me, but he took a breath, looked at the sky and blew it out, returning his focus to me. I pretended he was fine, great, no puking, he's a doctor.

"Get the glue in the muscle, then hold the wound together. Superglue is similar to cement, it will dry chemically, it doesn't really need a lot of air, it will just take longer. Next this." I held up the stapler. "Don't let go of the wound. Try to staple while holding the skin together so you don't lose the bond you get with the glue."

"Oh God," Now he put his head between his knees. "You actually *do* have a stapler, I thought you were kidding."

"No, look, doctors staple now, it's very common, this is sterile. It's our best bet to avoid infection." I felt the steam run out of me and closed my eyes. I leaned my head back against the tree and breathed slowly. "You can do this Lucas."

"I know Pumpkin, I will. Don't worry." He had my hand now, and I smiled, he called me pumpkin, it was our pet name, and I was grateful he was trying to cheer me up.

"OK, Cowboy, do about half an inch, maybe three quarters apart, I can't remember how many are in here, and I don't know how much is torn down there. Once you get it stapled, put this on, it will help create a barrier and assist in healing." I held up the plant. "Slice it open, with a clean blade, mash it up, it will turn to a chunky gel, then smear."

"Smear got it."

"For the rest of me, use these." I held up the alcohol pads. "Wash the wounds. Let them dry, then scrub with these, let *that* dry then apply plant." I held up the Aloe again. "And then wrap me up. The important part in the wrapping is to assist in keeping the skin closed, make it tight, but not so tight you cut off blood flow. OK, done." A wave of dizziness engulfed me and I swallowed hard, trying to keep my vision locked on Lucas.

"You ready?" I gave him a weak smile I knew had to be ghastly, but couldn't summon better.

"Yes, I'm ready." Lucas rose and fetched his knife from his bag, went down to the raft to wash the blade, and brought back a cup of clean water. Carefully, he pulled the layer of dresses off of my leg. I saw him grimace and turn green again, but he kept going, exposing my hip and waist. He slowly began pouring the cup of water into every scrape and scratch, then down my leg into the deeper cuts.

I gritted my teeth and moaned quietly, but knew I had to stand it. He knew too. He didn't stop, not even when I gasped as the water hit the deepest cut on my thigh.

Three more times he made a trip out into the rain, to Ducky, bringing back water. Once he handed the cup to me and I drank, grateful for the refreshing liquid on my burning throat, and sweet taste of rain.

Lucas handed me a stick and said, "Bite down. It gets worse from here on."

I nodded and took the stick, put the wood between my teeth and closed my eyes. Lucas tore open the iodine and began pouring the dark yellow antiseptic into the wound. The flash of lightning that struck me was so fierce I couldn't scream, or breathe, or think. And then the stars again, and blackness.

Chapter 15

When I woke up this time, it was dark. The rain had stopped, but the mugginess remained.

The birds were quiet, just insects left chirping, and the distant sound of waves hitting sand.

I felt Lucas beside me. The heat of him, but he wasn't touching me. I reached out, fumbling in

the dark toward his shadowy form, groping where I sensed his arm would be.

"Sophia. How are you?" He shot up and was at my side, holding my hand. "I was

worried" He murmured. "You passed out and didn't wake up, even during the stapling." His

hand was on my face, on my brow, checking for a temperature, stroking my hair. "I thought you

had a heart attack." I could hear the stress in his voice. Sense the worry.

"I'm alright. I'm thirsty." I put my hand over his and ran it up his arm, searching for his

face above me. "Thank you Lucas. I know that couldn't have been easy for you."

"Hardest thing I have ever done in my life" He bent down and I felt his kiss on my brow.

"Hold on." He whispered, and then he slipped away.

In a moment he came back, holding the metal cup to my lips, helping me sit forward to

drink. I felt like I was parched through to the bone. My skin was wet from the air, but inside I

was dust, desert.

"Can I have more please?"

"Yes Oliver, I will get you more." He left again and returned with the cup full.

I finished that one and lay back again. The bandages around my waist and hip were tight

but not restricting. "How does it look?"

Lady Sun

He knew I meant the wounds, the surgery.

"It looks better. You will scar." He said softly. "Some of the cuts are pretty jagged, but they pieced together decently. I used a lot of glue. Wherever did you learn to use glue for cuts? Are you sure that's safe?"

"I read a lot. It's actually an old military trick. Superglue was invented for military field medicine. At least I read that somewhere. I hope it's true because it's too late now."

He chuckled. "Well I'm grateful, my head wound feels like it was stitched by a surgeon. I'm betting you dumped glue in there too."

"Yep, hey, what happened?" I opened my eyes even though I was hardly able to see him in the dark. "You didn't catch the reef thank God, but your head was split open, blood everywhere. It was pretty ghastly."

"The metal box attacked me. When the raft flipped over I think it panicked and just lashed out in fear."

I chuckled and was grateful when it only hurt a little. "Well it could have been worse. How's your wrist?" I hadn't looked earlier, but it occurred to me now that it must be hurting some.

"Some rope burn and bruising, nothing that won't heal. You rest Sophie. Go back to sleep. We will check my work in the morning, and I'll hunt us down some food."

"Food, oh blessed food. That would be lovely." I closed my eyes again and reached out for his hand as he lay beside me. He was careful not to touch me, or jostle me, or bump my bandages. But he clasped my hand tightly, and I heard him whisper just as I fell into the deep black again...

"I love you..."

*   *   *

Morning brought the sun and heat. The wet jungle was steamy, and muggy, and the air made me feel like I had to constantly swallow. Like a slow drowning. It was almost solid with humidity. I recalled forecasts predicting rain, or snow, calling for seventy percent humidity, ninety percent humidity. At one hundred percent wouldn't we be swimming?

It was one hundred percent humidity this morning. I swam to a sitting position, groaning with pain and soreness, but strangely happy. It only took a moment for me to recognize where the emotion stemmed from. *Lucas loves me. And I love him.* If we ever got home we would figure things out. Be together. But for now, my mind was on water, because even swallowing the wet air, and the one hundred percent humidity didn't sate the thirst, and sandy, scratchy feeling in my mouth and throat.

I looked longingly toward my suitcase, knowing it held inside it my toothbrush, and tooth paste. Brushing would make me feel half normal, a glass of water, and maybe a doughnut wouldn't be too much to ask for either I figured. I had, after all, endured much. The universe owed me some payback. Balance the scales.

Lucas was nowhere to be seen, he must have snuck off at first light, maybe in search of breakfast. Perhaps there was a *Dunkin' Donuts* around the corner. I groaned aloud. I needed to not think of food. It was obvious I had lost weight. I didn't need clothes to tell me that. My hip bones were pokier than when I had boarded the plane in my sassy white pants and navy tank. My face seemed thinner too, my cheekbones closer to the surface. I ran my hands up over my face, rubbing away the sleep and exhaustion.

I'm a planner, a doer. I have a very hard time sitting still. If I must sit still, I will knit, or sew, or fold socks, or read. Winter time at home is full of sitting still projects. But here I had nothing to do, and even though I wanted to take out the matted clump of braids, and brush the sand out of my hair, dig out my toothpaste and brush the sand out of my mouth, I wanted even more, to heal up. To not feel any more pain and be able to walk again. I wouldn't risk ruining Lucas' handiwork of stapling and bandaging me back together. So I lay back, and looked up into the green palm fronds above me, and waited for Lucas to return.

A half an hour went by before I heard his footsteps through the underbrush. He appeared from behind me, holding something in his right hand and wearing a huge grin. Seeing I was awake he quickly put his hand and whole arm behind his back.

"I have a surprise." He knelt at my knees and I couldn't help but laugh. He looked like a kid who had just got his allowance and spent every penny at the candy store.

"Yay, I love surprises!" I do, I think anyone who goes through the trouble to surprise someone else, really cares, and is thinking of them unselfishly. Unless the surprise is bad, or when someone jumps out from behind a door and makes me pee a little in fright. I hate those surprises.

Lucas pulled his hand around from behind his back with great ceremony and plopped my very wet, and dirty, fishy smelling, purse in my lap.

"Oh my God!" I squealed in delight. I knew I sounded like a baby girl piglet but this was the best surprise ever. "I can't believe it! You found it, where was it?"

"It was wrapped in a big clump of seaweed a couple hundred yards down the beach from Ducky. I almost didn't see it, but then it caught my eye." He leaned over and kissed my forehead. "I thought it was a dead animal at first." He chuckled. "Kind of smells like one."

"Oh this is almost as good as donuts!"

"Well I did say I would find us something to eat. I haven't opened it yet, a woman's purse is a mysterious and forbidden thing to men." He shrugged and sat back, his face still split with a grin and I was thrilled to see him smiling.

"Thank you Lucas." I reached out and ran my fingers down his face, tickling his beard with my nails. "Let's see if anything survived the dunking."

I opened the zipper with some effort. The metal teeth were full of sand and the leather was slimy, and wet, and hard to grip. But finally, I had success and was able to peer inside. After seeing the wet contents and the mass of sand, and water, that still remained, I decided to just dump the whole mess out beside me, and see what could be salvaged.

The empty water bottles were there, my makeup kit, the flashlight I knew better than to even try to see if it worked, three candy bars, one bag of nuts, all seemingly safe in their plastic wrappers. I knew we couldn't be sure they hadn't been ruined until we opened them, but I crossed my fingers and quickly scanned the rest of the pile. The other odds and ends that made up the mysterious and forbidden contents of my purse were all there. My hair clip, a rubber band, a very wet wallet, a ball of string, a lighter, nail clippers and of course the beer, the mixed drinks and the vodka. The Mia Tai had broken, large pieces of pink colored class littered the sand, obscuring the smaller items, but the sight of the beer made me laugh.

"Oh my God! We are so going to celebrate tonight!" I reached out one hand high in the air and Lucas promptly high-fived me.

"Dibs on the beer."

"Oh no, we share big boy. We each get a beer, and you can have the Peña Collada, I'll have the Mudslide. If you help me, maybe we can go down to the beach and celebrate at sunset, just like I wanted to.

"You wanted to celebrate on the beach at sunset?" Lucas looked slightly confused. He had one of the beers in his hand, reading the label that was half peeled off and soggy.

"Not here, on the castaway island in the Maldives. That's why I have this hoard." I waved my hand at all the alcohol. "I wanted to have a tipsy tan, and a drink at sunset on the beach in paradise."

Lucas laid the beer back in the sand and leaned forward to kiss me. He lingered a minute with his forehead against mine, then said, "We will celebrate. I have a lot to be grateful for. Let's play it safe and not re-injure your leg. I'll carry you down to the beach."

I wrapped my arms around his neck and caught his smell. That scent of home and fields and leather. I inhaled deeply then laid my mouth against the warm skin at his throat, kissing lightly.

"So do I. Have a lot to be grateful for." Lucas leaned back, sitting on his haunches, his fingers now tangled with mine. "I love you Lucas"

His face transformed, and he smiled. His eyes were warm, and full of tenderness, and even a hint of happiness I noticed, then he said very directly and sincerely. "I love you too."

*   *   *   **

I was happy. Filthy, and grimy, and my leg still burned, but I actually felt truly happy. Lucas and I had devoured the bag of nuts and split one of the candy bars. It was a strange one I had never heard of, called a *Yorkie*. It had a bright blue wrapper, and the slogan on the side said*; it's not for girls.* Of course that only goaded me to buy it. No one can tell *me* I can't eat candy. I had actually thought the guy at the checkout was going to give me a hard time, but he hadn't, and now I relished the chunky chocolate bar, eating with defiance. Take that you Brit's, it *is* for girls after all.

Lucas had brought me water, and I downed two cups before I felt better. Then he filled up the two water bottles, as well as his tall thermos, and left me to 'go hunting.' Apparently, even though the manly chocolate was good, he insisted we needed some protein. I didn't argue with him, I do love me some protein.

Lucas had dragged my suitcase close to me and promised to check my bandages later in the day. I didn't want them to stick to any scabs forming, and I hoped that later he would take me to the beach where I could remove them. The sun and breeze would air out the wounds and assist in scabbing. I planned on replacing the strips at night for sleeping. He had said it was a good plan and vowed to be back soon before he kissed me goodbye. On any day of the week in suburbia, it might have been a normal domestic scene.

I opened my case and found my toothbrush and toothpaste. I brushed and scrubbed and spit and rinsed three times before I judged my mouth was up to sparkling standards. I drank some more water and began the very long task of taking out my braids and untangling my long hair.

Once the braids were finally free I began brushing out the sand and tangles. It took some time and a lot of patience as my waist and hip didn't like the stretching, also, I was only able to hold my arms up for a few minutes before I began to fatigue. I knew I was not in good shape when I finally sat, panting, my arms tingling and tiny black spots darting across my vision. I relaxed for a few minutes then forged on, determined to feel human, and this was the only sitting still project I had.

I poured a bottle of water over my head, letting it run over my face and down my hair across my shoulders, taking a mini shower while sitting in the sand on palm fronds. I brushed out my hair once more, intent to remove all of the sand and any remaining tangles, then rested for ten minutes, and repeated the process. By the end of it all I had scrubbed my face clean with one of my dresses, gotten my hair pretty darn clean, and completely tangle free, and deemed myself almost human again.

I wanted to get dressed but didn't want to disturb the bandages, so I settled for slipping one of the sundresses that had served as a blanket over my head. It was a creamy gold with delicate white daisies embroidered around the hem and had a full breezy skirt that would fall to my knees if I were ever able to stand up. The dress had no sleeves but gathered a couple of inches below my throat and then a gold rope tied behind my neck leaving my shoulders bare and free to catch the breeze and cool my skin. I couldn't pull on panties but I did fish out a pair of white sandals and slipped those on. I knew I wouldn't be walking anywhere soon, but it made me feel prepared nonetheless.

All said and done I felt better, and completely exhausted, but my stomach wasn't grumbling and I was semi clean and almost completely dressed. It seemed weird to not be wearing underwear.

With the tasks finished I soon became bored. I downed the last of the water and lay back to rest, the warm air lulling me, drugging me. Soon I drifted off, to dream of white beaches, dark pirates, and a tall cowboy with wide shoulders and a soft mouth.

*   *   *

True to his word, Lucas came back with a feast. I had been awake for a little while, whistling at the birds that were a cacophony of sound around me. I was trying to master a particularly pretty call when he strode into our little hut-shelter carrying a rather large fish.

"Wow! How about that, is that a tuna?" I was incredulous and really excited. This was going to be a fantastic meal. We would need a fire, and maybe a coconut, we could open it and use the milk to flavor the meat, wrap it in some palm fronds and roast it over coals. I was cooking up recipes in my head, my mouth watering in anticipation when I realized Lucas hadn't replied. I tore my eyes away from dinner and looked up to his face. He stood there, staring at me. He took in the dress, my clean face and hair that now spilled around my shoulders, slightly curling in the humidity. I put a hand to the thick mane, thinking *Llama* in my mind and gave him a little smile.

"Lady Sun."

I was confused, had he seen the ship? Were the pirates here on the island? He saw my eyes widen and must have read the panic there because he quickly dropped down beside me and set the fish aside.

"No Sophia, not the yacht, you. You're beautiful, your hair," he reached out to touch it and then pulled back not wanting to get fish on me. "It's golden, and full, like rays of the sun. *You* are Lady Sun." He smiled gently. "And yes, it is a tuna, Blue fin."

My heart settled back to normal, and I basked in the complement. "Thank you."

He just nodded and turned back to the fish. "Let's get you down to the beach. I bet you would enjoy some sunshine and a view"

"Oh yes, thank you, I'm dying to get up and explore, but don't want to pull the stitches."

"Staples." He corrected. "How do you feel?"

"Better today. My leg is a constant fire still, but it hasn't made me cry, or scream, so I think that's progress."

He looked concerned and then sighed. "Well we will check the healing once we get you into the sun. You look like you're dressed for a party. We're really overdue to enjoy our vacation so what do you say we start a fire, roast some fish and have a drink on the beach?"

I would have jumped up and down and clapped my hands in joy if I could. I settled for the clapping and laughed "Oh hell yeah, let's have a party!"

Lucas laughed with me, smiling wide at my cursing, and reached over and scooped me up into his arms. I squealed a little with pure delight. He was like a deserted island prince, But Lucas needed no armor, even though he was my knight.

Very gingerly Lucas carried me against him careful not to jar my leg. It had protested with a brief threat of lightening, but settled down again and now it was back to the normal raging fire.

We broke free of the tree line in only a few of Lucas' long strides. He set me down on the pure white sand just inside a patch of shade, and there before me spread out like a perfect postcard, was paradise. The waves crashed onto the white sand, and they were lovely now that I wasn't mad at them. The bay stretched out in a brilliant aquamarine blue, shimmering like a liquid gem, until it reached the coral reef where greens and deeper blues tied in. Then out to the ocean that no longer scared me, now that I wasn't floating aimlessly on it. Intermittently, a palm tree dipped out from the jungle, leaning and grazing its fronds along the sand, creating such a picture of tropical perfection I felt myself tear up.

"Why would anyone ever leave this place," I whispered. "It's so beautiful, it's stunning. Lucas," I reached up for his hand and pulled him down beside me. "We should stay forever. Have you ever seen anything so perfect in all your life?" I was overwhelmed with it. So pristine, and warm and inviting, now that the fear was gone. Lucas was fine, I would be fine. We were in heaven.

"Only one thing."

"Hmm?" I had forgotten what I had asked.

"I have seen one thing more perfect than this."

Lady Sun

"Oh," I felt the thrill of the island sink a little and turned to look at him. He was looking at me, steadily and purposefully. "Montana." I said softly. "Home."

"No Sophia. You." He ran his fingers through my hair. Then he grabbed a handful at the nape of my neck and pulled my mouth to him. He kissed me hungrily, and I kissed him back. We were suddenly both starving for each other, and the taste of him ignited in me a fire completely unrelated to pain. I put my hands on his shoulders and steadied myself, ending the kiss with a gasp, and a yearning to strip off our clothes and fulfill the burning need in me. But we could wait. We had time. I would heal, and we would make love every day in this paradise. We had no choice. Love it or hate it, we were here. And I loved it.

Lucas smiled against my mouth and I chuckled, the laughter coming from deep inside, warming me with joy.

"Let's feast."

"I thought we were." His breath tickled my lips.

"Oh no." My grin was huge. "Let's eat roasted tuna, with coconut milk, then let's get drunk and watch the sunset."

Lucas ran his hand over my hair again. "OK, Lady Sun, we'll feast in paradise."

Chapter 16

Lucas had swiped my red lighter that morning before he had gone on his hunting trip. He tapped the sand out of it on a rock, releasing any trapped water that may have made a home in the little silver wind break. He had then laid it in the sun to dry. Intent on making a fire, he now began combing the beach for driftwood. Gathering armloads of twigs and sticks, all worn smooth and bleached to a creamy white from the sun, he placed them about fifty feet in front of me. The stack soon began to grow as he returned with yet another armload.

"Gonna build a signal fire?" I was laid out on my back with my head elevated on a life vest Lucas had fetched from our palm hut-nest. My legs were thrust into the sun, my body from the waist up, tucked into the shade of a leaning palm. The warmth felt luxurious. Now I could sit in the sun with the shade as an option, it had the psychological effect of making the sun rays that toasted my skin feel yummy, rather than the scary headache inducing result, when floating out at sea. I imagined I was at a spa, enjoying the view, basking. *Oh lord it's good to bask.*

"It will burn up fast, I thought we would like to be prepared. This will make some good coals to roast the fish, we can enjoy our drinks and luxuriate while on vacation."

"Oh ho," I chuckled, "I hope you feel the same way five years from now when no rescue comes, no boats, or planes, or long distance scuba divers. You'll be stuck with me, no alcohol, and fish to eat every day."

"You don't seem concerned." He took a break, plopping down beside me in the sand, and stretching out his long legs. His feet a sat a good four inches past my toes that were sprinkled in

Lady Sun

white sand, like sugar on a doughnut.

"I'm not." I put my arms under my head and studied him, he was shirtless, with a pair of khaki shorts that had to have twenty pockets on them. They reached past his knees and I figured stuffed full, his pockets could probably hold all the contents of my purse. *No wonder men didn't carry purses. Their clothing could hold an assortment of knives and wallets and keys, cell phones and an array of manly items, without ever worrying where you misplaced your bag.*

Lucas' feet were covered with a pair of brown deck shoes that looked comfortable and well worn. He was already showing a decent tan, and I was determined to catch up.

"I figure," I continued as I admired his physique, "that we can't leave, we can hope for rescue, but being here, well, making the best of it really isn't that hard. We'll have to find food, water, stay safe, don't do anything stupid that will get us killed. But Lucas, if we're to be stranded anywhere on the planet, I can't really bitch and moan about paradise."

Lucas sighed and looked around us. "Yeah, I have to agree. I mean we did actually pay to go to a deserted island alone, so I guess we got what we paid for."

"Oh yeah, and then some, plus, even though the 'alone' part was a total attraction to me, I'm thrilled I'm not. Relieved, grateful, thankful, blessed. I wouldn't be this chipper if you weren't here."

"Really? Well thanks." Lucas grinned widely and his eyes sparkled a deep blue in the shade of our palm. "I'll admit you were a bonus to the package too Sophie. You're right, being here alone would be a whole other story."

"Hmm…" I closed my eyes and let the sun soak into my skin. The shade was moving, and I gauged five more minutes and I would have to readjust, scoot down the beach a little more.

Lucas had carefully unwrapped my bandages before he went trekking for the firewood. My cuts and scrapes and gashes looked pretty ugly, and it was a bizarre sight to see my leg decorated with staples, but it was clear they were on the path toward healing. The breeze off the water and the warm sun encouraged the skin to dry out and the smaller cuts were already hardening. I was concerned about my thigh, it seemed pretty red and inflamed, but I didn't know if that was normal. There was nothing to be done for it anyways, except the now familiar hoping and praying. So I put the worry aside and opted for looking on the bright side.

"How much have you explored? You didn't find a resort, a hospital, a *7-eleven*?"

"Nope, none of the above. I've walked a good portion of this beach, but haven't circled around to see the other side. This morning when I found your purse in that big mass of seaweed, I found some tangled fishing line. The test was much stronger than what I had, so I spent some time untangling as much as I could. I got about fifty or sixty feet of it, and a good sized hook." He waved lazily at a gnat-like bug that was buzzing around his face. "When I went in search of food I noticed the peninsula, a little ways past that bend on the beach." He pointed his long, tan, arm south east. At least I thought it was south east, being south of the equator, all my compasses were upside down and backwards in my head. I determined I would do some serious calculating on that issue later and looked to where Lucas was pointing. I had to shade my eyes with one hand, squinting against the glare off the bright sand. My sunglasses were back in the trees with my purse.

"One side of it drops pretty steeply into the ocean, so I took a chance and rigged up a pole and sat to fish. It's pretty hard to cast a line without a reel but years of fly fishing taught me some technique." He shrugged and smacked at the gnat, leaving a red mark on his shoulder and a tiny black corpse that he flicked off to land in the sun, just outside our line of shade. "The tuna practically hopped on the hook, begging to be brought in. I was wondering if it was luck or if these waters are a great fishing spot."

"Only time will tell I suppose. Speaking of the tuna, we should get to roasting before it starts to turn."

"Hmm, doubt it will turn in the hour or so since I caught it, but as you so command my lady," Lucas leaned in and kissed me, "so shall I do your bidding." Then he tipped an imaginary cowboy hat at me, and rose to go in search of more wood, sugar sand sprinkling off of him as he strode away.

Yes, he definitely made this not only a tolerable experience but a delicious one.

Lady Sun

*   *   *

A few more trips, and a few more armloads dumped on the pile, and Lucas deemed we were ready to begin. He brought out of the jungle, an old, brown, palm frond and laid it in my lap. "Shred that up as small as you can for tinder, I'll go get a coconut and a fresh frond for roasting."

The dead brown leafy thing in my lap would have been crisp, and dry, and perfect for tinder if it hadn't rained recently and then sat on the muggy jungle floor. But I shredded it into threadlike strips and laid the pieces in the sun beside me to dry. In ten minutes I had a nice size pile of light fluffy tinder that was growing crispy, just as my legs were turning pink.

I decided my tan time was over and lifted my weight up on my hands and dragged myself backwards. I managed about six inches per scoot, but soon I was in full shade and still had the benefits of warmth and wind.

Lucas soon returned with an armload of palm frond, green and succulent looking, and a few coconuts still in their tough green, casings. He deposited the ingredients beside me in the shade and went off to get our dinner. Returning with the tuna, he laid it on the fronds and then sat beside me to begin attacking the coconuts.

I had begun a tally of our blessings as I lay in the sand, encouraging my wounds to heal, and I counted Lucas' knife as one of our greater ones. He carried a small armload of the brown hairy balls that are an all too familiar sight if you ever watched Gilligan's island, and dumped the pile beside me. There were many green coconuts still in the trees that had yet to ripen fully, I had never had young green coconut, and Lucas didn't seem too keen on shimmying up a palm to fetch any. He had gathered these from the jungle floor, choosing the freshest he could find.

Lucas began smacking the ridge of one of the round balls with the hard backside of the blade, all the while turning the coconut until he had smacked it all around the equator. One more turn with some sturdy smacks and the fruit cracked in half.

"Oh yay!" I was thrilled there was no loss of digits, no throwing against rocks, or working up a sweat. Lucas made it look easy. "How did you do that without an ice skate?" I laughed and reached out for the two halves, careful not to spill the coconut milk that balanced in one of the creamy white bowls of sweet meat.

"My mom, she's a baker, or rather, she bakes a lot and cooks from scratch. I've watched her smack open these tough nuts in three blows." Lucas then chuckled as he said, "And Sophie, you watch way too many movies."

"Well, you clearly understood the ice skate reference so I could say the same. Besides, there won't be a worry of too much of the tube here. Your mom sounds like a fun lady."

"Oh yeah, loves to laugh and cook and feed her kids, she's a lot like Paula Deen, but without the southern accent."

Lucas moved to the pile of firewood and began digging a pit in the sand using his hands. When he deemed it the perfect depth and size, he strolled off into the jungle hunting for rocks.

I started thinking about our earlier conversation. Being stranded and making the best of it. I really couldn't summon up any fear or dread, but I did wonder how my mother was doing with my farm. It was a handful to take care of alone, and I knew the animals and their finicky ways. All the personalities and the dispositions, they were my friends, so I didn't mind, I enjoyed tending them. My mother, though, didn't have a farm, because she didn't want one. A week was all I could beg out of her, she was the only one I trusted to do it right even if she didn't enjoy it. I hoped she called Lily to come and stay and help her. I hoped they were OK, they must be beginning to miss me now.

I would have to figure out the time difference, but I thought I was due back today. Flying back I would almost be arriving the day I left. Even though the return flight would be just as long as my flight out had been, the time change would work in my favor. When I didn't disembark from the plane at the airport would Anna panic? I tried to imagine the steps she would go through. She would call me first. With no service, no battery and a thorough dunking, my cell would not get that call. After a couple tries she may inquire with the airline, see if I booked a later flight. If she didn't find me on any manifest that night, or in the near future, she would probably call the family.

My family consists of my mother, and my two sisters. I had a brother, Jared, but, he had passed away two years ago. A car accident. Then of course there is my Aunt and my cousins. So my mother would call Clara, my older sister, who would then call the airlines, and the travel agent in Malé. Once she learned of the missing yacht, she would call the authorities. I was wondering if they had already been notified, when Lucas returned, lugging an impressive armload of rocks.

"Hey, do you think the travel agency knows we're missing?"

He began layering the bottom of his fire pit with the rocks and seemed to think on the question for a minute. "It's possible. Jok had said they had expected more visitors to the castaway isle. So with the yacht not being returned they might go and check to see if we made it."

"Seems logical," I agreed. "In which case, the authorities are looking for the yacht, and for us. So maybe our families have been notified."

Lucas finished layering the rocks and began piling the now dried palm fronds in the middle of the pit. I watched as he built a tee-pee of twigs over it and then another tee-pee of sticks to cap it off. Then he sat back on his heels and looked at me.

"Possibly Sophie, maybe our moms are wringing their hands, our families figuring out what to do, who to call, where to search. We can't know. And we can't do anything to help them."

We both fell silent then, both of us lost in our own thoughts. The sun was lowering in the sky, and the shade felt nice, less of a wet oven, more relief. The topic of rescue and stressed out family depressed me. I wondered how Lucas felt. He had his ranch to get back to, and memories of a failed marriage that lurked there. I had my life in Washington that consisted of basically the same thing season after season. I loved my life there. Or I had, until the thought of leaving this beach, struggling through the next season, actually depressed me.

"Do you want to go back?" I asked the question softly, almost as if it were a taboo thing to say out loud.

Lucas rose and strode over to where the lighter still lay on a log in the sun. It should be bone dry now and the fluid absolutely combusting to be set free.

When he returned he knelt in front of his well laid pile of sticks and said, "Ask me after we eat and I have a beer in me. I'll likely be more honest."

I nodded my head and watched with bated breath as he put the lighter to the shredded palm and flicked the metal roller, hoping for a spark to hit the flint.

Apparently hoping and praying do actually work, if you cross your fingers on both hands, scrunch your eyes tightly shut, and whisper; *please, please, please, please*. On the third flick of the *Bic* I heard a soft crackle and smelled smoke. I cracked one eye slightly and witnessed the miracle of fire.

"Fire! Oh thank the heavens above, and the *Bic* Company, and your awesomeness, we have fire!" I reached out to Lucas and we high-fived, he had a grin splitting his face from ear to ear and I could see he was proud of himself.

"Well played island man. Now to the feast!" I carefully set aside the coconut halves that had grown warm from being held in my lap, and reached for the succulent palm fronds. "Do you want to gut the tuna, maybe slice it into steaks, it will be pretty hot once we pull it out of the fire."

"Good idea," Lucas quickly gutted the pretty fish, sliced the meat off its body into four healthy steaks, and handed them to me to wrap. He then picked up the fish guts and wrapped them in one of the fronds. "I'll keep this for bait, I can bury it under a rock so the crabs and birds don't get at it."

"We have crabs here?"

"Oh yeah, tons of them, really crazy looking too, they're huge. I saw a bunch down at the shore this morning."

"Huh, I can't wait to discover what else this island holds."

Lucas smiled and fed the fire some more sticks. "Soon. Your leg should be able to take weight in another day or two. Then we will explore."

The flames were greedy, and I saw that Lucas had once again been right. The wood would go fast. I was glad he stocked up.

I began laying the tuna steaks on the palm leaves, then I carefully soaked each one with the coconut milk. Finally, I dug out some meat, which proved way more difficult than I had thought it would be, and added the white chunks to the fish before I finished wrapping them. It was easy to tie the fronds to themselves to keep the wraps intact. I placed the meal to the side and watched Lucas down at the water, washing the fish from his hands.

He was still something of a mystery to me, but the learning of him was so enjoyable I didn't want to rush it, push him. I compared the experience to an excellent meal or an exotic dessert. You take each bite and taste it. You eat slowly, sipping it with wine. You enjoy the experience, the flavor, the texture. Lucas wasn't a chew and swallow kind of meal. He was a rare cuisine I intended to enjoy every bite of.

The fire soon made a bed of coals, and Lucas laid the bundled steaks on top of them. He fed the fire all around the coals and hot rocks below, but didn't bury the tuna in sticks and flames. After ten minutes he turned the bundle over and kept at his rock oven until finally he deemed the steaks ready to eat.

My mouth was watering with anticipation, and my stomach was clenching, and growling like a beast. With two sticks Lucas picked up a now darkly singed frond bundle and set it before me.

"While it cools enough to touch I'll go get our drinks."

I almost didn't hear him. The beast was clawing to get out. *Eat, eat, eat.*

Finally, Lucas landed beside me in the sand, handed me a bottled water, a beer, and the Mudslide. I saw that he lined up the same for himself except his third was the Piña Colada.

"Oh this is going to be good." He leaned over, and with his knife cut down the center of the green, fish/palm calzone. "Can we eat the palm leaves?"

"They do in Hawaii, I'm gonna give it a shot." I picked up my half, noting that the tuna was cooked perfectly, white around the edges with a little pink in the middle. Like fine sushi from a master Japanese chef. I lifted the wrap to my mouth and took a bite.

"Oh my god!" I moaned and rolled my eyes. I tried to relish it, enjoy it, chew slowly, but the beast in me was set free, and I devoured the entire thing, palm fronds and all within five minutes.

Each of the four steaks had been huge. Knowing the size that Blue fin tuna could reach I had guessed that Lucas had caught a young one, but even so it had been an extremely large fish on the scale of a trout or a bass. But even as stuffed as I was, I almost wished it had been bigger. I lay back and let the beast settle, my stomach stretched to thanksgiving proportions.

After a week of surviving on water and random candy bars, huge amounts of stress and dehydration, the tuna was a blessing. Add to that, borderline sunstroke, and being beat to hell on Paradise Island's coral reef, my body and spirit had needed the fuel and I didn't regret a single bite.

Lucas had clearly enjoyed the feast as well. His tuna-coconut-palm disappeared as quickly as mine had and then he too lay back on the sand beside me, the coals of our fire smoldering at our feet.

"Oh yeah, that was crazy good." He reached out and took my hand and we just let our bodies bask in the feeling of finally being full.

"Hey," Lucas said after a few minutes.

"Hmm… yeah?" I lay almost comatose with the warm air, full belly and general feeling of contentment.

"The sun is about to set."

I pulled myself up and reached for my beer. I wasn't going to let my full belly stop me from enjoying my first real sunset on land. The bottle wasn't a twist top so I handed it to Lucas who did some quick magic with the lighter and handed it back.

"I could never figure out that trick."

"Well at least I know you'll keep me around as long as there's beer to open." He winked and lifted his bottle. What should we toast to?

I turned to watch the blazing ball of fire sink slowly, dousing its light for another day. The sky set free it's dressage of reds and oranges, yellows and pinks, making paradise glow with holiday flamboyance and magical mystery.

"To surviving in style."

Chapter 17

The next two days drug by. It didn't rain again and when I expressed my concern about refilling the drinking water, Lucas showed me the metal can. He had dumped all the water that had gathered in Ducky, into the can, almost topping it off. It had to be almost five gallons. I was instantly relieved, but we both agreed to ration anyway, not knowing how long we would have to go until the next rain, or if we would discover fresh water on the island.

Lucas didn't explore without me. I wondered at that at first, thinking it was a sweet gesture to wait until I could walk. But when I asked him why he hadn't gone off into the jungle in search of a Starbucks, or a tree house, he explained that was on his mental list of stupid things.

"What stupid things?"

"When you mentioned that we might be happy here, enjoy the stranding, hunt for food, find water, and not do stupid things that would get us killed. Well, I started to make a list of stupid things."

"Finding Starbucks is not stupid, that is on the list of survival skills."

"Wandering into the jungle leaving your injured woman alone is pretty stupid though."

I had sighed and basked in being called his woman, deciding sacrificing the Starbucks was worth it.

"So what other stupid things are on your list?" We had been laying under the stars, opting to sleep below the tree line so we could see the sky and wake with the sun.

"Swimming with sharks."

"Agreed, really, really, stupid."

"Befriending cannibals."

"Is that an option?"

"Robinson Crusoe seemed to think so."

"I don't think Friday was a cannibal."

"Well he suggested eating people, so I'm going to go with cannibal. Crusoe was lucky, at any moment Friday could have snacked on him, so I propose a house rule, or island rule; no befriending cannibals."

"OK, I second."

"Stupid item number four; No swimming without a lifeguard."

"Oh come on, really?"

"Between your reef attack, my metal can attack and jumping off a yacht, I think we've both had enough water drama. Let's not test fate. Swim where I can see you and let you know when the sharks close in."

"Oh, then it circles back to stupid item number two."

"Sure, but not just sharks can getcha, there are sting rays and jelly fish."

"Sea urchins." I added, trying to be helpful.

"Well if I step on a sea urchin you can just pee on my foot, it's rarely life threatening."

"Why do I have to pee on it, you can pee on it."

"Are you saying you would refuse to treat me medically?"

"Peeing is not medical treatment and besides you would have better aim, I would just, well, spray. House/island rule; either of us steps on an urchin and you get to administer the pee medicine."

Lucas had laughed and curled into me. "I'll second." He kissed me thoroughly and then whispered, "Good night pumpkin."

It was now two days after our drinks on the beach. I was champing at the bit to do anything but lay around while Lucas got to fish and collect firewood and coconuts. After finding a couple of brown coconuts rotted with bugs in them, he began climbing the trees to get the fruit and walked around practically flaunting his ability to move upright. Well now I was beyond ready.

Today was the day I got to walk.

Lucas was off in search of a crutch for me. I examined my leg one last time. At night I had been applying aloe, to help with the tightness of the skin so the wound wouldn't tear, and to assist in healing. In the daytime I let it air out. My waist and hip looked fine, the scratches and scrapes would fade in time, but my leg still looked angry.

The wound was closing nicely, the staples did their job, it didn't seem infected, and the pain was more than cut in half now. It was so shocking to look down and see one leg so smooth, a little tan now, but with creamy skin, the other a mangled mess in comparison. But I sighed and was grateful we had dodged the bullet of infection. I most likely would have died on the island and Lucas would have been left alone.

I wrapped up my leg with the long strips of my dress. Lucas washed the strips every morning, using some of our precious clean water. They were bone dry by the time night fell and it was time to wrap up again. I was wrapping it now to keep everything together while I attempted my stroll. No need to risk a remission due to wounds opening.

I sat on the beach in my now usual spot, staring at the same perfect, pristine, view. I wasn't bored with it yet. Not even a little. After we had finished our beers and my Mudslide, Lucas' Piña Colada, I had asked him again if he wanted to leave. The weighing of home and loved ones worrying, and the happiness we felt here, was a difficult one to sort out.

We talked long into the night, sharing our motivations behind why we both had chosen to live in seclusion, to live on farms and be self-sufficient. Neither of us missed the city or desired to go there, even to visit. Our dream vacations had been to escape even further, to an island where there were even less people.

And then we landed here, where there's such beauty, it's more than feasible to survive, and we could survive happily with each other. Before we drifted off to sleep Lucas and I had both admitted we didn't want to leave. The biggest pull back to the states were our animals and our guilt over our families concern. But given that we had no power over the fact that we were here, we decided not to indulge the guilt or worry, but to take each day and be grateful that we had survived and we had love.

Looking out over the water, patiently waiting for my crutch, I wondered now, if we did spot a boat or a plane, would we signal them? Would we hide in the jungle? Would we be this happy together if we had to struggle through the seasons, pay bills, feed cattle, give sheep shots, chain up, and shovel snow? Would store bought tuna be as delicious? Would our love be as passionate?

Lucas strolled toward me now with a crutch held in the air in triumph, and I felt deep in my heart that I would love him even in the snow. I hoped and prayed, as now was my habit, that seasons and bills and the real world wouldn't make a difference to him either. But I was too afraid to ask.

I smiled and waved and focused on *this* day. Today I would walk. Today Lucas did love me.

A line from *Gone with the Wind* popped into my head and I opted to agree with Scarlett, I would worry about it tomorrow.

*   *   *

The crutch worked perfectly. It was actually more of a sturdy cane with a knobby end that was easy to grip. Lucas lifted me to standing, and I adjusted my weight, taking a moment to center my balance. I took a step, bearing heavily on the cane, applying very little pressure to my wounded leg. Then another step, and another, and I was laughing and hobbling down the beach.

It was difficult going with the loose shifting sand, so we took it slow, meandering toward Lucas' fishing spot. We paused now and again, taking in the view of the thick jungle on one side, and the rainbow hues of blue ocean on the other. We neared the peninsula and Lucas guided me to a log in the shade where we sat to relax. Here the beach turned sharply. If we followed the bend around the corner we could see the other side of the island.

"Please Lucas, come on, you're such a jailer!"

"Really Sophia, you sound like a teenage girl who wants to go on a date past curfew." He flipped my ponytail and stuck out his tongue. He had been becoming more easy in his manner as the days went by, not the man on the *Lady Sun* who wouldn't even talk to me, but still sexier than ever.

"Well you are acting like my parent trying to tell me what I can do. You're not the boss of me Lucas Lael."

Lucas threw back his head and laughed, "Oh, OK Sophia, you win this battle. We can go exploring. But we rest when I think you need it, and no going into the jungle, too many things to trip you up. Let's just keep to the beach and round the bend, see if there's a resort or a Starbucks."

He leaned over and kissed me, one of the things I loved about him. He loved to touch, to kiss. I wrapped my arms around his neck and returned the kiss.

"I promise I'll be good, and I will more than repay you for indulging me."

"Mm… you should have led with that. But promise of payment seals it. Off to explore!"

We drank a bit of water from the bottle Lucas carried and then made our way toward the water. We agreed it would be much easier to walk on the wet sand near the surf than struggle along near the trees. It was another typical hot, muggy, day, which also contributed to our lazy stroll. We reached the wet sand, and I took a pause, assessing my leg, the pain level, trying to tell if I had put stress on the staples. Amazingly, I felt great. The wound still hurt like a beast had gnawed on me, but it was tolerable, and I attributed it to healing. The wounds way of letting me know it was still there, but as long as I was nice to it, it would be nice to me.

I turned my face in the direction we were heading. Having sorted out my inner compass, I judged that we had landed on the Northwest side of the island. I couldn't really judge the shape, as the shore line, and the jungle itself, blocked any view further than a hundred yards or so. But now, once we rounded this northeastern bend, we would most likely be heading due south, or southeast, depending on how sharp the bend turned. I felt better having some bearing and picked up my pace in anticipation.

"You know we will most likely be seeing the exact same view as we do here, just a different direction."

"You can't tell me you aren't excited to see though, to know." I grinned at him and punched him in the shoulder, the one that had been wounded when jumping off the Lady Sun. In seven days it had healed almost completely, it was now just a pink line along his bicep. "Come on Luke,"

"Don't call me Luke."

"Come on Lukey, you have to have some adventurous blood in you, you know 'to explore strange new places, to boldly go where no one has gone before!'" I held a fist to the sky in an interpretation of Captain Kirk in my mind.

"Sorry, I'm not a Trekkie, or a Lukey, just Lucas. And I love adventure, as well as exploring. I wasn't trying to quash your inner Columbus, or Cap'n Kirk, or whatever, I'm just sayin' the view most likely won't change."

The timing couldn't have been more perfectly ironic. We had been walking a half circle beach and came to the beach that ran north /south. It *was* different. And in that moment everything changed.

Chapter 18

"I know where we are."

"What?" Lucas grabbed my arm as I sank to the wet sand, steadying me to float gracefully down, rather than plop, which would have most likely popped a staple.

"I know where we are Lucas. I've seen this before."

"Where? What are you saying, you've been here?"

"No, I viewed it from space, on *Google Earth*. Look," I waved my arm at the view in front of us. Our island stretched out like a long green snake with white sand fringe. But there, just in view, was another island separated by only a short span of water. It was directly east of us, rounding the bend had brought it in view. The water on this side was calm, no waves, clear as glass and a lovely pale, pale, sea foam green. Further out it became a light aquamarine, and then a deep blue, but not like the open ocean on the other side of the island. Because this wasn't open ocean, it was the center of an atoll. "See that island, beyond it there is another, and another after that, if we follow this beach I'm betting we'll see another island south of this one. This atoll is a giant circle of islands similar to the Maldives but on a smaller scale."

"How do you know this? I mean couldn't we be back in the Maldives?"

I shook my head. "I don't think so. The uninhabited islands there are small, privately owned by resorts for people like us to get away on. But nothing the size of this." I waved my hand down the long beach, it had to stretch a mile before a clump of jungle blocked our view. "This is too valuable, they would have developed it. From the Googling, and research, and satellite snooping I did before I came, I'm pretty sure this is Peros Banhos."

"Seriously Sophie how can you remember that, or even *know* that, sometimes I think you swallowed a librarian or had a microchip implanted in your brain."

I smiled and said, "Hey you know the Super bowl is in a few weeks, who's your money on?"

"Completely off topic. Bengals and the Patriots."

"Seriously, the Bengals?"

"Yeah, what of it?"

"When was their last super bowl?"

"1988."

"What was the score?"

"20/16 San Francisco."

"Have they ever *won* a Super bowl?"

"No, but I have hope."

"I rest my case."

"You were making a case?"

"Look Lucas, you remember nonsense that interests you, and I remember nonsense that interests me. I happened to spend way too many hours searching for deserted islands when I planned my trip. Peros Banhos was a really interesting story as well as one of the more beautiful places on earth. So yeah, I do think that's where we are, but there's one way to know for sure."

"OK, how."

"We find the island with the house on it."

*   *   *

Lucas seemed interested to hear the story of the island so I began telling him what little bits I could remember. I do have a great memory, but it is far from photographic.

"So from what *Wikipedia* told me,"

"You know for a lady who runs a farm," Lucas interrupted right off the bat, "You sure are plugged in. So far I know that you shop on *Amazon*, You *Google* everything including earth, you quote movies and make pop culture references as if the cast of *Lost* are your good friends and you seem to have *Wikipedia* pretty well memorized."

"Hmm, well I have no excuse for using the tools of education and entertainment at my disposal, do you wanna hear Wiki's story?" I could tell he was only teasing me, so I didn't take offense. But I did give him my stern school teacher face, which he obligingly bowed to.

"Yes oh wise Wiki, tell me your story."

I cleared my throat and continued. "So, Peros Banhos is in an atoll chain that is smaller and more scattered than the Maldives. I think it's called Chagas or Chagos, I just remember it means *wound* in Portuguese, which, at the time, sounded ominous."

"Still does."

"Yeah, I agree, especially since we're now residing on 'wound'. So it turns out, the UK owns this area now, and I do know that the US has a naval base about a hundred and fifty, maybe two hundred miles from here, at the lowest and largest island. Diego Garcia. You might've heard of it, it's like our jump off point for fighting in this region."

"Yeah, it sounds familiar, but it might just be because it sounds like a Spanish super hero."

I laughed, "Yeah, Diego is also a cartoon character my nephews love, but anyway, so, the islanders that lived here were kicked off the islands in the seventies. I thought it was pretty brutal, like the good old US putting the Indians on reservations."

"Typical."

"Uh huh, so then when the islanders took them to court, the UK, to try to reclaim their islands, they responded by declaring the whole area a preserve. The water, the fish, the birds, all of it. The reefs here are some of the healthiest in the world and it became one of the largest preserves on earth."

"So the natives won't have a chance to come back, even if they did, they wouldn't be allowed touch anything so they couldn't survive."

"Exactly. Sneaky, like smallpox in blankets."

"Huh, so there are houses here?"

"Well yeah, that's what I was getting to, the atoll Peros Banhos, and another atoll about twenty miles to the east, Salomon, were settled. They had a church, a school, huts, and a manager's house, a pier for loading off coconut crops and coconut oils and stuff. It's been forty years now, so the jungle has reclaimed most of it, but they are on the furthest southern island if I remember correctly."

"Wow, that's just crazy. I feel really bad for the natives, but I'm curious to see the buildings."

"I didn't dig up much online about the area, I was focused more on the Maldives at the time. I do remember reading that the area is patrolled, and yachts can get permits to anchor and explore the islands, they just can't disturb anything."

"No fishing?"

"Especially no fishing, or at least I'm sure no commercial fishing. I don't actually know. That's all Wiki told me."

"So now we can either explore and set up camp here and hope a yacht comes to this island, or we can make our way to the other island with the house and expect visitors."

"Yeah pretty much, the whole atoll is like sixty miles around or something like that, I remember it was a good size. Salomon was a lot smaller, that's why I figure we're in Peros Banhos."

"OK, I believe you and your friend Wiki. Let's head back and gather our things up, tomorrow we'll move to this side of the island. It's more protected and looks like this area is going to be great for fishing."

"I agree, plus the water is shallow and clear, we can swim and not worry about sharks."

"Island rules still apply though."

"Island rules." I sighed and took a swallow of water. "Maybe tomorrow we can penetrate that jungle and see if we can find something of use. This is a decent size island, the natives had to of used it to live on."

"Let's sit and form a plan. Our best bet for getting home might be to get to the other island and wait for tourists."

And there it was. The unspoken question. We could stay. We both realized with the size of the atoll and even with a patrol it would be easy to hide in the jungle until we were old and gray, avoid all ships that anchored, build a hut. Eat tuna, make love. Very *Blue Lagoon*, but without the scary parts. Or we could do the mature, responsible thing, and move to the southern island, flag a ride home. Deal with the red tape, and the fallout of the pirates, and the *Lady Sun*. Go home, feed our horses, our cattle, and visit each other now and again. Maybe Lucas would move to my farm. *Not likely. He would want me to move to his ranch.* I wasn't against it, but the details to work it out would be nauseating and tedious.

Now I was thinking too far ahead.

Lucas and I began our slow stroll back to the ocean side of the island. I was lost in my own head. I wanted to ask him what he thought we should do, what he thought it would be like when we went home. But I was afraid the answer might ruin this perfect little bubble of paradise and denial we had built. So I stuttered along beside him, keeping my thoughts and worries to myself.

*   *   *

By the time I was settled in to my life vest couch in the shade of my leaning palm, the sun was beginning to dip closer to the water, preparing for its evening bath. Lucas had by now, quite a healthy pile of firewood, so he picked up his fishing pole that was propped against a tree and gave me a quick kiss before heading off to hunt down dinner. We had been eating fish every day for three days now. I had employed the same recipe I used for the tuna, and each meal had been delicious, but I caught myself thinking of my spice rack often. Salt and pepper and garlic, lemon peel, or even a whole lemon. I planned to scour the island for different things I might be able to use to spice up the dishes, and I also wanted to experiment with obtaining sea salt. I mean we were surrounded by an entire mine of the stuff. As long as we had fresh water to stay hydrated, I would like to liven up our palates with salt if nothing else.

I began shredding some palm fronds, it wasn't difficult to find dry ones now, and by the time Lucas returned I had the fire crackling and the sky was putting on its evening show.

He had caught a grouper this time. At least that's what he called it. I had never seen one before nor had I eaten one, but he cut up fillets and wrapped them in fronds and began roasting.

He was unusually quiet, and as I mused over what the reason might be, I realized I was also not conversing much. *He* was probably wondering about *my* silence. Finally I huffed out a breath and faced it. *Just jump in Sophia.* I gave myself a push, and the words came out in a rush.

"Do you want to stay? I mean here, not just this island, but here. I know we said we were going to enjoy the fact we were stranded, but in a month or a week, maybe tomorrow, we could possibly go home." I paused, looking at my feet in the sand. I didn't want to see his expression, he might think I was nuts and I couldn't handle the judgment. Especially now that I couldn't take it back. So I forged ahead, talking to my feet, trying to explain myself, sort through my fears.

"Lucas, I love you. I love this, our fire, your grouper and I will love whatever you catch tomorrow. I love the sunsets that are just mind blowing gorgeous, and the sudden storms that bring us drinking water and a free outdoor shower, even though I do miss my shampoo. I can't imagine going back, trudging through snow, and the world, maybe... changing us." I looked up at him finally. He was sitting very still, watching me stare at my feet and blurt out my confession.

"Why can't we stay?"

Lucas left the fish to cook and sat beside me, taking my hand in his. "Sophia. I would stay here with you. I would build you a castle in the jungle, we could figure out a way to thrive here, but there are more concerns than just food and water. What if one of got sick, or injured, we've already used up a good portion of luck in that area. What would we do if we went a week and were unable to catch any fish? I can't promise you that the sunsets would balance it out. Life here would be a survival every day. No *Google*, no books to read, no way to Wiki an interesting shell you found or call home, talk to your sisters, your family."

"I know, and you have your ranch to worry about, and all the things that make time go by in the real world, but Lucas." I faced him and held both of his hands. "In my heart, this feels like home, *you* feel like home. I wouldn't be able to stand it if we went back, and we lost this. Our connection, our paradise, it's what movies are made of."

Lucas wrapped his arms around my shoulders and hugged me. I lay my head on his chest and listened to the beating of his heart. The embrace was so comforting and so still, it seemed more intimate than a kiss. I felt protected and complete.

"We can stay. I would stay." His voice was low against my ear. "But you should know that if we did leave, I would never let you go Sophia. We would figure it out, find a way, but we would always be together."

I felt a warm tear slide down my cheek. And we sat there with our arms around each other as the sky turned dark and the first star winked on.

Chapter 19

In the morning we packed up. Lucas drug our two suitcases behind him, and I strapped on my fishy smelling, but now dry purse, that had been re-stuffed with its original contents, minus the booze.

I still had the flask shaped bottle of vodka but was saving it back in case of emergency. It was our only form of disinfectant and would be more useful as a medical supply than to drink while tanning.

We trudged through the sand and around the bend, discussing our plan as we huffed in exertion through the now familiar muggy morning air.

"So do you think we can make it around the entire island today?" We had settled on a course of action, agreeing that we would set up a temporary camp on the east beach, then we would pack a lunch and walk the beach around the entire island, if the beach permitted. Lucas intended to map it as we went, to try to get a sense of its size, and to see if we could make out any other islands in the atoll.

"Well we can always camp along the way if we get held up, but your leg seems to be doing well, so we should make decent time."

"Yeah it's hurting way less than yesterday. The exercise probably did it good." I had rubbed it down with aloe the night before and still had the wrapping on. I intended to let it air out some once we dumped our load at the new camp, then re-wrap it for the trek.

"Maybe it's the magical island air." Lucas heaved his smaller suitcase up to one shoulder and carried mine in his other hand. Dragging them clearly hadn't been working.

He was shirtless again today, and I had a hard time not drooling. I could adjust to the beauty of the island, startling though it was, but Lucas' skin shining damp in the hot sun, always set me to feeling like a virgin schoolgirl. Or a wanton floozy. It was a toss- up.

"I think it *is* magical. Muggy, and always really, really, warm, but *magical*."

We arrived at the east beach and started looking for a good spot to set up. About fifty yards south we spotted the perfect alcove. The line of jungle dipped in to the west just a bit, providing shade and a windbreak. Plus it was level, and the sand was a bit firmer.

I had dawned two life vests when we set out, ignoring Lucas' teasing about the air not being *that* muggy, and now my neck and back were sweating, the orange turtle neck effect practically choking me.

"Ah, home sweet home!"

"For now. We'll most likely find a better camp than this." Lucas dropped his load onto the sand.

"Ah, hotel sweet sandy hotel."

Lucas chuckled. I stripped off the vests, and my purse, and lowered myself carefully to the ground.

"I won't be long. Two trips should do it." Lucas deposited the suitcases on the sand next to me and turned to head back for the rest of our things.

"Why do we have so much stuff? Do you think we should have a yard sale? You know, do some spring cleaning."

Lucas just waved as he strode away but I heard him laugh, and it made me smile. I loved his laugh.

I set to work putting together a lunch for our trek. I packed all three water bottles, which Lucas had filled that morning. (Our can was getting low. I sent out a brief wish for rain with only one hand crossing fingers. I educated that two hands would bring a hurricane or monsoon.) Then

I wrapped up the leftover palm-fish-burrito from last night. The grouper had been huge, so we had

enough for another full meal today.

With our stomachs shrunk we didn't feel the desire to eat as much as before our adventure

began, plus little choice in the matter really. We ate what we found, then hunted for more. Or

rather Lucas hunted. I worked on my tan and the new awesome calendar I had created on a large

piece of bark Lucas had found for me. *Oh, I hope he doesn't forget the calendar!* I added our last

candy bar to the picnic and sat down to wait.

I was wearing shorts and a tank today, my wrapped leg fee of any material, and I began

taking off the bandage, scooting to a piece of sun where I could set my thigh to air out. I studied

the staples glinting in the rays of light. It looked like I would be able to take them out tomorrow.

*Maybe once we find our permanent camp I will be stitched together enough and I will remove

them.* I relaxed and sipped at the water bottle.

Twenty minutes into my tan, Lucas returned carrying the metal box and the remaining six

life vests. All of them had been salvaged. Six tied to our luggage and the box, and our two

personal ones had washed ashore. *Fat lot of good they had done*, but having sex with life vests on

totally killed the mood, so of course we hadn't been wearing them when the island sucked us in.

A quick kiss and Lucas was off again.

"Don't forget the calendar!" I called out behind him. He threw up a hand in

acknowledgment as he jogged across the sand and soon disappeared around the north bend.

According to my wooden tab keeping board, today was January, ninth. I had flown out on

the thirtieth and arrived in Malé on New Year's Eve. We jumped off the *Lady Sun* that day,

floated for three days and four nights and then washed ashore here. We had been on the island for

five days total, today was the sixth. So that made today the ninth. I was glad I had started

counting, it was already pretty fuzzy. If I had a journal I would keep one just for posterity. I have

no idea how Robinson Crusoe managed it. He was on his island for twenty odd years. That's a lot

of journal keeping… and a lot of aloneness.

Lucas popped back in sight carrying the rolled up raft. When he reached me he dropped the raft and plopped heavily down beside me. "I hate moving."

"Oh, me too, you know we should just rent a *U-Haul*, save the walking."

"Oh you're just all giggles today. Excited about our hike?"

"Am I that transparent? I'm not a good sitter stiller. So yes! I'm very excited. I packed a picnic." I held up the satchel I had made from one of his shirts. He didn't wear them anyway, and I wanted to encourage that trend.

"Good planning." Lucas took a hearty swallow of water and stood back up for the final trip.

"Forgot the motor huh?"

He shook his head as he strode away, muttering, "I hate that useless motor."

He may call it useless, but he had already come up with an idea of making fuel from coconuts. If we were able to patch up Ducky, he figured we may be able to motor to the other islands. I didn't ask if he thought we could motor to the Maldives. That sounded terrifying. Storms, and no navigation, in my mind it would be a death wish.

At last the motor, and my calendar were added to the pile to be unpacked later. We refilled the water bottles, I re-wrapped my leg, grabbed my cane, and together we set off to explore.

*   *   *

Ten steps down the beach Lucas reached out and took my free hand. "Sophie, we should talk."

My heart skipped, but not in a good way. It was clear he meant 'serious' talk, and I hadn't heard that tone in his voice before. I decided I would say nothing and just let him say what he needed to say. Maybe it was his plan for the castle in the jungle, or he wanted to tell me his life story beginning to end. I nodded and kept hobbling forward, our hands growing sweaty in the heat. He didn't let go though.

"About last night…"

Oh god it was one of *those* talks. I steeled myself for judgment, for him to tell me I was

nuts and what kind of woman wanted to stay on a deserted island with a man she had known just

over a week. *Yeah that did look bad*, but I shook off the self-judgment and left it to Lucas.

"I've been thinking about our conversation, about staying here. The feasibility of it, and I

have to agree that the idea is tempting. But we both know that long term it isn't the right choice."

I kept my silence. I pictured in my head a year from now, two years, and I saw me, thin

and tan and living in a jungle tree house. Lucas and I closer than ever, relying on each other,

reaping life from the island and the sea. A small voice in my mind whispered, *what about*

sickness? I ignored it. *What about luxuries like soap, and shampoo, toilet paper, tampons.* My

mind paused at that one. Island life without tampons would be rough. But I was stubborn, and I

tuned it out, but then the voice whispered *what about Anna.*

It was easy to think of my family as a whole, to dismiss that whole as capable of enduring

the loss of me. But Anna. The princes, my niece. That cut deep and I let the thought settle into

me.

"You and I are responsible people, we have others who rely on us, businesses built by us,

sitting waiting for us to return. I think the fact that we're both strong and capable is one of the

main reasons it's such an alluring idea to stay. The weight of responsibility lifted. But you know

Sophie, we would just be transferring it. Although there's no snow here we would be dealing with

elements just as harsh. We may not have to chain up, but we have to hunt for food, truly hunt, and

water, so far, is a gift of chance and weather patterns. Sophie," Lucas stopped in the sand and

turned me to face him, "we could easily die here, with *one* mistake. I won't be responsible for

that, and even worse, I won't leave you alone to fend for yourself if God forbid, something

happened to me, and you were left here alone"

I hung my head and let his words sink in. He was trying to reason with me before I got too

attached to the idea of staying. He was being sensible, and logical, and even loving. And I had been indulging in selfishness, dreams, and illusion. Today was pretty, but tomorrow might bring a hurricane, or even pirates. If this last week had taught me one thing, it was how fragile our lives were, and that luck alone had kept us alive this far.

"I know," I studied Lucas' face. I saw real concern and a deep patience. He wanted what was best for me, but didn't want to drag me kicking and screaming. He was waiting for me to come around to reason in my own time.

"Lucas, what will we do when we get home?" I lifted my chin and faced my real fear, the one that was at the root of my desire to stay. Beyond the beach the sunsets, the fun part of the adventure, I wanted *him* and the thought of losing him tore at me. It made me panic, and scramble to keep him, even if it meant the stupid choice. Staying here.

"Help me understand, help me see how it would be when we get home. We met nine *days* ago. We know very little of each other in the scope of our lives away from here." I spread my hands to encompass the island. "But I do know how I feel when I am with you. My attraction to you is beyond physical, more than your body, and the passion we share, although it began that way. But I love that you work with your hands, I respect your choice in lifestyle, ranching, not indulging in the rat race. I ache for you, for what your ex-wife did to you. You have proven in these nine days that you are patient, resilient, loving, funny, and smart. So I'm very afraid of losing you when we land in the states. That this island is all we have." I sighed and turned to face the water, focusing on something other than his piercing eyes.

"I know we have to leave." I said softly. "I also know that you are irreplaceable, and no man would ever measure up to how I feel when I'm with you."

"You want to stay because you think that's the only way we can be together? Sophie, look at me." He turned me back to him. "You are an amazing woman, if I haven't made it clear already, let me say it again. I love you too. No other woman would have gone through what we have, and let it roll off her back, you doctored me and then taught me to doctor you while you were bleeding to death in front of me. And the next day you put on a pretty dress and made jokes. You're beautiful and funny and I was never even close to this level of love in my marriage. The thought of Cassie doesn't even hurt anymore, you have completely healed me. Filled my heart to overflowing. So yeah, it's crazy that we've known each other nine days, and yes, we have more to learn, *much* more about each other. But I am in this with you, here *and* at home. We will figure it out. You can come to my ranch, bring all your animals, or I would move to be closer to you if that's what you wanted, I could lease out the ranch and we can go from there."

I was crying now, my damn faucet turned on full force and he grabbed me and pulled me against him, hugging me tight.

"We will have so many adventures when we get back. The biggest of all would be a giant wedding." Lucas brought his mouth down and kissed me, then he sank to his knees in front of me and I couldn't stop crying. "Sophia, you can't believe I would ever let you go. Marry me, say you'll be my wife, we'll bring our giant families to your farm or the ranch and throw a huge party. You'll wear white, I'll wear a tux."

I lowered myself to the sand in front of him, my face wet with tears and my heart full and lifted.

"Oh my god Lucas, how can you be this perfect? You have to see why I would give up everything to stay here with you."

"I don't want you to give it up Sophia, I want you to *have* everything. Please say yes." He kissed me and we sank down to the sand.

"Yes." The word was swallowed in a kiss and I laughed against his mouth, wiping at my eyes and face. "Yes Lucas Lael, I will marry you."

His mouth crushed mine again, and I realized as his hands began pulling off my clothes that he had been afraid too. He had been as lost, but he found the way back and showed me the direction I needed to go. Towards him. Into him.

My fingers unbuttoned his shorts, and he carefully stripped my clothes from me, turning then to his own. We were twenty feet from our campsite but we didn't care, this moment was all that mattered, and it swept us away.

Chapter 20

Survival is a word. An idea. An image of cavemen with sticks. Survival is something we think of when we must make a cruel choice. The adage 'Survival of the fittest' all the justification our conscience needs to stay quiet.

Survivors are cancer patients, or victims of car accidents. Hospitals are full of survivors, people that made it through a stubbed toe or a heart surgery.

Surviving though, as and action, not a metaphor, but as a purposeful act, with intent. Well *it* should have its own word. Brutal, or terrifying, or visceral. A word that encompasses *those* things, because we soon began to realize that Lucas had been right; Luck was our water supply, and fickle fate our food.

*   *   *

Lucas had lost the hook. Well technically it wasn't lost. A fish had it in its jaw, or belly, somewhere. A large fish, and the hook drug behind it, the majority of the heavy test line. Now we were down to a small hook and short line that would have never pulled in the tuna he had caught that first day. Or had it been the second? I strolled back through the sunny days, trying to remember our first meal. Yes, the first day we had washed up and screamed a lot. Or at least I

Lady Sun

had. Lucas bled a lot. And I suppose I had shed a fair share of red too. The second day was the tuna. I wished we had a tuna now. Now we were twenty days in. Well, twenty since the flight, so a couple of weeks here on the island, give or take.

I still loved the view. Hungry or thirsty, it didn't matter, the view was perfect and there is no denying beauty. Bad mood, good mood, injured, hungry or horny. Beauty is.

We emptied the water can two days ago. Now my sole purpose in life was to find water, to squeeze water from the air.

Lucas's purpose was to find food. To spear it or trap it, to find a way to keep two bellies full enough to have the energy to do the same thing again the next day, then the next.

Coconuts were plentiful, but they are also laxatives. We had to be careful not to eat too many, we quickly became dehydrated and crampy. I drank aloe juice that first week to aid in healing, getting vitamins in me for my skin and blood. I kept at it, still, scraping at the inside of pokey leaves with my teeth each morning, now that I had no water to mix it with. I convinced Lucas to chew at a leaf as well, he complained at first, but now, we ate a breakfast of aloe gel each morning.

Today, I sat on a log in the shade, just inside the tree line. Lucas stood out in the shallow water with a spear he had sharpened to a point and hardened in the fire.

I loved watching him stalk fish. His form and grace were distracting, and I always watched where he couldn't see me. I didn't want him to alter his natural state of being. I knew he was worried and stressed, it was clear in the set of his shoulders that never fully relaxed, but still, I took this moment to enjoy the view, and then stood up and moved on to my task.

I was trying to access my inner Wiki, I knew I had read somewhere of a simple method of distilling sea water. It was the most plentiful thing around us, and looking at all that clear water but knowing we couldn't drink it, was really starting to piss me off.

The natives of these islands, surely stored rainwater during the rainy season to last through the dry seasons. It seemed the logical fix to living on an island with no fresh water source. *Unless you knew how to distill it.*

I kept at the problem, juggling common sense knowledge, with references from books and episodes from *Myth Busters*. Finally, I came up with a plan I thought would have the most likelihood of working. I would present it to Lucas when he had speared dinner, or failed to spear dinner, but I knew he wouldn't like it.

I had, until now, been collecting condensation from our bottles and some plastic I found and scrubbed clean. It amounted to very little each day and would not keep us alive. I had dug into the sand at an area in the jungle we discovered, where there were holes that looked like the natives had done the same. Hoping to find fresh water that resided near the roots of the jungle forest. That brought more results, but still only enough to soak up, and squeeze into the pot, yielding half a bottle for two hours patient labor and the water was dirty. I was worried we might get sick drinking it. There had to be a better way.

I had faith my plan was pretty solid, but I was lacking an item to pull it off. Before I proposed the plan to Lucas, I decided I would scour the beach for debris. See if anything washed up lately.

Over the last week, after we decided to make camp in a clearing in the jungle, about two hundred feet in from the tree line, Lucas and I had developed a kind of schedule.

Every other day or so I would walk the beach, shopping for new and exciting things. This usually meant discovering a dead animal, most commonly a bird, and getting freaked out by the ginormous crabs that we had yet to attempt to catch and eat. One, because they were fast, and wily, and we didn't have a net, and two, because they looked so creepy I wasn't sure I could eat one. Lucas was sure, but I hadn't reached the ravenous stage where they looked tasty butter or not. In a day or two they might, though. My stomach was shrunk and angry with me.

On my shopping trips I had found a shoe, it was a child's flip flop, crusty and yellow. A few plastic bottles that had miniature universes growing in them. Seaweed that sometimes looked like it hid cool stuff in its mass, but usually ended up to be the dead animal find of the day. I found a hat, which I loved, it was made of plastic straw, and had a wide brim. It had been stuck on the branch of a twisted stick. After scrubbing it down with wet sand and rinsing it in the salty ocean, I thought it was dashing, and now I wore it every day, the side of the rim with the hole in it facing the back. It helped cut down my headaches, and now I always kept a searching eye out for a hat for Lucas. He spent more time in the sun than I did and was now a nicely tanned brown.

As I wandered the beach, Lucas looked up from squinting at the water and flashed me a smile. His teeth were shocking white against his tan face, and his beard, with its calico red and gold colors, was getting longer. He raised an arm and waved.

I raised mine back, "Going shopping." I called out as I gestured north up the beach. He nodded and then turned, going back to squinting for fish.

Later in the day we would make a fire, or explore more of the island. We had penetrated a good portion of the jungle already, and Lucas dutifully mapped what he saw. He had the long beaches and shape of the island on paper, and a hint of the other islands, and their distance from us, to the south and east. The rest of the evening would be spent working on the castle.

Together we had been building a hut at our campsite. The main reason being, if a storm came, we wanted secure shelter. We stopped feeling pressured to work on it after the first few days, when no hint of a storm, or a sprinkle showing itself on any horizon. I thought it was so funny, in a not funny way, that I had been upset that rain would have ruined my vacation. My travel agent assured me that this was a good season to visit, and I had wanted to tan, and relax in the sun. Now the *lack* of rain was ruining my survival, and relaxing in the sun rarely happened. The tan came as a side effect to the fact that really, there was no choice but to let my skin turn whatever color the ball of fire in the sky decided that day. Most days it was pink or red. Another month and maybe I would hit that golden goddess shade.

I strolled along to the north, keeping my eyes on the sand, my sunglasses thankfully sparing me the glare. My leg had finally stopped hurting a few days ago. Now I rarely felt a twinge. Lucas had used his multi-tool to pull out the staples the second night in our new camp. The healing had accelerated and now I barely saw any of the marks along my waist and hip, and just an angry jagged line down my thigh. That one would scar, but at least it healed, and there was no permanent damage. It would have sucked to have to walk with a cane for the rest of my life.

I reached the bend at the northern point and turned west, trekking slowly back to where we began. When I reached the spot where I had crawled up on shore that first day, I sat down and looked out to the west, over the ocean. Far enough that way, past Africa and another, bigger, ocean, and there was home.

I was ashamed now for ever wanting to stay here, embarrassed that I ever uttered the thought aloud. Although it ended well, and I was thrilled with how much closer Lucas and I had become, I felt silly forever thinking this would be a gentle life, a vacation forever.

I had always laughed at the people who couldn't do without the creature comforts, the conveniences of the twenty first century. No one I knew went a day without posting on *Facebook*, or using a cell phone, or flipping a light switch, turning the thermostat up and down. If I never saw *Facebook* again I'd be fine. I could do without the light bulbs, even electricity. I didn't care for air conditioning, and fire was warmth enough. But the essentials, the things that kept us human and not beasts. Those things I missed. Not a bed, or blankets even, not my stereo or T.V. I missed food, water. From a faucet or a creek, just access, to indulge my thirst.

I missed my family, the animals. There were no animals here, besides the thousands of birds that screeched constantly, and the freaky crabs. I missed my garden. The seeds that I plant and tend and they grow into tomatoes, lettuce, and corn. It would be a short list, the things I would take to a deserted island. Because when you strip away the distractions, and you sift through what's left, you find that only a few things really matter. Only a few items are truly needed. The rest is just want.

I pulled myself up from the sand and continued down along the beach, heading south on the ocean side. I didn't get far before I saw it. It was still drifting in, the waves kicking it to the sand, then pulling it back, sweeping it up, and tugging it back, like a moody woman, not knowing if she wanted it or not. But I did. I wanted it very much.

* * *

Lady Sun

As I approached the stretch of beach level to where Lucas still stood in thigh deep water, I saw him look up. He began laughing and shook his head, and then just stood there and watched me as I placed my queen size, fully inflated, air mattress in the water. I stripped off all my clothes and waded in, pushing the mattress ahead of me. When I reached him he was still grinning, staring at me and then at the raft.

"So how much did you spend this time?"

"It was on special I swear." I climbed onto its warm surface and lay on my back, my floppy hat shading my face and my sunglasses still propped on my nose. "Seriously, the store was having a blowout, I got it for a steal." I grinned back at him and then crooked a finger. "Come join me Cowboy, you work too hard."

With his grin still in place Lucas climbed aboard, careful not to get too much water on our new Blue Ducky. He stretched out beside me and lowered his sunglasses from his head, shading his eyes with them. He had told me when I asked him about it, that he couldn't wear them while searching for fish to spear. They were too dark and he couldn't see through the water well. I told him he was going to go blind with squinting at the sun on the water all day. He had shrugged, and we left it at that.

"Oh, this is better. About time we had a float on the water day."

"Hmm, yeah, reminds me of another float on the water we had." He turned toward me and ran a hand over my bare breast. "We had some fun on that yellow waterbed."

"Oh, yeah, that *was* fun." I turned and reached over to run my fingers along his hot skin. "As I recall you couldn't keep your hands off me."

"Oh really? If memory serves, you were lusting after *me*, I would have beat you off with a stick, but I didn't have one." He reached for my other breast.

"Sure, I remember that, you kept saying 'No Sophia, get your sexy self to your side of the raft.'"

He laughed again and then leaned down, and his warm mouth covered mine.

No matter whether we had food, or water, or if he spent the day roasting in the sun, or working on our castle, Lucas always tasted sweet. Like he had sipped at honey. I deepened the kiss and we let our hands explore each other, awakening senses, and sending chills through limbs.

"Hmm..." I moaned and pressed against him. "Think we could be naughty and not fall off of the raft?"

Lucas looked around to gauge the space he had to use.

"I'm willing to give it a shot if you are." And his mouth was back, working its way down my throat, biting lightly, making me arch into him.

Our attraction to each other was never sated. Hunger and thirst never deterred us, we made love every day. Without fail, we always found a moment, always reached for each other in the night. Now we enjoyed each other in the blazing sun, moving slowly, making small swells around the raft. Taking the one true pleasure that the island still afforded, no matter how stingy it was with other sustenance.

Love sustained our spirits.

*   *   *

We floated lazily for a while, basking, and letting our fires die down to coals again. After a bit my front began to feel the warning of pink growing to red, and I flipped onto my stomach, Blue Ducky sloshing about and rousting Lucas from his near nap status.

"Hey, so I have an idea I need to run by you."

Lucas rolled over and rested his head on his arms, his eyes closed behind his glasses. "OK, shoot, but we need to get into the shade soon. Without water we're just torturing ourselves out here."

"Well, that's what I wanted to point out. We're surrounded by water. I have an idea of how to get it out of the ocean and into us, minus the bad stuff."

Lucas opened his eyes. I could barely tell behind the dark lenses, but I saw that I had his attention.

"Go on." He said as he reached one hand over the front edge of the mattress and began slowly paddling us toward shore.

"Well here's the thing, I think we can set our metal can up on some big rocks, like, ten inches high or so, at each corner. Then we put the metal cup in the center, and fill the can with sea water about halfway up the cup, so it doesn't float." I explained. "Then we start a fire underneath the can, and bring the water to almost a boil, enough to steam it off, but not enough to move the cup. Next, we arrange something hard, like metal that won't burn or melt, above the steam. If we indent that something, the steam will hit it and run to the dent that points down at the cup, and viola, we just distilled sea water. Once the cup is full, we let it cool, and put it in a water bottle, and start over. What do you think?"

Lucas sat up as the raft drifted toward the sand and stared at me. "Honestly Sophie, It's brilliant! I can't believe I didn't think of that, how did you come up with it?"

I thought about *Wikipedia,* and *Myth Busters,* not sure which one had taught me the trick, but didn't want to suffer the teasing so I said, "Oh you know, desperation being the mother of invention."

"I'm pretty sure its necessity, Pumpkin."

"Well fiddle or faddle, I think it will work, we just have the one problem…"

"Yeah, what to use for the steam to funnel into the cup."

"I have an idea for that too."

We climbed off the raft, each of us grabbing a corner and pulling it up onto the sand. This was the part he wouldn't like.

"What, did you find something on the beach that will work?"

"No, we already have something. The motor."

Lucas looked confused for a second, then it dawned on him, "You want me to take it apart."

"Yes." I knew he would do it. We had no choice, water was too important, but Lucas was determined to find a way to use the motor, he was experimenting with making fuel with coconuts, but so far hadn't gotten the recipe right. We both agreed we had to get to the island with the pier, south of here, but for all we knew there was miles of water and islands to cross to reach it. We both thought Ducky could be repaired, and I intended to start checking her to find her wound and see if we could patch her up. I had voted for making oars, but without food and water, we wouldn't be able to row for long. So we were stuck here until we could fill the water bottles, carve oars, or create gas from fruit.

Lucas hung his head for a minute and I felt really bad for him. He had been excited with the idea of refining coconut oil, I figured it was a kind of man thing. But finally he sighed and took my hand, heading to the castle.

"We can start now. I'll pull off the part you'll be able to use, and you can rig up the oven and the can. Maybe you'll have some bottles of water ready by the time I catch dinner"

It wasn't until Lucas had the gas tank on the motor practically off, that I realized there was a better solution.

"Hey, why don't you remove the lid from the can, give it a good smack with a rock in soft sand and we have our funnel!" I was relieved I had discovered something that would work better and would save Lucas' pet project. We had too few things to give us hope here, and I didn't want to take away his dream of motoring around the islands.

Lucas set the motor down and just looked at me, then he reached out his hands for the metal box and I set it between his legs where he could begin attacking the hinges. Thank goodness for multi-tools.

"So how is the coconut fuel coming along?" I was trying to apologize for making him take apart his baby.

"I'll check it in the morning." He looked up and smiled, "No worries babe, I won't blow us up, or burn down the jungle."

"Oh I know, I wasn't saying… you know I totally support your plan, your efforts, I'm just sorry I got you to cannibalize the motor."

"Well that's easily screwed back together, I'm glad you thought of this," he jerked his head toward the can "before I did permanent damage."

"Well, I'm off to find big rocks."

Lucas looked up from his work and winked. "Stay within yelling distance, K?"

"K." I wandered off to make my invention real and hopefully, we would drink well tonight.

It worked like a charm. It took a long time, but in a couple hours of steadily feeding the fire and watching with strained eyes through smoke, and heat, I saw the steam rise, gather and run then drip, drip, drip, into our cup. By the time the sun set, and Lucas was back with a smallish fish, I had two water bottles filled, assorted burns on assorted fingers, and a raging headache from the smoke, and heat, and thirst.

Lucas cooked the fish and made me sip at one of the warm bottles of water I had made, and when we were finished eating, he carried me to our castle and tucked me into bed. We debated on bringing the mattress in for use as, well, a mattress, but we determined it was more valuable as a flotation device, and didn't want to risk puncturing it. So he secured it on the beach and we settled into our life vest pillows and I let sleep take me, to erase my headache and bring me into day twenty one.

Chapter 21

The following day Lucas and I divided up the chores. Over our breakfast of aloe gel, and now, island temperature water, we came to the conclusion that now that we had the ability to distill salt water, we would fill the three bottles we had, as well as the empty Mudslide and Pina Colada bottles. We also agreed we should fill the two beer bottles and Lucas would carve corks for them. With this impressive hoard of hydration we could embark, finally, to try and reach the southern end of the island chain. I had wracked my brain and scoured all of my Wiki tidbits and I guesstimated that the diameter of the atoll was around twenty miles.

"Really, twenty miles? That's a ton of water to cross Sophie, I know you have a strange mental trap for information, and trivia, and anything regarding the cast of Lost, but twenty sounds pretty far for an atoll."

"Well that's the number I keep coming back to. I know it's almost twenty miles between this atoll and the Salomon atoll because I had to do conversion math. Oh! That's it, twenty *Kilometers*, the islands are part of the UK, so they use metric, so how many miles is that, I forget the swappy conversion math."

"Swappy conversion math? Didn't you go to college?"

"Yes I did mister I can make diesel from coconuts, but soon after schooling, those conversions went A.W.O.L. from my brain. So remind me how many miles is one kilometer."

"It wouldn't be plural babe, it wouldn't even be one. It's a little over half a mile."

"So that means it would be ten, maybe eleven miles from the top to the bottom. Given we
Lady Sun

aren't at the peak of the circle or traveling a true diameter, we would only need to go about eight miles. That's fantastic, right?"

Lucas put his knife in his sheath, he had carved two perfect wooden plugs for the beer bottles while we sat there calculating. "Well, it sounds way better than twenty, but if we don't find a way to make this motor work for us, we'll be rowing that distance. Rowing eight miles will be very, very, very, far from easy."

"We can take shifts." I was looking on the bright side. This was progress, the planner in me was fanning the flames of hope. "And you can fish while I row, and vice versa. How long do you think it would take?"

"With the motor, we might cover eight miles in an hour and a half or so, depending on if the engine liked the fuel. Rowing, going nonstop, five hours, or two days. Hell, maybe a week, I just can't know until I see you row." He gave me a wink, and I tossed an empty coconut shell at him.

"Well I'm off to the distillery. Let me know how it goes."

Lucas planned on trying his last batch of coconut oil fuel. If it worked we would make more. If not, we would make oars. Then we would patch Ducky and pack up the castle, load the rafts and head off to southern isles, and hopes of some tourist or security guard finding our stranded selves, so we could go home.

And plan a wedding. This thought I rarely let out. I was too excited about it. I kept the dream in reserves for when I was truly in need of cheering up. I didn't want to wear out the shininess of it, the butterflies that tickled my stomach at the thought of walking down a country aisle toward Lucas. So I tucked the pretty scene away, and set off for the metal can on the beach, and to hunt down more wood.

*   *   *

I had just topped off the last beer bottle, and was wiping the sweat from my brow with burnt fingers, when I heard it.

An engine.

I stood up quickly and ran down the beach, looking out at the clear water, my excitement and breathing momentarily blocking out the sound. I stopped running and stood very still, held my breath, and shaded my eyes. Where was it? Where was the sound coming from? Just as I pinpointed its location it stopped, puttering out softly and definitely. The jungle. *Lucas had started the motor!*

I tore back up the beach, huffing and puffing and kicking up sand behind me. Once in the trees I ran down the path we had forged over the last two weeks, racing toward our tiny palm castle. As I burst through the clearing, Lucas was there, striding toward me. His face was lit with a huge grin and he was practically bouncing with excitement.

"Did you hear it? I got it started!"

"Yeah, I heard it all the way down to the beach, how did you manage it? That's just amazing!"

"Well," he started rattling off the process he had gone through as he grabbed my hand and tugged me toward the motor sitting propped against a log. "At first I thought it was a problem of condensation, the air here is no help at all. Then I thought maybe it was clogged with sediment, I mean that first batch I tried had been pretty cloudy, so I cleaned the whole damn thing out. The filter and the…"

"Lucas, just tell me, will it work?" I was squeezing his hand, kneeling down at the motor, stroking it lovingly, *Oh baby you are going to save me from so many blisters!*

"Yes, Sophie, I really think it will." His excitement hadn't abated. "Turns out I had been right, the oil needed to be filtered again, so I strained it and then spent almost a half an hour yanking on that damn rope, and, hey!" He pulled me up and hugged me.

I squeezed him back and gave him a congratulatory kiss. "Well done island man, now we won't have to row until our hands bleed."

"Yeah, thank God for that because I think I threw out my shoulder yanking on the rope."

"Oh poor baby." I began rubbing his impressive sized shoulder and asked, "So what now?"

"Well, have you finished filling all the bottles?"

"Yep, all topped off, Cap'n."

Lucas saluted and I high fived his upraised hand.

"Well then, I need the can, I'll have to get to crushing more coconut and straining the oil, but I need to store it in something. I don't know how fast this oil will burn compared to diesel so we'll want to be prepared. It will take about three days, possibly four, to get enough to fill the tank, and then store some aside."

"Oh wow, so I guess *I* can tackle the project of Ducky. Find the leaks, find something to patch it with and start blowing her up. That will take about four days too." I rolled my eyes.

"You'll be fine, you have great lungs."

"Mm hm. Uh, those aren't lungs." I batted his hands away from my breasts. "Well, I'm super proud of you Cowboy, I never doubted you'd be the man who could make an engine run on hairy fruit."

"Thanks babe. Get to blowing. I'll catch us some food."

While Lucas went fishing, I rolled the yellow raft out on the sand. With my floppy hat securely on my head and my sunglasses on, I began visually scanning every inch of Ducky's surface, looking for her mortal wound. There was nothing on the topside that seemed obvious, so I flipped her over and began my detailed perusal again. Finally, near her rump, I found it, an indented part of the plastic that had a tear the size of a half dime. It must have caught the reef at a shallow point, due to the drag of the motor and luggage and can, all being hauled behind her. If Lucas hadn't wrapped himself in the rope and balanced out the weight distribution she probably would have flipped over. Then the motor *would* have had a moisture problem.

I had enough superglue left to patch the small hole. I just needed to find a patch that would be waterproof. It was time to go shopping again.

I hunted down Lucas, who was off standing on a sand bar, two hundred feet from shore, his pole held out in front of him, his glasses propped on his head.

I whistled and raised a hand, he looked over and I called out "Shopping!" and pointed in the direction toward the north end of the beach. He waved and went back to fishing, his mind probably still on his achievement. It *was* impressive. I had so much respect for him and his ability to figure things out, make things. He was the perfect model of a man.

I always went to the north bend to shop. Less traffic, easy parking, and great deals. The ocean brought a ton of deliveries each day. If you were patient, and sifted through the debris, you could always find something.

Today was a good shopping day. I found a gallon juice jug. *Tropical fruit punch* said the label that had half washed off, the other half bleached almost white from the sun. One side of the jug was pink from floating on the water, the other side was red, the original color the manufacturer had chosen for the jug that once contained fruit punch. "Well now you're a gas can and they're usually red too, so you work perfectly. Don't worry, you'll like being a gas can, you'll smell like coconuts."

I set the jug deep into the sand where I could pick it up on my way back and kept shopping. I really needed a piece of rubber or heavy flexible plastic for my patch. I was sure the ocean would give it to me if I just looked hard enough. I poked at every tangle of seaweed with sticks, ignoring whatever bird corpse the mass held, then I strolled further to poke at the next pile.

As I approached a large mass of seaweed that lay pretty close to the tree line, I saw two strange things that didn't compute at first. One was a glove. How could a winter glove be here where it was so warm? It must have had a very long trip, also, why wasn't it on the bottom of the ocean? It isn't buoyant. The second strange item the seaweed had, was a pillow in its green grasp. I couldn't even begin to imagine how a pillow could be there, and as I drew closer, I wondered how it could be so white still. It was pristine clean. Finally, just as I was ten feet from the glove, the pillow moved and I let out a very girlish screech.

It was a bird. A bird that had been tangled in plastic, which was tangled in seaweed, and now it was here, looking like a pillow with its glove friend, feeling out of place. The bird flapped its wings at me and attempted to fly away, instinct trumping pain, but then it flopped back down, anchored to its instrument of death, plastic. I saw then that the bird's leg was almost sawn in two. It wouldn't survive if it did get free.

"I'm sorry pretty pillow bird. You had a bad time of it didn't you." I crooned to the pretty lady. I assume all birds are ladies until they tell me otherwise.

I sat down in the sand and as I looked at the bird, thinking of its predicament, trapped like I was, but with a shorter leash, I reached out for the glove. "Hey!" I spoke aloud, talking to the glove, (I had long since agreed with myself that I could talk to whatever I wanted as long as Lucas didn't hear. If no one knew, then I wasn't crazy, just friendly.) "You're not a winter glove," I admonished the not winter glove. "You're a diver's glove! Hey, do you have a friend, a blue raft, I bet you and Blue Ducky fell off the same yacht. I'll introduce you when we get back, but I am afraid your life will be short. I will be cutting you up for a patch." I smiled at the glove and briefly wondered if I had scared it, but then realized that thought *was* crazy so I turned to the bird.

"OK pretty bird, this is how it's going to be. You are going to die there a miserable, and painful, scary, death. *Or*, you can let me come closer, and make it swift and painless, and you can go to the great father bird in the sky." I decided not to tell pretty bird I planned on eating her. That was just mean. But I *am* a farm girl. I eat my chickens and their eggs. It's the circle of life, and pretty bird would be a nice change from fish, plus, there was the added bonus that it wouldn't be murder, it was actually a mercy.

The bird hunched down as I slowly crept forward, I murmured, and hummed, and it tried at the last second to break free, fly away, but I caught her and folded her wings to her body. Kneeling in the smelly seaweed I pet pretty lady and said a brief prayer, because suddenly, I felt really sad for her. I never really felt sad for my chickens, or even the cow when harvest time came. But I connected to pretty lady. She just wanted to go home.

Before I could cry and get too emotional to follow through, I reminded myself that I felt no remorse for the tuna, and I was being silly. I snapped the bird's neck, and she lay limp, set free at last. I sent along another prayer and began untangling the trapped foot.

Glove, bird, and jug in hand, I rounded the north east corner and headed back to camp. All in all it was the best shopping trip yet, even better than the blue mattress, for we had a meal, we had a patch and we had a gas can. A hat trick. I whispered a thanks to the universe, always one to be grateful, even when the universe is stingy. I mean a cruise ship would have solved all my problems, but I would take the bird, and the jug, and the glove, and I would move forward, continue with the plan. Stay alive, get to the south island, and certainly there would be a yacht anchored there, or a regular patrol for evil doers here in the preserve.

I was optimistic.

Lucas was in camp scaling a very interesting looking fish on a rock. "Hey Cowboy, you feel like a chicken dinner?"

Lucas looked up, and upon seeing the bird his eyebrows rose. "Well that sounds good, uh... it hasn't been dead long has it?"

"About fifteen minutes."

He looked at my face. "You killed it?"

"Yes I did."

He nodded thoughtfully. "Can you pluck it?"

"I've plucked many a chicken and a few turkeys, so yeah, I'll start heating some water." I turned to retrace my steps back toward the beach.

"Hey, Sophie,"

"Yeah." I stopped and turned back to him.

"Well done Pumpkin." He nodded to pretty lady.

I didn't smile. I knew I would enjoy the meal, and the circle of life was something I accepted, but I didn't feel like I should be praised for it. At least not today. So I just nodded back and tossed him the jug. "Gotcha a gas can. It was on sale." Then I went to pluck our dinner.

Chapter 22

Instead of four, it only took two days to get ready to go.

The next morning, I patched Ducky. Lucas cut a square from the glove and I used the last

of our superglue.

I spent the rest of the morning blowing up the yellow raft through the emergency tube that

looked like a rubber straw poking out near the back. I took a good many breaks as I began feeling

light headed after exhaling a few lungful's, but I sat in the shade with my chore and drank an

entire bottle of water. Now that I possessed water making skills, I intended to stay as hydrated as

possible. Toward late morning my yellow friend was completely inflated, and I was very dizzy. I

took a few minutes to admire my lung's efforts and then went in search of Lucas.

A little further into the jungle past our camp, Lucas had set up his fuel refinery. That is to

say, he smashed coconuts there.

When I walked into the refinery, I was surprised at the giant pile of coconuts he had

amassed.

"Have you been playing monkey all day?" I waved at the pile and sat down on the ground

across from him.

"Oh those," He looked up from his smashing and shook his head. "No, most of those I've

been collecting the last two weeks, I only topped it off today." He went back to his crushing

chore. Literally. The method for achieving oil from these hard nuts was to dig out the white meat

and pound the coconut as fine as possible. The crushing action released the oils from the meat,

Lady Sun

then, he would strain the oil from the debris of white pulverized mass, and drain that oil into a plastic bottle.

The most precious and awesome find on the island yet, was what Lucas used to pulverize the coconut in. A large tortoise shell. It would hold about six gallons of water if I so chose to fill it up. We had come across it on the first day we took a picnic to traverse the circumference of the island. It sat high up the beach near the trees, Lucas had spotted it and we went to investigate.

It was smooth and picked clean from birds and insects and appeared to have been there for some time, not a hint of flesh or turtle was left. It was truly beautiful and very useful.

"Watcha up to?" Lucas glanced up at me and continued with his rhythmic pulverizing.

"Well, Ducky had a full recovery, the doctors said she's cleared to float again."

"Hey that's fantastic news, I hope the hospital bills don't bankrupt us."

I chuckled and waved my hand around his refinery lab. "So how can I help?"

"Well," He nodded to the pile of coconuts, "open those and dig out the meat, if I can get a good amount crushed, we can set it out to dry and in the morning I'll work on extracting the oil."

Lucas had discovered that trying to get the oil out before the meat dried, polluted the oil with the coconut water contained in the nuts, I call it milk, even though it isn't white, Lucas calls it water. We both drank it happily though. It's full of electrolytes and was the only thing that had kept us from collapsing when water was scarce. The meat though, we had cut way back on.

"OK, be right back." I went back to the beach and grabbed the now very well used metal can. I had scrubbed it furiously the night before after dunking pretty lady in hot water to loosen her feathers so I could pluck her. I didn't want any bird diseases, so I had sat in the water with a fist full of sand scrubbing away all traces of germs.

This morning I had boiled some water, enough to refill the two water bottles Lucas and I had drank, now I intended to use the can to collect the coconut water. Our diet of fish and palm and aloe and one bird was severely lacking in vitamins. I planned to mix the coconut milk in our water supply and be grateful for any antioxidants it offered. Sports stars paid big bucks for coconut water/milk in the states, I wasn't going to waste a drop if I could help it.

That afternoon Lucas and I sat in companionable silence while I smacked coconuts, collected their juice in the can, scraped out their meat with the screw driver on my multi-tool, and added to the ever growing pile of crushed coconut in the tortoise shell.

After the second day of Lucas muttering about drying, and separating, and straining, and purity, he finally had the tank full in the motor, and a quarter of the gas can filled. He sported a few cut or mashed fingers as well, that I had washed out and bandaged. Every cut in the jungle was a chance at infection. I kept a close eye on my burned fingers and any cut or scrape we acquired during our daily activities.

In the late afternoon of our twenty third day from home, Lucas announced we were ready to pack.

I was floating on the raft with the fishing pole in hand, the line cast out in the clear water, fish guts as bait. *Come on Cannibals, come and take a bite.* I encouraged our future dinner.

Lucas waded out to me and took the pole. "Why don't you get into some shade babe, you're turning the color of a coconut."

I had finally, after spending too much time boiling water on the beach, achieved golden goddess color. Within minutes of said coloring, my skin rebelled and started running straight toward African native. Now I was a blonde who spent too much time at the tanning salon color. "At least I'm not orange or red though." I smiled and gave him a kiss. "I guess if we're packing to leave in the morning I'll boil some water, and we can drink a bunch tonight, then I'll refill them in the morning while you load the ship."

"Ducky is a ship now?"

"Yeah, I promoted her. I offered her a purple heart for being wounded in the line of duty, but she wanted to climb the career ladder, you know how it goes, always harder for a woman to get rank."

"Uh huh, what's your rank?"

"Superior Master."

"Oh that's appropriate."

I waved and began wading toward shore.

"Hey, what's my rank?" He called after me.

"Cowboy, First Class."

The ship was loaded, we were hydrated, and all the water bottles were full. Lucas had loaded the blue raft with our suitcases. He strapped the life vests to them once again and set them perfectly balanced in the center of the dark blue mattress. The mattress was then tied with our one rope to the back of Yellow Ducky, a good four feet of slack between the two vessels. With no loops to secure to on the blue raft, Lucas had tied a tight knot around the blow port, it was the circumference of a gold dollar, meant to hook up to a portable pump. It seemed pretty secure, and I felt confident it would hold. Without the weight of the luggage we ran the risk of the raft catching air and blowing around, or tangling with the motor, plus this left more room in Ducky to move around.

Lucas insisted we both wear life vests. '*We're not taking any chances*' and '*we have pushed our luck already*' becoming all too familiar quotes from his lips.

So I indulged him and prepared for the sweaty uncomfortable ride, the vest chafing at me in the first five minutes.

We cleared out our Hut, I wished I could take a picture, but my camera had taken a bath in the ocean when my purse went to sea, so I would have to be content with a mental picture. As with the rest of the island, I still had not gotten a single picture of Lucas either. *Time enough for that when we get home…*

With everything secured, and rechecked, twice, I climbed aboard and sat in Ducky's nose, flashbacks of three weeks earlier making me tense. I focused on the naked flashbacks and relaxed, trying to find a comfortable medium of at ease, but not horny. Lucas would need to concentrate.

The motor was topped off with the yummy smelling fuel, and Lucas took hold of the rope pull. I crossed my fingers on both hands scrunched my eyes and whispered the magical; "*please,*

please, please, please, please." and on the twelfth pull, the motor sputtered to life.

The yanking had gotten us to rocking and drifting, and as soon as the engine began purring Lucas directed us out away from land. "OK Sophia, you need to navigate, turn forward and keep an eye out for sand banks, shallows, or reefs.

"Aye, aye, Cap'n."

I twisted around and faced the water ahead. I imagined I was the figurehead of a great exploring ship, the form of a mermaid or Athena.

We traveled at a decent clip, the motor purring, and the thrill of it, the exploration, the hope of getting home, lifted my spirits to the sky.

I couldn't really sight see, I was determined we achieved our goal without mishap. We had enough mishap to last a good long time. I scanned the water and directed Lucas if shallow water was ahead, or when we were headed toward a sand bar, which there were actually quite a lot of. This atoll had a shallow center, I almost thought we could walk across it.

We spotted a few small islands, tiny compared to where we had left, and I was suddenly grateful, seeing what we could have landed on made me appreciate what we had.

The water did grow deeper suddenly, a channel between two islands, but Lucas navigated it like a pro, and we were then passing the island that had been to the South of us. While I studied the water ahead, Lucas studied the land masses, probably marking them down in his mind to update his map.

He had been right, something I was getting used to and also beginning to rely on; it took just over an hour to reach the furthest southern island. We knew it when we saw it because one; there was an old crumbled down rock pier, and two; the great big ocean beyond proved free of anything but deep water.

Lucas guided our yellow ship to a sandy shore that was nearly identical to the one we had left, and we towed in Blue Ducky to our new home. *Temporary*, I stated in my mind, *very temporary*.

I gazed out in all directions as the raft bumped against the sand, hoping to spot a yacht, a boat, anything, *give me a sail or another life raft with a homing device*. But the waters all around were calm and clear.

"Soon." I whispered. I was certain the tourists would flood in soon. After all, this was the most beautiful place on earth. Of course the tourists would come.

That night, as we lay on the beach surrounded by our luggage, the raft, and the air mattress, something did come in from the ocean. It wasn't a tourist or a patrol. It was a storm. I named it Hurricane Fury, and she stole both of our rafts.

Chapter 23

We had no light.

We had made the decision to camp on the beach after Lucas spent the afternoon fishing. Then we had cooked a dinner of a tasty white fleshed fish neither one of us recognized.

I had pulled up the luggage to the tree line, and only poked into the jungle fifty feet or so, just to look around. I hadn't spied any houses, but I did find trails that visitors had left. Or they may have been old well-worn paths from days gone by. As the sun set, I dug a fire pit, collected rocks, and wood, and started a nice bed of coals to roast on.

Lucas had taken the motor off of ducky and set it by our luggage and we set the inflatables up near us, but we hadn't tied them down. Why would we? A good breeze was all we had been gifted with for nearly a month. It wasn't hurricane season, so when Fury blew in, dumping rain like a madwoman, we dove for shelter in the trees. Trying desperately to find any spot that would keep the torrential wind and rain off of us. In the confusion and rush, we left everything behind.

"What the hell is this?" I screamed over the rain. "I thought the equator didn't get hurricanes!"

Lucas kept a firm hold of me, the deep blackness of the clouded sky, and the noise of the storm, would make it easy to lose each other.

"I don't know, we need to find better shelter, this is going to last awhile!"

We struggled further into the trees, tripping and stumbling on the wet jungle floor. I had one hand in Lucas' large strong grasp, my other hand clung to his waistband. I trudged behind
Lady Sun

him with my head down, rain running down my face, soaking my clothes and skin. We were making snail's time, looking for something we weren't able see. The wind tore at the trees, and the noise added to the confusion of blackness and chaos. I held faithfully to my seeing eyed cowboy, hoping his senses were sharper than mine.

Twenty minutes of struggling through underbrush, tripping over rocks and knocking into trees, and Lucas finally came to a stop in a copse of tightly packed palms. It was similar to the clump he had taken me to, to sew me up, but these trees seemed larger, older. They grew so thickly together we just fit, huddled at the base of the trunks. The storm here seemed angry, because it vibrated our shelter and whipped at the tops of the trees, but less rain got through. The heavy layer of fronds diverted the water to the sides of the copse. We were splattered intermittently whenever a good gust of wind opened the canopy to the raging storm above, but it was bearable, and better than being stuck on the beach in the madness of it.

Lucas and I settled in, wrapping up in each other and leaning back, feeling the life of the storm surge and sway through the trunks behind us.

"We'll be OK."

Lucas spoke into my ear. Not shouting, but speaking loud enough to cut through Fury's voice. He held me tightly to him and I just nodded against his chest. *What doesn't kill us makes our mettle.*

Hours went by. I tried to sleep, hoping to pass the miserable time away in a dreamless blackness, perhaps waking to rescue or at least a steady drizzle. The lashing and noise and the constant wet, refused to let me even nod off. I huddled my wet body against Lucas's equally soaked form and tried to think of happy thoughts.

I didn't really know how many tourists came to this area. I also didn't know what time of year was 'tourist' season. I had been assured that January was the best time to visit the Maldives, but we were south of the equator now, I wasn't sure by how much, but maybe a couple hundred miles. The weather below the equator moved in its own way, completely separate from the northern hemisphere, that, at least, I knew. The whole thrill of the water in a flushing toilet circling opposite directions in Seattle or Sydney being a well-known trivia fact.

So what was great tanning weather to the North, may well be great storm weather to the South. From all the news coverage on the monsoons in the Asia's that had recently flooded out villages and rivers, I knew that a good portion of the big storms started near the equator. Then if conditions were right, they grew in size and ferocity as they approached warm shallow water and land. Fury was most likely a tropical storm that was gearing up to head to Africa or Madagascar or somewhere south, where we in the northern part of earth, rarely covered when it came to sensational news.

I hoped it was just getting worked up and would move on. These little islands wouldn't hold up well to a full force hurricane, and we most likely wouldn't have a chance at survival out in the open. *Not even any rope to lash myself to a post.* An old poem my mother used to tell me came to mind, of a ship at sea hitting a storm and a father lashing his daughter to the mast for fear of losing her overboard. When the storm passed, the entire crew was lost, and her body washed ashore...still lashed to the mast. My mother tended toward the dramatic and I wished now I were there with her. At my farm, sipping a cup of hot coffee, watching the snow fall, looking forward to spring. But I was here, now, lashed to Lucas, on a small island in a storm, like a ship at sea.

I guessed that only boats would venture to the island chains this far out. And only yachts or experienced sailors would travel over great lengths of water to reach a small island chain that offered no services, no shelter, or water, and one you had to jump through hoops and cut through red tape to even approach.

The entire area being a reserve meant that visitors had to apply for a permit even to anchor off shore. The fines were pretty steep, from what I understood about maritime law and trespassing on a reserve, their boat could be confiscated. So chances of rescue were looking worse and worse. Storms and restrictions would mean weeks, maybe even months, before someone ventured this way.

We had to hope for a patrol, one of the law-keepers of the preserve who checked for permits, but I had no idea where they would be stationed out of. How often they patrolled the islands, *which* islands, this atoll had a dozen or so. Would they come ashore? Would we even see

them? Perhaps they would only circle the outer circumference, looking for any boats in the

vicinity. I was pretty sure no one would venture in to the center of the atoll and risk getting caught

up on a reef or sandbar. The reef that circled this atoll was pretty far out, we may never even hear

them even if they came every day, or see them if we weren't ocean side. I was starting to panic a

little. My stomach was in knots and I clung tighter to Lucas.

The rain was warm, and even with the wind whipping about us I wasn't cold. I never fully

dried out because the wind brought rain down from the fronds above, but I was grateful at least,

that even without shelter, we would not freeze to death. We had more of a chance of starving if

the storm lasted for days. There would be no fishing, and eating coconuts would only make

matters worse.

I knew I was working myself into a state of distress. Worrying and freaking out wasn't

going to help anything, and I knew too, that given what we now had to deal with, I needed to calm

down. I was starting to feel nauseous with the dread that was creeping in. I took a few deep

breathes. Tucking my head down on Lucas' shoulder, I forced all the worries out of my mind that I

had no power over, and instead turned to thoughts of my future. Our future.

Lucas was the first truly wonderful thing to happen to me in a very long time. I had

wanted to be married. I had wanted a farm and a hundred babies and horses and the country

version of a picket fence life. Jon, though, had wanted to live in the city. We had moved from

Seattle to Portland, visited cities all over America, but he was never satisfied. It wasn't until a few

years in that I had realized it was impossible to satisfy Jon. He was a perpetual complainer,

always wanting more or different. Always competing with the Jones'. Nothing was good enough.

I had begged him to move back to Spokane where my family was. I hated the rain of

Seattle and the cold shoulder of Portland. Jon refused to live in the country, and along with that

refusal had included children. I was devastated, I could let go of the dream of a farm, but not the

want to mother. I loved the princes and Audrey, and craved so longingly for my own children, but

Jon insisted we wait. And wait. And wait, until it became a battle between us. When he cheated with one of my friends at a work party, the fight wasn't worth it. I left and bought my farm and started over.

It had been a struggle and a fight. I scraped together pennies and worked my hands to blisters putting in fencing, repairing the barn, hauling hay, cutting firewood, but finally the dream was real and my farm was just now starting to support itself. In another few years it would start turning enough of a profit I could relax, and hoped to finally find someone. Preferably someone with the same values and life goals. A man who wanted to live in the country and have a hundred children. Well, I would settle for two or three, but I wasn't getting any younger. And now here I was, stranded with the perfect man who loved me. Lucas enjoyed farming, and horses, and… God, I hoped he wanted children. We would have to talk about that. Figure out what our future held. I was willing to move to Montana, my animals didn't care where they lived, and Lucas had the ranch. It wasn't far to visit home, so compromise was easy, but children was not something I could compromise on. I prayed Lucas wanted the same.

The nausea wasn't abating and a roll of sea sickness flooded my stomach. I hoped suddenly that the fish we had eaten wasn't poisonous, being sick now was close to a death sentence. I pulled away from Lucas and sat up straight. Crossing my legs Indian style, I began taking slow breathes, physically assessing myself. I didn't feel cramping, no sharp stomach pains. I was thirsty, but not dehydrated. Another wave of nausea and I sat forward, hoping to not throw up on myself.

"Sophia are you OK?" Lucas reached out, putting his hand on my back.

"Just a little sick, it will pass. It must have been the fish." I didn't want to alarm him, and was thankful for the dark and distraction of the storm, he wouldn't be able to see my green face. "It will pass." *Not a big deal, no cramps, that's good, not food poisoning. Then it's probably… Oh my god.*

I suddenly knew, and the realization brought all the butterflies to the surface and I heaved forward to my hands and knees, throwing up the fish and water from my stomach. *How could I not know, this whole time sitting here thinking about children, my instincts screaming at me to notice.*

    I'm pregnant. Of course I was pregnant. What had I thought? I could have sex constantly for a month with a virile cowboy and not get pregnant?

    I had been on birth control with Jon but hadn't taken a pill for two years. I suppose I had plenty of excuses. Six years of not getting pregnant after having sex, trained me to not think about it. And of course I had a few distractions, pirates and floating at sea and the island and hoping to not die or starve to death. Sex wasn't about procreation with Lucas it was about affirmation of life, and passion and expressing love. But of course it was also about procreation, whether I had acknowledged it or not. Nature didn't care about psychology, nature only wanted lots of babies, and Lucas and I fell right into the genetic design. We created life to insure the survival of our species.

    Lucas was at my shoulder, his hand rubbing my back. "Hey Sophie, take it easy, tell me how you feel, are you feverish?" I could hear the concern and fear in his voice.

    "I'm good, I think the fish just wanted out. I'll be fine." I sat back wiping my mouth and patted his hand. "Don't worry, no fever, just stress probably. You feel OK?"

    We were still talking loud, the storm hadn't lessened even a little. He just pulled me to him, stroking my wet hair from my face and wrapped his long, strong, arms around me.

    "Don't worry."

    He somehow managed a soothing tone, as if he were settling a scared child, and I curled into him. I knew he would make a fantastic father. I just didn't know how to tell him, or if this was even something that he wanted. I decided to wait until the storm passed. Wait until we had our bearings and a plan. Then I would tell him and hope to God he didn't hate me.

    I prayed he didn't judge me for being irresponsible, or for adding another burden to an already impossible situation. What should have been joyous, was just another thing to balance in the struggle to survive. I hated that I finally got what I wanted, this man, this child, and I couldn't celebrate them, cuddle on a couch with a movie, make love in a bed, paint a nursery, shop for strollers. I was here, hoping the storm didn't take us away and drop us into the ocean. Hoping that if it passed we would find food, water, shelter, rescue.

God gives with one hand and takes with the other.

I closed my eyes, knowing I wouldn't sleep, but needing the shelter of ignorance. I would pretend all was well until it actually was.

Chapter 24

The sky lightened imperceptibly at first. The shelter of the trees blocking any true view to the storm above. After what seemed like years of huddling together in a wet mass of arms and legs and clinging clothes, Lucas and I finally pulled apart and began looking around at our surroundings.

Fury was having a great time, her party still in its peak, and although we could now see in shades of gray, it didn't brighten our reality at all.

Lucas turned to me, assessing my condition. I hadn't thrown up again. The nausea passed, and I believed I had a handle on my stress level. With any luck I might keep my stomach from hurling up whatever was left of the fish it contained and be able to pretend all was well.

"How are you?" He didn't raise his voice, I could read his lips even if I hadn't heard him, his face was so close to mine. I gave him a bright smile that I knew looked totally fake, but tried to put some heart into it.

"I am having a great time. Nice shower!" I waved my hand at the sky and then to my soaked condition.

"Yeah," he grinned back, "like a free Laundromat. We need to start building some shelter. Are you OK to help?"

I nodded and clamored to my feet. The rain had soaked my clothes, which had been pretty dirty to start with, but we were both muddy and had sand and debris clinging to bits of us, the wet serving as a great glue for anything we touched.

Lucas rose too, and we ignored the kinks in our muscles and uncomfortable situation of wet clothes rubbing raw places on our skin as we began hunting down beams to begin castle 2.0.

"Gather as many palm fronds as you can and stack them here." Lucas pointed to a sandy spot near where we had huddled through the night. "I'll go see if I can find something sturdy for our roof."

I just nodded and began gathering wet, brown, palm fronds, that littered the jungle floor. Fury had helped in a way, by bringing down quite a few green ones during her party. They would work much better at keeping out the rain.

As the morning began to lighten, my pile grew bigger and bigger. I remembered how Lucas had constructed castle 1.0 and in my searching, gathered whatever sturdy branches I could find as well. Lucas scavenged further than I, coming back with branches that were practically logs, stacking them in a pile next to the fronds, and then striding off to the islands *Home Depot* for more lumber. At one point he came back with an actual beam. It was a four by eight, that had been treated to withstand the humid air of the region, and was in decent shape. It ran about twelve feet in length, and I saw that one end was splintered where it had broken off of its other half. I raised my eyebrows as Lucas let it fall to the ground.

"That's a strange square tree."

"I found the house." He gestured behind him. "About a hundred yards or so that way, it's pretty beaten up, not safe at all, and the jungle has grown over most of it, but this was laying in its side yard."

"Too bad you didn't find a Hilton. I would love a bed and room service!"

He reached out and tousled my hair. "I'll build you a Hilton Lady Sun, and we'll order big juicy burgers. And by burgers I mean rain water and maybe some coconuts."

I clapped my hands and gestured to our pile, "Let's do it!"

We worked through the morning and into the afternoon. Lucas's beam worked perfectly as the main support for the roof. He set it, notched between the clump of palms, and then began placing the longer logs running from its length down to the ground. I began weaving fronds through the logs, creating a base for the rest to come. We saved the green ones for last as they would divert water better that the dried up ones. As Lucas secured the last layer of thatch on the outside, I took a handful of sturdy fronds and began sweeping out the inside of our new castle.

It ran about seven feet long by about six feet deep. The back curved a bit, and the roof/back wall sloped steeply, but once we tucked ourselves into it, it was perfectly dry inside. Well, no water got through, but the entire thing was wet, having been built with wet material, even so, I felt better.

We had achieved shelter, and we were out of the elements for the most part. Lucas created walls on either side with the smaller branches and extra thatching, so the wind only occasionally gusted through the open front.

I sat down on the hard packed sand and dirt floor, and Lucas poked his head in. "I'm going to get our bags. Stay here OK?"

Lucas rarely ordered me to do anything, except to stay within yelling distance, or to be careful, so I could tell he was concerned about me to actually command me to stay.

I nodded and shooed him with my hand, "Bring me back a taco. I'm starving!"

He gave me a thumbs up and strode off into the trees we had stumbled through the night before.

To be honest I wasn't feeling well. I had trudged through the construction, appreciating having something to focus on, but the queasiness remained and I was exhausted. My breasts were tender, which now that I realized why, I noticed they were much firmer than usual. My breasts always grew tender for a week or so each month in anticipation of my monthly visitor, so I had grown accustomed to ignoring it, But this tenderness was different, my breasts felt full, and heavy, and itchy. Of course the itchy part was most likely the sand and wet, but I decided it would be a good idea to take it easy and let Lucas haul the luggage up. If Fury hadn't taken it.

It only took Lucas about twenty minutes or so to find the beach and return with our two suitcases. Now with some light, and a little less confusion, making his way to the shore had to be less tricky. He deposited the bags inside the castle, and then promptly went off again. I began setting to the task of untangling the life vests from the handles, looking forward to forming a mattress and maybe napping once Lucas brought back some water. As wet as I was, I felt incredibly thirsty.

Another half hour later and Lucas came back with the metal box and my purse. He climbed into the hut and stretched out his long legs.

"Both water bottles were gone." He sounded angry, "the raft, the air mattress, and your calendar."

I almost swore aloud, but didn't want to feed his bad mood. The trial of this adventure weighed on him, and I knew his concern for me added to his stress.

"We have the thermos in the suitcase, and no need for the raft anymore." I reached out and ran my hand down his arm. I hated talking so loud it made both of us sound mad. "Why don't you go set out the can to gather water and we can drink from the thermos, take a quick nap, you have to be beat."

Lucas turned and looked at me. He saw I was trying to put him into a better mood and sighed. "No worries, Sophie." He reached over and dug in his suitcase, pulling out the thermos full of the water I had distilled the day before. He took a long drink and then handed it to me. "I'm going to go get us those tacos. You rest, I won't be too long."

He leaned over and kissed me gently. It was a strange contrast to be surrounded by noise, and rain, and feel so uncomfortable, and lousy, but our kiss was gentle, and soft, and sweet.

"Be careful." I ran my hand down the side of his face, his eyes looked tired, this last month had taken a toll on him as well. His clothes hung loosely, his muscles more defined. Always handsome, but wearing down. *We both are.*

Lucas kissed me again, a quick one this time and then he was gone, off to take care of me. *Yeah, he will make an excellent father. Assuming we survive this.*

* * *

The storm seemed to last forever. The rain would come down in sheets, drenching and stinging. Staying out in it for any length of time was torture, the individual drops attacking any exposed skin like angry insects. The warm water transformed into avenging needles made of two parts hydrogen, one part oxygen, and one hundred percent angry. The wind never ceased, it would gust, and batter, and then change its tempo to howling, or whipping, but it never once stopped, or tried out a gentle breeze attitude. It was righteous in its pissed off-ness, and I wondered, as I sat huddled and miserable, cranky, and starving, just who had offended the weather enough to raise such wrath. Then along the same illogical line if thinking, giving the weather even more animate value, I wondered further -- what someone had to do to conjure a storm as punishment.

Noah's flood came to mind as the only example I could summon toward human cause and effect in righteous weather. But of course hurricanes, and snowstorms are common. I knew this, I could reason away the cause of my current situation by arguing the logic of seasons, and jet streams, and moisture content in the clouds etc. But being inside Fury somehow made the storm feel alive, as if it breathed around me, yelled, and threw its tantrum, and cursed in wind tongue.

Watching the hurricanes, snowstorms, or floods on the weather channel didn't compare to reality. Nothing compared to the visceral fear, and torment, of being stuck it a makeshift shelter, on a castaway island, in the middle of a very large ocean, lost to the world, while this logical storm dealt out its punishment to whoever had pissed it off.

"Wasn't me." I muttered. "I recycle, I don't sin, well, not big ones." I shrugged my shoulders to no one at all.

Lucas hadn't come back yet, and my rambling of trying to find reason in the storms wrath was my way of distracting myself from worrying. *How long had he been gone?* I quickly shook the thought away. I knew that wondering would lead to panic, which would lead to me freaking out, and I promised myself I wouldn't freak out. Calm was my new motto. So I pretended I hadn't wondered at all about Lucas' whereabouts and went back to musing over how to piss off the weather.

The best I could come up with was damage to the ocean. Since weather and the oceans were so tightly married, it stood to reason if you pissed off one, it would affect the other, but as far as I knew the most I had ever done was peed in the ocean. Considering fish did that all the time, I couldn't see how the storm would have any beef with me.

Probably another oil spill out here. One country or another was constantly fouling up the waters with the black sludge we ran the world on. I'm just collateral damage to the wrath. *Figures.*

I knew full well that my entire train of thought was based on giving the planet and the oceans *and* the weather, the benefit of being sentient beings. As well as the ability to reason out dealing wrath and punishment at all. But it served to entertain my ever growing stressed out, and miserable state of being, so I didn't bother chastising myself for the silliness. Hell, maybe I would become a full blown pagan before the island or the storm released me and return to society with the insistence of sacrificing virgins to volcanoes to spare future crops from blight. Right now I just wanted Lucas back safe with me to suffer and starve together in our twig hovel. *Maybe he'll return with a feather bed and Chinese takeout and we can snuggle up and watch an old episode of friends on our imaginary TV.*

Christ I really was losing it. Ten more minutes. I would give Lucas ten more minutes to return, and then I would indulge my banked back panic, and head out into the bitchen' storm to hunt him down. Oil spill vengeance be damned.

I had counted sixty Mississippi's eight times and was rounding fifteen Mississippi's when Lucas' very wet head appeared in our castle doorway.

"I have a surprise for you."

I crawled across the wet sand of our new home's floor to reach out and hug him. He was soaked completely through, his shirt clung to his chest, and his khakis shorts were covered in mud, and sand, and dripped like a faucet. He crawled inside the shelter, plopping down on the hard packed sand and leaned back against one of the palms that made up the back side of the lean to.

"Is it jewelry? Cuz babe, I would rather a nice box of almond chicken and chow mien over diamonds."

"Well not chow mien or chicken, but almost as good, plus, no sodium." Lucas began rummaging under his wet shirt where I now noticed were some conspicuous bulges.

"I like sodium, sodium and I go way back." I knew I sounded pouty, but the thought of Chinese food had me reminiscing.

"How about an orange instead." Lucas held in his hands two perfectly round oranges.

I was speechless.

I live in two food realities. One is the fantasy, where I relived in my mind every cheeseburger I had ever eaten, every hot dog or chocolate cake. A world where I had faith, one day, my tongue would taste flavor again. Spices, like salt that wasn't ocean water, and pepper -- those two shakers everyone takes for granted. And garlic bread, oh my God, and spaghetti and meatballs, smothered in cheese. Oh yes, my fantasy-food-reality is totally tricked out with a state of the art kitchen, and an unlimited pantry.

My other reality is acceptance. I knew I would eat fish. The fish would vary, but it all tasted like fish. If you want to make fish fun, you need spices, like salt and pepper, hell even lemon would be nice, but in reality, all fish tastes like the ocean, which is fishy. I knew I would chew some coconut, but not the fun kind like an *Almond Joy*... oh man, chocolate and coconut are the bomb. Or those snowball cupcakes that *Hostess* makes, covered in marshmallow, rolled in coconut and sold in fun colors like candy pink or green on St Patrick's Day. Yeah, *that* coconut is on my list of awesome. But straight from the shell after four long weeks of coconut, and knowing each bite would bring on cramps and bathroom breaks, when your bathroom is a hole dug in the sand. Yeah, that coconut gets old real quick. Like day three.

I knew I would have warm water. Never cold, never icy, never refreshing. Just mouth temperature water to keep me from dehydrating, not really to enjoy. My food reality is that I may eat a stray bird once in a while, a bird that back in the States I wouldn't have considered food. I may get up the gumption to catch a freaky looking crab and eat it, sans butter, or beer, or shell crackers, just a rock and teeth.

So when Lucas held out the orange, it glowed. It confused me. It was two realities, trying to meld. I looked up at his face, tearing my eyes from that heavenly fruit, taking a chance that when I looked back he would be holding a fish. *Oh god not another fish.* And he was smiling. The set of his shoulders was relaxed, and his grin was genuine, and full.

"It's real Sophia. I found an orange tree, an orchard actually." And he pulled out another lump from under his shirt.

A banana. A freaking gorgeous, still green, rock hard, banana. I started to cry.

As I sobbed and tore at the rind of the heavenly orange, Lucas told me of his discovery.

"I went back to the manager's house and started to explore. I figured there was no way I could fish in this." He waved his hand indicating the storm that still tore at the jungle but did show signs of lessening. Finally.

I hardly noticed Lucas, the scent of the orange was almost over powering. The sticky juice got under my fingernails, stinging little cuts on my fingers, and warming me from the inside. Before I even took a bite, all I could smell was orange, citrus, sunshine, and sweetness. That fruit became the center of the universe, and I reacted to it viscerally, my mind focused on getting to the meat inside, my body hunched over it like an animal protecting a kill.

"There's actually a little village here" Lucas' voice was secondary to all my other senses, but I registered him, it was the least I could do after he brought back sweet sustenance.

"Some of the buildings are still standing, some with a few walls, or just foundations, and none of them safe to enter. The jungle has taken it all back, but there is a church there."

I looked up at that, in my mind picturing a modern structure like you see in the States, basically a warehouse for people to congregate in, the mental image didn't compute.

A church? That can't be right. And I lifted the now peeled orange to my mouth and took a bite.

Oh holy of all holies.

I'm sure everyone has tasted an orange before, but *this* fruit I was chewing, wasn't what you get at a store. This was warmth, and sweetness, and tangy, and honeyed. It was so full -- the flavor, that my mouth, and tongue were inadequate relayers of deliciousness to my brain. I was brought back to the conversation by a 'Mmmm..." sound and realized I was sitting cross legged in front of Lucas, my mouth full of fruit, *Mmming* to myself in heavenly appreciation of an orange.

Lucas was sitting in front of me, smiling patiently.

I swallowed and took a breath. "A church? Really?"

Lucas chuckled and shook his head. He began peeling the other orange as he continued his story. "Yes, the church was built of stone, or coral, so it's completely intact, other than the roof, but I think I can rig something up from remnants of the other buildings. But that's not the best part."

"Better than a church?"

"Yes, Sophie, we can have a real shelter, and the orchard, there was orange and banana and a few other varieties I couldn't identify, but behind the church, there's a well."

I stopped eating and moaning and looked at Lucas. "A well? So you're telling me that you went out and found shelter, food, and water. Is that what I'm getting here?"

"Yeah Pumpkin." Lucas took one of my sticky hands in his. "It may not be a resort, but we will have four walls and a roof. There's food from the orchard, and maybe more, I haven't explored that much, and water. We may only be able to use it for washing and such if it's not clean, but we might be able to rig up a more permanent distiller where you won't have to burn your fingers and slave over a fire."

I rose up to my knees and fell into him. I wrapped my arms around his neck and held on. "A home. We can build a little home until rescue comes." The relief was absolute and overwhelming. Fury was kicking her way out to sea to go torment some other island, or blow out all together, and when the storm cleared, we had a chance to not only survive, but live.

The stress of the last month, the pirates, the life raft at sea, the endless ocean, the reef that tore me open. The hunger, and thirst, the worry that no one would come, and then the baby, the storm. I had been winding tighter, and tighter, trying to maintain a positive attitude without cause. And now, we had a chance. We could make it until someone found us.

I might gain back some of the weight I had lost. I could stay out of the sun, let my skin heal and not burn. I would harbor this life and it could flourish. If I was careful, very careful, everything might possibly be OK.

For the second time in five minutes I began to cry. I clung to Lucas and let the tears soak into his wet shirt and cried silently, wondering how I would tell him. *When* I would tell him. Perhaps I would sleep on it and wait. Perhaps I should wait until rescue came. No, that wasn't fair. I knew that it was just as much his child as mine, and it wasn't my news to keep from him. I resolved then as Lucas held me in his strong warm arms, with the taste of orange on my tongue and hope in my heart, that I would tell him in the morning.

We finished the water together. We each ate a banana, and then, exhausted, and filthy, and sticky, we wrapped around each other and lay down on our familiar, and quite squished, life vest bed, and fell into a deep sleep.

Chapter 25

I dreamed of wide open fields and children playing in a creek. I dreamed of Lucas riding a horse across the Montana range and my belly swelling with life. In the dream my family surrounded me, and we celebrated with tables of food, and music, and campfires. My niece's and nephew's laughter rang like bells against the sky, and I felt full, and content, wrapped in love and safety.

I woke up with a prayer on my lips, that Lucas would love this little life inside me. For although it was surely smaller that a sesame seed, it owned me, heart and soul, and I wanted so badly for we three to be a family.

But the dream had ended, and this new day brought me out of sleep, and into itchy sand in my still damp shorts, the urge to pee, and a slight tickling of nausea.

"My kingdom for a toilet and a shower." I rolled into Lucas and stretched, trying to work out the kinks that never truly receded. My days were filled with kinked muscles, bug bites, burned fingers, and an empty stomach. My mind was constantly distracted with the pre-occupation for finding water, food, a comfortable place to sit, and to eat *one* mouthful of fish that didn't crunch with sand.

"So the shine has finally worn off?" Lucas pulled me closer to him and nuzzled his bearded face into my sandy, tangled hair. "You would trade all this for a porcelain throne?"

I wiggled out of his embrace, sad to leave the comfort of his arms, but my bladder ruled me, and the nausea was less a threat, more a promise. I didn't want Lucas to see the ugly side of

my news. I wanted him to think of me as glowing, and healthy, and capable of growing a strong,

healthy, baby to bounce on his knee.

"Yep, vacation time is over, I'm off to the trees. Would you mind checking us out and

calling a taxi, we don't want to miss our flight."

"Mmhm. Sorry Pumpkin, that plane has flown, ship has sailed, train has left the station."

Lucas propped himself up on an elbow as I scooted out of our hut into sunlight. "But I can order

room service, how do you feel about an orange-banana salad?"

I shook my head wearily and smiled. Lucas was my rock. He was my giggle, and my

warmth, my shelter, and my food. Without him I wouldn't have lasted a week. Well, most likely

not a day, considering the reefs attack on my leg. "Sounds perfect. I won't be a minute, then we

can tour the village and begin our new life of luxury."

*   *   *

The church was gorgeous. Well in all honesty it was rather creepy, like a scene out of an

old *Frankenstein* movie. The walls were completely overgrown with vines and creepers, the door

was half rotted and hanging from its rusted hinges. If ever there had been glass in the arched

windows, the islanders must have taken it with them in their mass exodus, for there was no trace

of it now. The roof had long rotted and collapsed and then began its return to the earth as the

rotted beams and boards wasted away. Some on the interior of the structure, some along the

outside walls.

But to my eyes, there in the bright sunlight after the storm, the church looked like a gift. It

had potential. With some elbow grease, and some ingenuity, we could have a rather decent,

maybe even romantic, shelter.

Lady Sun

Plus, it was on holy ground. That couldn't hurt.

"New island rule." I stood with my hands on my hips, eyeing the collapsed and ramshackle structures on deserted island lane.

"No cussing in the church?"

"Oh yeah, that, plus, no tetanus shots. There has to be a minefield of rusty nails in there."

"Agreed, proceed with caution." Lucas held out his large warm palm toward mine and I absently shook it as I eyed the possibilities.

"I wonder if bed bath and beyond is having a sale on curtains."

Lucas pulled me to him and gave me a light bear hug squeeze. "Well decorating can come after we figure out a roof, but first, let's investigate the well. If it's halfway decent I can get something rigged up for a shower."

I squealed and did a little bounce, "A shower? Oh man, you had me at 'let's'."

Both of us had a much lighter mood than we had maintained on the other island. Although the storm was a daunting welcome here, the village, the fruit, and the potential well, had us both walking jauntily despite our bedraggled states around to the rear of the church. A promise of a shower was motivation enough to have me willing to sing and dance and flaunt my sunburn, my sand rashes, my bug bites, and my now very scrawny form.

Lucas had fared a bit better with his tan, his skin halting at a nice golden caramel, and refusing to burn or peel. *Good genes.* The thought immediately leading me to the news of our combined genes I had yet to figure out a way to broach. *I mean really, shelter, and water, a shower, at least let me be clean when I say 'hey, you my baby daddy'.* So I shoved the niggle of guilt aside and continued my assessment of said baby daddy as we picked our way through the overgrowth behind the church.

Lucas may sport the perfect tan, but he too had suffered from the flies, and mosquitoes, and sand gnats. We were freckled with the itchy bites randomly placed all over exposed skin, (and a few on skin we only exposed occasionally, but had been too distracted on such occasions to notice any blood sucking visitors.)

He had lost weight too. I knew we looked a sight, my clothes no longer fit me, and Lucas was constantly hitching at his waistband to keep up his shorts. He wasn't gaunt yet, but there wasn't a speck of fat left on his frame. We were past our bodies using our reserves, and now we were consuming ourselves. We both knew the discovery of the orchard, the fruit being added to our fish, bird, crab, coconut diet, was a life saver. Literally. And now water. *A shower.*

 Lucas led me toward a stone structure covered by a piece of corrugated metal which in turn, was covered in afore mentioned vines and creepers. He pulled handfuls of vines away from the metal, freeing the well covering from the jungle's grasp, then slowly, he slid the metal from the coral rock base to reveal the dark shadows it had been covering.

"Moment of truth." Lucas flashed me an almost nervous grin and picked up a stone from the base of the well and let it drop into the shadows.

Not even a second passed, I hardly said "One Mississippi." and there was a splash. I whooped and jumped up to high five my Cowboy, but he was too distracted to notice the upraised hand. I high fived myself and then leaned over the lip of the well. "It must be pretty full!"

"The island is probably no more than twelve feet above sea level, this well isn't deep. I'll measure it later, but for now we need to be sure it's fresh water." Lucas pulled out his metal cup from one of his many pockets and leaned over the lip of the well. Reaching down, his long arm extended into the dark shadow, he scooped up some liquid and pulled it into the sunlight.

"You aren't going to drink it are you?"

"No, just taste it. Fresh water will float atop salt water, but the storm may have gotten things stirred up." He put the cup to his lips and took a small mouthful. After a moment of letting it sit on his tongue he spit it out and smiled. "It's fresh."

"Yay!" This time he reciprocated my high five, and then poured the cupful back into the well.

"It tastes clean but we can't be sure, it would be safer to boil it before we drink it, but it will work fine for cleaning"

"A shower?"

"Yes my lady, your kingdom for a shower. Sorry, haven't found a toilet yet, but who knows, the day isn't over."

The next hour was spent fetching the metal can and filling it, thermos-full, by thermos-full, until I deemed it was enough to clean me. Then Lucas returned to the castle to retrieve my cleanest garment, which happened to be a pale, blue, sundress I had only worn a few times, and had yet to be torn, or stained, or burnt, or smelling of fish.

I stood in the packed earth of what had been the main road -- the only road -- through the village. One thermos at a time, I poured the clean water over my head, scrubbing with my fingers at my scalp, rubbing with my palms, every inch of me, to remove any speck of sand. Then I poured more, and more water, until the can was empty.

Lucas appeared, holding my dress as I stood drying in the sun on the road. He grinned at my nudity and leaned down to kiss my clean lips.

"I brought your *Keds* since you'll want to explore," I had been wearing my flip flops which kept flipping or flopping off, "and your brush, and toothbrush and toothpaste."

"Oh you're the best, thank you." I held out my arms for the pile and began dressing as he walked away, metal can under his arm, to fill it for his own shower.

When he returned, I sat on a rock, brushing the wet tangles out of my hair, and then braiding it to hang down my back, hopefully to remain sand free for one day. I watched the sexy form of Lucas as he repeated my earlier attempts at cleaning. He was such a sight and still took my breath away. Tall, and wrapped in muscle that was now leaner, and more defined than when aboard the *Lady Sun*, but no less impressive. The sprinkling of hair on his chest glistened with water as he dumped a thermos-full over his head, the rivulets running down his stomach, over hips and thighs and calves, drawing my eyes to revel in every inch of his perfect form. *Damn he's a stunning man. Good genes,* whispered again, and I took a long steadying breath. *Let him get dressed, then I will tell him.*

My palms were beginning to sweat, and having finished the chore of braiding, I decided to inspect the orchard while Lucas finished his shower. "I'll be right back, just off to fetch a bite."

Lucas nodded, and I strolled in the direction he had indicated earlier where he had discovered the orange tree.

Sure enough, not a block from the church, back from the road, there was a group of formally placed fruit trees. I couldn't help but laugh out loud. There had to be about twenty of them. I saw two orange trees, a lemon tree, *oh man, that will help the fish situation,* three or four banana trees, a bread fruit and a few I would have to inspect to see if I could identify them. I began filling my skirt that I pulled up to form an impromptu sack, with oranges and bananas, and bread fruit. I scanned the rest of the orchard, trying to determine which trees had been planted purposefully, and which, were part of the jungle.

They all varied in size, and color, and form, the decades having given them time to mature and spread their roots and branches. Just as I was about to turn to go back to Lucas with my breakfast hoard I recognized one of the trees.

"Oh my freaking holy wow!" I almost dropped the hold I had on my skirt as I plunged past branches to get to one particular tree that loomed over the smaller ones. "Avocado!" The California girl in me was doing a dance inside while the starving island Sophia was pulling down perfectly ripened fruit from the branches. My aunt had an avocado tree in California, we called it brain food because it was chock-full of carbs and fat that was good for the brain. You know, the good fat as opposed to the bad fat the scientists are always touting. Plus I absolutely loved guacamole. I stopped myself at four even though the starving mother in me wanted to be a glutton. I wrapped my large breakfast in my skirt and headed back toward the church.

Lucas now sat on the rock I had vacated, slipping his deck shoes on. I sat down on the sandy/ grassy/weedy ground beside the rock and let the fruit roll from my skirt.

"Wow, you found avocado"

I nodded and held one out to him. "Yep, things are going to be much tastier from here on out." Lucas lowered himself to the ground to sit across from me, his back against the rock. "Well let's dig in, build up our energy, we have a long day ahead. This evening I'll see about catching some protein to add to our fruit."

I nodded as I peeled my banana. I planned to have the orange next, then an avocado, and tackle the huge breadfruit for lunch... with maybe another avocado. As I chewed I pieced together in my head how I wanted to broach the sticky subject that hung over me, but nothing I came up with in my mind sounded good. Most of my sentences began with *"hey guess what?"* Which sounded flippant, or, *"I have something to tell you."* which sounded ominous.

My mind wandered through my options as I finished my orange and started peeling the avocado. I was careful with my breakfast, trying to keep my dress relatively clean, and the mess confined to my fingers, which I could now wash when I was done. I noticed Lucas had been as quiet as I was and looked up to see him gazing at the church with a calculating eye. *Ah the hunter-gatherer-protector is figuring out a roof.* Of course he is. Just one of the many reasons why I loved him.

In that moment I knew what to say. I saw this man sitting across from me who had saved me from pirates, bandaged my wounds, fished in the blistering sun every day to feed me, worked to shelter me, and made love to me in every moment with his kindness and strength. I owed him the truth. No embellishments, no fancy words.

"Lucas." I set the remains of my avocado aside and wiped my fingers in the grass, attempting to free them of stickiness but not bring back any sand. I failed, and resigned myself to be patient and deal with cleaning them later. I sat up straight and folded my messy fingers in my lap.

Lucas had pulled his eyes away from the church and was looking at me. He swallowed the last bite of his avocado and tossed the peel into the brush. "Yes?"

He looked so sweet and relaxed. Our bellies full, our bodies clean, there was no better time than right now.

"I'm pregnant" I said it softly, but clearly. Looking him square in the eyes, not wanting to miss any reaction, no matter how slight, hoping beyond hope that after the shock, I would see joy.

Lucas blinked. He stared back into my eyes, his body absolutely still. Then very slowly he leaned forward and took my sticky hands in his large warm ones.

"Please say it again, so I can be sure I heard you right."

"I'm pregnant." I repeated myself slowly, calmly, and then added, "I only just realized it yesterday. I'm about ten day's late, give or take."

He said nothing. He held my hands in his and looked at me with such a queer expression, one I couldn't quite place. Then he leaned forward and kissed me very gently on the mouth and stood up.

I rose to my feet, worried now and not sure what to say, what to do, I couldn't take the words back, I didn't want to. There was no way to hide facts, sooner or later he would know. But I feared again, that he would turn away, that he would take his heart from me and shut down, reject the future we might have together. *Oh God, I'm going to lose him,* lose the man I loved with all my heart and I could do nothing.

Lucas turned slowly and began to walk down the overgrown road toward our hut. He wasn't hurried or even distraught. He was thinking, sorting, mulling through the words, the implications, the world shifting news, and absorbing it. Figuring out his place in it.

I let him walk to the end of the road and disappear into the trees. Then I followed him. He may need to think, but I needed to talk, the minute he was done with his thinking I planned to be there to hear whatever conclusion he came to.

I kept him in sight but didn't rush to catch up. He clearly needed space and I could at least give him that. He walked slowly through the trees, then past our hut and on toward the beach where we had landed only days before. When he reached the sand he continued down to the edge of the water and then stood, looking out across the perfect, glassy, aqua, pool.

I wished I was inside his head with his thoughts. I wished I was there beside him, wrapped in his arms, celebrating the news. But I knew it was a big deal. For more reasons than I cared to think of in my own mind, it was a big deal and no joke, or smile, would make it any less weighty than it was. I lowered myself to the sand and waited. Sitting in the shade of the jungle, watching my future form in the mind of the man not fifty feet from me

The sun had moved across the sky, shifting my shade in its journey, giving me a rough estimate of almost an hour before Lucas turned and walked up from the water toward me. He slowed as he approached, looking me over, assessing me I think. My health, *my worth?* I wasn't sure, but his eyes were kind, and he lowered himself to sit in the shade beside me.

We were both quiet for a while, the minutes passing, but without tension, just a settling in together, with this new reality shared. Then Lucas reached out and took my hand, he squeezed my fingers gently and held my hand in his own, placed in his lap, creating a bridge between us. I squeezed back and remained silent. Looking out at the blue and the sun. At the perfect scenery that held us trapped like a trick, so very pleasing to view, but the price of it, for us, was painful beyond words.

"Cassie and I married young." Lucas spoke softly, his voice sorting through the words as the thoughts formed, his intent to share the struggle he was sorting through, clear in the halting way he continued with his story.

"We had both wanted the ranch, or so I had thought. I wondered later if it had been my dream I forced upon her. If that had been the reason things started to fall apart." He shook his head, looking down at the sugary sand in front of him. He paused long enough for me to wonder if he would finish. Then he took a breath and blew it out and forged ahead with purpose. "We spent our money and time and energy on the ranch. The first years were a struggle, but I found such satisfaction in it, I think I didn't notice that we weren't as well suited as I had thought. Cassie went into the city often, she joined book clubs, and made friends, and would go out for drinks with them at clubs. I stayed and held down the ranch. Of course she would invite me, and a few times I went, but I never enjoyed it. It was loud and I don't dance and everyone was just hell-bent on getting drunk and hooking up. I couldn't understand why she wanted to go. She was married, I wanted the married life. But like I said, we were young."

"After the first few years, the ranch began to turn a profit. My brothers and sisters were having kids, at family gatherings I would see them with their babies and they seemed so alive and happy, forming their own units, traditions. I had always wanted kids."

"On our fourth anniversary Cassie threw away her birth control pills. We made a whole celebration of it, certain, that month, we would get pregnant. She stopped going out, started nesting and planning. It was our happiest year. But every month her period came, and after five or six months I started to worry. By our fifth anniversary I wanted us to go and get tested, find out what was wrong. But she didn't. She said it was up to God and she was happy to let it happen.

At the time I didn't find it odd. I started putting more energy into the ranch and she stopped nesting and began joining new clubs. Quilting and knitting. She even took a few classes at the community college, beauty school, creative writing. But she never really showed any interest in what I had thought was our dream, first the ranch and then children."

"Years went by, and one day she came home from a routine checkup and told me she had been tested. That she had asked the doctor to test her fertility, her egg count, I can't remember half the tests she told me at the time. But I did hear the end result. She was fine. Fertile as could be. She said I was the problem."

"Something changed after that. I wasn't sure if it was her or me, but we grew distant. A month would go by and we wouldn't even notice that we hadn't made love."

Then, not long after, she announces that she found someone else, a professor of one of her classes and that she was pregnant. The divorce went pretty quickly after that.

Lucas paused and then turned to me. "I realize now with clarity, that she never loved me. Since meeting you I've felt more in my heart than I ever did for her and have felt more loved by you than I ever did in my marriage. I know she lied. I know she kept taking her birth control. She must have caught on before I had that we wouldn't last and she just bided her time. Let me take care of her, pay for her until she found something better. She used me and conceived of the most hurtful thing she could have done."

"I have always wanted children Sophia." Now Lucas smiled, he turned and looked at me, reaching up to brush my cheek with his fingers. "I believed all these years I would never have any. I am so grateful for you, for pushing me to call you Pumpkin on the *Lady Sun*, for being strong under pressure, and being my partner through this ordeal that would have broken any other woman. And although I already knew you had my heart, that I would marry you if you would have me, I dreaded having to tell you I couldn't give you children. I had planned to wait until we were home, and perhaps you would look past it and want to adopt, or try a surrogate or whatever it is that people do. But I would have done anything to keep you. And now," Lucas placed his large palm across my belly, "now I have everything. I have you, and we have a family, I couldn't love you more than I do right now, for making me whole again."

Then he leaned toward me and put his mouth on mine. The kiss was gentle and sweet and perfect. I wrapped my arms around his neck and he lifted me onto his lap. Lucas cradled me there as if I were precious and fragile, his hands stroking down my waist to my legs, running his fingers up my thighs under the hem of my dress.

I couldn't think of what to say. I was shocked at the level of cruelty, how hurt he must have been, but more than that, I was drowning in relief and thankfulness. Lucas loved me still, he loved our baby and we would be fine. Everything would be fine. I let my heart fill with hope, and lifted my face to his, taking his mouth, tasting the sweetness of this man who was beyond perfection.

"I love you Lucas." My lips breathed the words against his.

He kissed me again, this time with more passion, less gentleness, "I know," he whispered. And lay me back onto the sand.

*   *   *

We took the day off. We set aside all our plans and worries, and returned to our castle with armloads of fruit, and a full can of water. Lucas started a fire and set up a rock stove to hold the can and set it to boil. Then we reclined in the shade of our hut, clean, and full, and spent hours talking. We began to plan, what we would do when we got home, where we would live. I wanted to move to his ranch meet his family, he agreed only if I would agree to keep my farm.

"We can use it for vacations, pass it down to our children," Hearing the words spoken aloud made me tear up, and I rolled over to wrap my arm across his waist. I lay my head on his chest and listened to his heart beat. A strong steady rhythm that set the tempo for our future.

"Children." I whispered. "How many do you want to have?"

"How many can you make/?"

I laughed and felt the rumble of his returned laughter in my cheek still pressed against him. "We both came from big families, I believe children should have lots of siblings."

"Ah yes, to torture each other."

"Exactly, and to love each other. Family is important. When we die they'll have each other."

Lucas wrapped me up in an embrace, holding me against him, and I felt his lips press to the top of my head. "We will be family." His tone was soft and held a note of awe.

"We already are. Tied together by shared genes that is swiftly growing to the size of a seed as we speak."

Lucas rolled to his side, forcing me to do the same, our face now inches from each other.

"How are you? Are you sick? Any pain?" The worry in his voice touched me and I reached up to smooth his brow.

"I'm perfectly fine. So is our wee one. We have more food now, and plenty of water, and the potential for a home, all we need is to hold out, be careful and wait for rescue."

Lucas' blue eyes were full of concern and overflowing with emotion. I knew absolutely that he loved me, that he would do anything to keep us safe, all three of us, and I felt lightened by the knowledge, and quite aroused. I moved forward and wrapped my leg over his, pulling our bodies together, I wove my fingers through the hair at the back of his head and pulled his mouth to mine.

We made love slowly, taking our time, not rushing, but exploring each other, tasting the warm places the sun had turned to gold. Sliding along each other in the late afternoon heat, our bodies slick with sweat and full of need, full of love. We teased each other into new heights only true passion can excel to, finding those old wounds from past hurts, and healing them with kisses and whispers of adoration.

As the sun began to sink into the water beyond the trees, we reclined in our castle, feeding each other fruit, wrapped naked in each other's limbs, not wanting to not be in contact, to not be as close as we could possibly be to each other. Then as the night claimed the island we fell into a sweet sleep, bringing an end to our twenty-sixth day as castaways.

Chapter 26

Day twenty seven was the same as the one before where the weather was concerned, but nothing like any other day of my life. I was happy. Truly and thoroughly happy. I was sticky from all the fruit we gorged on the night before, and sand clung to every inch of me, despite my shower in the village yesterday. I was hungry again and craving something I couldn't put my finger on, and probably wouldn't be able to satisfy anytime soon. But despite it all, despite being stranded, and dirty, and scraped up, I felt wonderful. "Love really does heal all."

"Hmm." Lucas muttered, he moved about castle 2.0 with purpose, gathering up scraps of things and stuffing them in pockets. He secured his knife in the largest one and looked around for the thermos, probably to fill it from the can that still sat on, now cold, rocks just outside the hut.

Love made me feel all warm and fuzzy. Apparently, it made Cowboy feel driven. I could tell he was planning on building a roof, and probably constructing a whole houseful of furniture, he most likely had a side note to whittle a whole bassinet from a palm tree on his lunch break.

"Whoa, slow down there Daddy, come give Mommy a kiss before you go to work."

Lucas stopped and looked at me, still reclined against the very dirty, and almost flat, life vest bed. A huge grin split his face, and he crawled over to lay a sloppy wet sounding kiss on my forehead.

"Let's shower, Mommy, and we can start the day shopping for strollers and diapers."

"Oh, dear God, we better be rescued before this baby is born." I moaned and sat up, rubbing sand off my cheek as I got my equilibrium. Morning nausea wasn't full force yet, but it

Lady Sun

did tickle at my tummy with any sudden movements. "I think I could handle you delivering it, just knock me out with a coconut and let me know when it's over, but living here with no diapers sounds like hell. Can you imagine the sand in places on a poopy baby butt?"

Lucas kept his grin in place and reached out to tousle my hair. "That won't happen Pumpkin, we'll be home before you know it."

Somehow everything Lucas says, I believe. I trust him completely, and I could tell that he believes it too. So if it was just more waiting, and bananas, fish, oranges, coconuts and maybe a freaky crab to pass the time while we wait, then yeah, I'll deal with it. If Cowboy could deal and smile, then I would let him convince me everything would be OK and there would be no island delivery, no sandy poopy baby butts.

"Alright, shower and shopping. Let's do it." I crawled out into the sun and followed my man into the village.

As it turned out, Lucas was the overly protective type. Logic did reason out that there was more risk for me, being here on the island, no doctor, no vitamins, no cheeseburgers pickles or ice cream. But he seemed to think walking would hurt the baby, or sitting anywhere near where I might get bit by a spider, or stung by a mosquito, which was everywhere.

He wouldn't let me help with the roof, which, OK, that was legit, but he wouldn't let me tend to the fire to boil water either. Or stay in the sun longer than a millisecond, or explore on my own, or leave his sight.

I finally resigned myself to finding a piece of shade where I could watch the progress of the construction of the church roof and weave grass and palm mats for the floors. I figured if we could have a home, we could have carpeting, and maybe not sleep on the sand with the bugs. So we slipped into the traditional man/woman roles and let the days slip by.

On day three, or rather day twenty nine, Lucas deemed the structure safe and secure, and ready for a housewarming party. I had a stack of mats I couldn't wait to spread on the floors, and a pile of unripe fruit to stock the pantry.

Lucas had cleared away almost all the debris from inside the church. He scraped out as much sand as possible and pulled the weeds from the interior walls. The arched windows let in plenty of light without letting in sun, and it was surprisingly cool inside. Well, cooler than outside by a handful of degrees, but it was refreshing to move from sweltering heat, to tolerable heat.

I lay out the mats while Lucas fetched our things, and I spent the rest of the day puttering inside, nesting and arranging. I had found an old wire line attached to a fallen down structure and ran it along one wall to serve as a clothes line.

"Tomorrow is laundry day." I spoke to no one at all. Lucas had left again to catch us some protein for dinner. I was worried he was pushing too hard. The discovery of the fruit was all well and good, but he was trying to bear all the burdens of survival and was burning far more energy than he was replacing in nutrients. "Maybe now he'll slow down," I continued with my one sided conversation. "Now that we have a roof and a place to call home. Maybe I can get him to take it easy and build back some strength. I'll have to insist on it, he *has* been looking tired."

We hadn't made love since the night I told him the news. I wondered if it was that manly fear of hurting the baby, or if he felt too tired at the end of the day. I hadn't brought it up, but now began to worry that he had been draining himself, maybe doing damage. "Yes, I'll insist on it." I repeated. My no-one friend remained silent.

It was fish with lemon for dinner with a salad of orange and breadfruit. Nutrient rich coconut water washed it all down. I had two helpings of fish at Lucas' insistence, I didn't argue, for I too was concerned about the baby's health. But that brought my mind around to my concern for Lucas. He did look run down, he looked tired and distracted and darker than before. I couldn't tell in the dim light if he suffered from a sunburn from working on the roof for days, or if he was flushed.

"Lucas, let's take tomorrow off. I think you should rest up." I broached the subject ready to stand my ground should he argue.

"Hmm, yeah." He lifted his head as if it were heavy and gave me a weak grin. "I agree, I think I need a vacation."

I gave a perfunctory chuckle to that, given that we lived in a place most people would pay a lot of money to vacation at. But his response concerned me, I hadn't *expected* him to agree. Lucas was the engine that could, he never stopped, he always kept chugging. I got up and filled his metal cup with water from the can in the corner and brought it to him. He reached up and took the cup from my fingers and drained the water in one long pull.

Kneeling down beside him I lay my hand on his brow, reflexively pulling it back in shock as if I had touched fire. "Lucas! You're burning up!"

He looked at me with glassy eyes, shaking his head slowly, his lips forming the words, "No." then he twisted to the side and threw up all over the new palm mat I had woven him.

When planning my vacation to the Maldives I had researched whether it was a requirement to get vaccinated against the myriad of diseases that might befall a person when traveling to the tropics. It was not, in fact, a requirement, but it *was* 'strongly suggested.' Of course in my opinion the government and doctors 'strongly suggest' you get a jab for crossing the street, and then another once you've reached the other side. But in this case, I had made an appointment with my doctor, and had received the bare minimum of shots covering the most common ailments I might encounter. If it hadn't been for Anna throwing facts at me, and constantly wringing her hands at my nonchalance, I most likely would have forgone the 'strong suggestion.'

Lucas apparently had.

I had no idea what he had contracted, and even if I *could* pinpoint it, there was nothing I could do with that knowledge. It might be malaria, or dengue, or some water born something, a mosquito carried parasite, a sand fly's deadly kiss, it could be anything. But no matter what it was, it terrified me.

I helped Lucas to the bed, which was layered palm mats with the ever present life vest pillows, and arranged him on the side next to the sandy floor. If he threw up again I could at least clean it up and not have to toss the mats.

I kept an inner dialogue going in my head to calm me. After only a few questions directed at Lucas with no answers in reply, I came to the conclusion he would be of no help in self diagnosing, and his silence unnerved me even more.

He was covered in a sheen of sweat, his tanned skin clammy to the touch, and hot everywhere, as if his muscles were coals wrapped I flesh. I wondered how long he had felt this coming on, if he had kept it from me in his barbaric manly way of *'I no get sick, me invincible.'* kind of attitude. I knew he would never want to worry me needlessly, but this was clearly a needful worry.

I fetched a shirt from my suitcase and wet it with water from the can, then I sat down on the mat beside him and began to bathe the sweat from his brow. I softly hummed to myself, hoping the sound would sooth him, and me, all in one go. I tried not to think what would happen if this were an illness that lasted for some time, or worsened to... *oh God.* The word *death* hung at the periphery of my inner ramblings, and I clenched the shirt in my fist.

Lucas would not die. That was impossible. We survived a seventeen hour flight against Anna's odds of crashing. Then pirates with guns and a bad attitude. We survived floating at sea, at the mercy of the great big ocean and Mother Nature, we scraped by the crash landing on the island with wounds that healed, risked infection and dodged the bullet. We have survived gnawing hunger and desperate thirst, how could this big, strong, beautiful, man be brought down by a damn fly or stupid mosquito? It wasn't fathomable. But as I tallied my list of all we had endured, *you've used up all your luck,* whispered in my ear. Like a devil on my shoulder, laughing and rubbing his hands in glee.

"No." I said it aloud to feed my determination. "No one is dying, we will survive this too, and we will go home." I ran the wet shirt down over Lucas' bare chest, attempting to cool the fevered skin. He had opened his eyes at the sound of my voice, looking up at me, but his eyes didn't seem to focus on my face.

"Start a fire." He whispered.

A fire? I leaned down to hear him better, my face close enough to feel the heat rolling off of him. "Babe, you don't need to be warmer, we need ice not fire." I dabbed at his face again, trying to sooth away the burn, knowing the material wasn't much cooler than the air.

"A signal fire."

I almost didn't catch it, his voice was soft and distant. Then he began to shiver.

The night lasted forever. Lucas swung between bouts of dry heaving, fever, and chills. For the heaving I stroked his back as he wretched air, his body pulling in on itself in contracting spasms. For the fever I wet him down, blowing gently on his chest, hoping to cool his heart, cool his blood, comfort in any way I could. For his chills I wrapped my arm around him and leant support, warmth. Love.

I tried through it all to stay calm. I spoke gently, mostly nonsense. I talked about home and my childhood, the silly games I had played with my siblings, the trouble I had gotten into in school. I talked about the farm and the animals, the weather and of snow.

I didn't talk about the baby, or the future, or us. I didn't want to trigger worries, and I knew I wouldn't be able to handle it. So I stuck to the light, fluffy, stuff, and murmured through the night, waiting for the sun to rise.

Start a fire. We had talked of a signal fire, weighing whether it would be worth the effort it would take. The nearest land by our estimation and the map in my book, was more than a hundred miles away. In order for any smoke to be seen we would have to bet that there was a patrol, or ship in the area, or even a plane. But we just couldn't know if anyone would see it. There was the small concern that it might be illegal to burn on the protected island, but in the end we had simply agreed it would be a futile effort, and so had never tried.

If Lucas had decided at some point to try a signal fire, and as his last effort to communicate before the fever took him was to tell me, he must have felt the hope of rescue was growing slim.

I had weighed all this through the night. As the man I loved burned with fever and retched any drop of water I gave him right back up. I decided that at first light I would make a liquid paste of banana, aloe, and water to hopefully give to Lucas. He needed any kind of nourishment and hydration I could force into him. I prayed he would hold it down long enough to gain some nutrients from it.

Then I would build the biggest bonfire I could manage.

Fury had brought down plenty of green limbs and fronds in the storm so I would have plenty of fodder to make some good smoke. If this was our best bet, then I would send as much black smoke high into the sky as possible. Perhaps Diego Garcia would have jets out on training and would see the smoke, or even a commercial airliner could call it in. No matter who saw it, I didn't care, I would build it, they would come. Kevin Costner taught me that much, and I believed Kevin.

Chapter 27

The sky lightened to a dusty pink before the sun crested the island's edge. I tied the laces

of my *Keds*, planning in my mind how to most expediently find an aloe plant, try to convince

Lucas to swallow my planned concoction and then to gather the fuel for my fire. "Should I build

it here, where I can tend to it? Or on the beach near water in case of emergency and it got away

from me."

"Build it on the beach."

Lucas' raspy whisper came from behind me. I hadn't realized I was muttering out loud, too

used to talking to myself, my subconscious let me ramble freely now.

"Oh my God, Lucas! How are you?" I rushed to his side and knelt in the sand to reach out

and run a hand down the side of his face. He wasn't sweating any more, but he was still

shockingly hot, his skin felt pulled tight like a drum, and smooth like fiery satin. "Can you drink?

I need you to drink some water Lucas."

He nodded and closed his eyes, running his tongue out to moisten parched lips. "Yeah a

little water maybe."

I quickly fetched the metal cup and filled it, grabbing three Tylenol from the med kit that I

had placed next to the bed last night. I had sat going through its contents over and over, hoping to

magically find a bottle of antibiotics, or a pill marked 'cure all take only in dire straits.' There

were twelve Tylenol left but I wasn't sure I should risk him throwing them up. I knew they would help with his fever, but wasting them to be puked onto the sand was too high a risk.

"Do you think you can swallow these?" I held the small white pills in my palm looking desperately into his hazy eyes that only opened a crack.

He looked at the Tylenol, it seemed to take a moment for him to register my question, then he gave a slight nod and began to struggle to rise.

"No, wait, I'll help you." I moved to sit beside him, and lifted his shoulders, raising his head enough to sip at the cup of water and swallow the pills without fearing they would stick in his dry throat. I knew it must be painful for him to swallow after all that heaving and retching through the night. I had experienced a few too many hangover mornings and was familiar with the drug-through-the-dirt-and stomped-on-by-elephants feeling.

Lucas opened his mouth, and I placed the Tylenol on his tongue and held the cup to his lips so he could sip at the warm water. Once he emptied the contents I placed the cup aside and lowered him back down to rest against the life vests.

"I'll get you a banana, you'll need something to keep the Tylenol from aggravating your empty stomach."

I rummaged through my stack of fruit and found our ripest banana, then piece, by small piece, I fed Lucas bites until he had gotten down almost half of the fruit. I let him rest a moment to see if he was going to keep it down, then gave him another cup of water.

"How do you feel?"

I knew it was a stupid question that could be honestly answered with some colorful curses, but I was hoping for more of -- what stupid ass disease do you have, and how I can fix it -- kind of answer.

"How do I look?"

I laughed before I could stop myself, the stress making it sound a little hysterical to my ears.

"You look like you partied way too hard and maybe was slipped a rufi in your margarita"

"Mmm." Lucas left his response simple and closed his eyes again.

Lady Sun

"Lucas, I need to run out for a minute. I need to get you some aloe and some coconut water, you sweated out a gallon of fluids last night." I lay my hand over his heart, taking small comfort in the steady beat I found there. "Please don't throw up the Tylenol."

He cracked an eye and gave me a weak grin. "I promise. I'll just wait here. K?"

I leaned down and kissed his hot brow. "OK Cowboy. Back in a flash."

It only took me ten minutes of searching the nearby jungle to find an aloe plant, and another five to gather up enough coconuts to gain a cupful of its precious electrolyte packed water. I didn't have an IV and didn't understand the water to sugar or salt ratio anyways even if I thought I could rig something. But I knew Lucas' fever would most likely return, and I wanted to get him as hydrated as possible before the next bout of sweats and chills.

When it came to tropical diseases I knew they took time to run their course. All I could hope for was that Lucas hadn't lost too much of his strength and stamina this last month. His body had already battled scorching sun, lack of food, and long stretches of thirst before we had begun the distilling.

"Please, please, please, please, please." I chanted the desperate plea under my breath as I hurried back to the church. Perhaps with the sacred ground, and enough sincere praying, God would actually hear me. I was completely certain that whatever sin I may have inadvertently committed in my life, this past month surely cleared my debt of penance.

"Please don't take him from me." I stopped just outside the still hanging door of the coral church with its new roof and hauntingly pretty facade. I clutched my burden in my skirt and closed my eyes turning my face to the sky.

"Please." I whispered, "Don't leave me alone on this island to bury this good man in a shallow sand grave. Don't ask that of me." I hadn't prayed since I was a child, and couldn't remember whether my mother had taught me the proper way of it. But my heart and soul was in the request, my fear and panic locked behind a flimsy door that threatened to break free and overtake me.

"Please, just let him make it long enough for rescue to come, then you can hand it over to the doctors and I promise I will pray more. I will be better, a better person, I'll try harder, anything to not be left here alone, to not lose him."

I had a feeling that begging and bargaining were most likely not God's favorite things to hear, but I didn't apologize. I just wiped the tears from my cheeks and finished the prayer with, "Thank you. Amen." Then I squared my shoulders and went into God's house to crack open my coconuts.

Lucas had kept down the Tylenol, and banana and water. He looked marginally better, but it might have been my hope-tinted glasses. The pills had helped to reduce his fever, and he was sitting up, leaned back against the wall when I came in. I knew he must hate being sick, he was not a man to take anything lying down, which was also one of the reasons behind my worry and barely restrained panic. If he could manage it, I knew Lucas would have kept any weakness from me.

He clearly couldn't manage it.

Using a hollowed out coconut as a bowl and a flat stick as a spoon, I mashed some banana with coconut water and aloe. Lucas sat sipping a cup full of water with my instructions to drink slowly but finish it all. He didn't argue and I could tell he was weak and exhausted. His greeting when I came in had been an apologetic smile and a whispered "Hey."

As I mashed, I kept glancing over at him, stricken by the extreme change in his appearance. His demeanor. Only two days ago he had been up on the roof in the sunshine, laying palm fronds and admonishing me for not drinking enough water -- in his opinion. Now he looked gray and weak and only opened his eyes to guide the cup to his lips every other minute or so.

"You said to start the fire on the beach." I rose and went to sit in front of him Indian style.

Lucas opened his eyes and set the metal cup to the side, I noted that he had finished every drop.

"Yes. In case of winds, and less trees to break up the smoke." His voice sounded better, no longer a whisper, but it still seemed like it took some effort.

"OK. I want to get you fed and comfortable and then I'll start building a pile for a signal fire."

"Don't wait for a plane Sophia. Light it and feed it."

I was silent for a minute. I knew what he was saying. He was admitting his state of health was bad. He knew he couldn't care for me, fish for me, protect me. Us. I knew I could fish, I could bear the burden he had lain down. But with the baby, and now this, whatever this illness was...

We needed to get *off* this island.

"OK. I will." There was no reason to argue it. I agreed with him. I would build it, and light it and feed it. I would come back at sunset and check on Lucas, care for him through the night, and tomorrow I would do it again. Send smoke and prayers to the heavens until one of them was answered by rescue.

*   *   *

The pile of palm fronds and tree branches stood taller than me. At least six feet to the top of the peak of the pyre I had slaved to construct. It was mid-afternoon, the sun directly above me, roasting me, as if I were on that pyre and had been accused of witchcraft, set to burn away my demons.

I had decided to build the pyre on the old rock pier. It had once been quite wide, maybe fifteen feet, its length I could only guess at though. It ran about fifty feet or so out into the water and then crumbled away. It might have been twice that length when originally constructed, but this was what nature, and storms, and ocean, had left for me to work with.

I had layered the immense pile with brown and green fronds. Enough dry ones to keep it burning hot, and enough green ones to achieve my goal of lots, and lots, of smoke.

Sitting at the end of the pier the bonfire would send my signal straight and true, into the blue sky, making our presence known to any who saw it.

"Here goes everything."

I reached my hand into the bottom of the pile where I had stuffed a large bundle of dry tinder and shredded dry palm fronds. My *Bic* was running low on fumes. It took a few tries for the spark to find the butane and when it did the flame was small, as if it too, had enough of this place, had spent its best and was ready to go home and be refilled. The tiny flame licked at the bundle of brown fronds and then finally, the tinder caught and began to feed on itself.

It grew larger and larger, belching out smoke before I had time to get to the end of the pier. I didn't want to be close to the flames if I could help it. The sun was enough torture. I found a spot in the shade to sit and watch the spectacle. I would take a short break and then begin gathering fuel to keep my S.O.S fed.

I drank from the thermos of water I had carried to the beach with me. I had left Lucas set up with the metal can half full of water, and his little metal cup. I hated leaving him, but I knew there was nothing I could do for him there. I knew too, that this attempt with the fire was the last meal to our starving hope.

Had Lucas not fell ill we could have waited, a week or two, maybe even another month before we would really start to deteriorate in our health. Before we would have grown desperate and worried. It sounds strange, but we had a can do attitude, the both of us, and so surviving had been something we adjusted to. We would have fished, and hunted for edibles, and boiled water, and waited. For we knew that someone would *eventually* come, it was just patience we had to feed. Just wait.

But now, there was no waiting. The baby had put us into overdrive, and now, well, I wasn't sure what the death rate was for tropical diseases, but I had a healthy imagination. I was so exhausted with the struggle to survive each day. To try and grin through it. I didn't have much energy left to battle my fears of what would become of Lucas, of me, of this tiny life inside me, if someone didn't come now.

Right. Freaking. Now.

I drug myself off my butt and went back to the hunt for fuel. Green fronds, brown fronds, branches ripped free during Fury's party. Old logs small enough for me to drag and heave onto the smoky mass of sparks and flames. I trudged back and forth, down the pier, back into the jungle, then back down the pier. Squinting against the smoke and heat, holding my breath, not wanting to breathe anything that could hurt me, hurt the baby. I had heard if you breathed in poison sumac smoke you would develop a rash in your lungs instead of on your skin. I couldn't risk something I had fed the pyre with getting me sick, so I would hold my breathe until little stars appeared in my vision, feeding fronds and limbs to the hot beast. Then retreat to the shade, rest a bit, and go again.

I was dead on my feet. I was starving, and thirsty, having finished my water hours ago, but I kept on. I didn't want all the work to end in naught if the fire burned down while I went for lunch. So I shut down and counted my steps, letting the rhythm of the numbers sooth me, until I looked up and the sun was setting into the water. Leaving me free to go home. *Go to church,* I thought, and I trudged back through the trees, to Lucas.

He slept. Drenched in sweat, his cup empty beside the mat. I couldn't tell how much water was missing from the can, so there was no way to judge how much he had drank while I was gone. But his fever was back with a vengeance, and from the looks of him he had been sweating for some time.

"Oh Lucas." I sobbed out his name and knelt beside him, I lifted his head and held a cup of water to his lips. He didn't wake, his head lolling in my hands like a dead weight and I let the tears run.

I kept back the panic, but my check valve had to release some pressure, and this was too much. I finished the cup of water, gulping it down just for the baby, then found the shirt I had used the night before to bathe him and ripped a piece from the back. I refilled the cup with air temperature water and arranged myself against the wall, placing Lucas' heavy head in my lap.

Dipping the scrap into the cup I opened Lucas' mouth with my fingers and let the water drip inside. He swallowed reflexively, and I did it again, then again. It took some time, but finally the cup was empty and I felt I had won a battle.

Leaning back against the somewhat cool coral wall I closed my eyes and sleep took me.

I woke to shaking. Lucas was shivering. His body shook so violently with the chills, his head had fallen from my lap. I crawled over to lay alongside his back, spooning his long frame against me, and I wrapped my arm around him to lay my hand over his heart. After a moment the shivering lessened, and I began to hum and old Simon and Garfunkel song. *Bridge over troubled water*, and soon I drifted off to sleep again.

The next time I woke it was to a burning sensation. Lucas' fever was back. Weak light came in through the windows, signaling the coming dawn. I had to get this fever under control, I didn't have a thermometer but I could tell it was ridiculously high. Even if he survived this, *when* I corrected myself, I didn't want any brain damage done. I loved his brain.

I crawled tiredly to the can of water and filled the cup. Using it to soak the rag, I washed every bit of exposed skin, blowing against his dripping body, sending every good thought I had toward him. I wanted to feed him more Tylenol, but had to wake him for it, he would choke if I tried to force feed him. I had an idea to crush the pills in water and ladle it into his mouth and decided since he hadn't thrown up through the night it was worth a try.

I filled the metal cup up a third of the way and dropped in three pills. Then using my flat stick/spoon, crushed them up until they were completely dissolved. I arranged myself against the wall as I had the night before, then I opened Lucas' mouth, with him putting up no resistance, and trickled a small amount onto his tongue. He swallowed again as he had before, and I sighed, hoping his fever would break if I could get it all into him. Very slowly and patiently I dribbled the milky white medicine into him until he had it all in, then I filled the cup again and repeated the process.

The sun shone brightly in the morning sky by the time I was through. I wanted so badly to lay down and curl up next to him, go back to sleep, wake up in my own bed to the smell of coffee and bacon. But I knew I had to eat, drink some more water, and go back to the pier. Do it all again.

So I did.

I hunted down some fresh fruit, stuffed myself full in respect to my baby, and Lucas' effort to keep me alive and healthy. Then I drank enough water to make me pee a gallon and went back to the church to find Lucas still sleeping. I brushed his hair off his brow with my fingertips and noted is skin was not as hot as before. I didn't really know if he was sleeping, or if he was in the grip of his illness, I didn't know how to differentiate between the two states. So I left, feeling a tearing in myself the further I got from him.

I cried almost constantly now. I couldn't think of a joke, or a witty quip that pertained to anything I was now living, and the tears just leaked out.

I returned to the pier where only a smoldering pile of coals remained of my labors of the day before. I began dragging and piling and heaving and resting. Repeating yesterday, excusing the tears with the internal defense that it was the smoke. I didn't care to argue with myself, so I let me fool me, and let the tears flow as they chose.

When I returned to the church, I now refused to call it home -- I didn't want to give it that power, this was *not* my home -- Lucas slept. At some point he had rolled over in his sleep, perhaps from thrashing, or shivering, but had ended up lying on his face. I rushed to him, crying out, the sight too close to death for me to handle it. I rolled him violently over, sending his arm flailing to the side.

He didn't stir. I could see his chest rise and fall with his shallow breathing and sweat slowly dripping from his brow. The fever and chills had taken so much from him, his face was hollowed out, his eyes sunken in dark shadows, his beard and hair matted and tangled. He didn't look like my Cowboy. He looked like a man who had been lost at sea, and starved on an island, and died of a fever, and was only just breathing to keep me from melting down.

But it didn't work. I melted. Way down.

I began sobbing so heavily I couldn't catch my breath. I wrapped my arms around his wasted body and clung to him, I wasn't thinking of anything. I couldn't form a thought. I was completely lost to the overwhelming rush of emotion. You can say it was hormones if you want, or hysteria, or too much sun, but I knew what it was, really.

Fear. The real kind. Not - I don't like spiders, or, snakes creep me out, fear, or afraid of getting a bad grade, or falling and breaking a hip. This was fear I would *lose* Lucas. I knew the chances were beyond high. He could, right now, stop breathing. It was more likely that I *would* lose him than *not*, now. I was terrified I would lose the baby. That the stress, the survival, or trying to, would trigger a miscarriage, and I would watch my baby bleed out of me. Alone, here on this stupid, cursed, island.

I was afraid too, that I would lose me. That very real fear that deep inside, survival wouldn't be enough. Going home wouldn't get me back, not after I had lost so much.

So I cried, and I gave up fighting not to. And then, thankfully, I slept.

*　　*　　*

I awoke to the sound of rain on a roof. *Thank goodness Lucas built one.*

All of me hurt, but I opened my swollen eyes and looked to see if it was February. Today was day thirty two.

The rain got louder, and I cringed, hoping it wasn't another storm, I couldn't build a fire in a storm, Lucas may not last long enough to wait it out.

Lucas. I looked beside me. He was there, no fever, or shaking, his chest rising and falling, but I could tell just by looking at him that he wasn't sleeping. He wasn't awake either. He was gone to someplace inside where sickness takes you. A retreat.

A surrender.

I felt nothing. I felt hollowed out. I rose and sat and placed my hands in their familiar spot over his heart. And then suddenly I *heard.* Not rain. Engines. A rotor. And I felt *everything.*

I flew to the door. *Flew.*

Outside I looked up, and in the dawns pearly light, there hung the most gorgeous thing I had ever seen.

A helicopter.

Chapter 28

Chaos hit me.

Not only from the large metal bird hovering over the trees, its angry sounding engines and rotors screaming through the peace of the island air, but from within. My mind was racing, my heart beating in a fierce rhythm, forcing blood through my veins to rival the noise and cacophony of the wind and dust and droning of the helicopter. It hung there for a moment, black against blue sky. My eyes squinting, my arms raised against the wind that buffeted me creating a flurry of leaves and dirt, whipping my skirt against my legs, my hair into a tangle around me.

As I stood in the chaos, wondering how I could climb the air up to the noisy black bird, get it to come down, to give me what I need. To save him, *please save him.* It turned and veered away. Toward the beach, toward the pier, and the wind, and dust, and noise, followed it as it disappeared past the trees surrounding the broken village.

My body took over. My legs were running, my arms pumping at my side. I was leaping over fallen logs, my weight nothing, for now it truly was. I was so thin now I could only wear my dresses, my shorts wouldn't stay on my hips. The skirt of my once pretty sundress flew behind me like the wings I felt I had as the jungle blew past my peripheral in my mad dash to the beach.

They had come. Rescue. *Had they seen the smoke? Had they already been looking? Was it a patrol? Would they speak English, would they have medicine, food, where would they take us?* My mind was separate now. My body did the work to get me through the trees, along the path, *don't trip, don't stop, don't let them leave, go. Go.*
Lady Sun

Inside, where the panic and fear lived, where the shell of me functioned to only just barely hang on to the shredded and frayed hope that I knew in truth was a lie, *there* was the storm. The questions that ran screaming and bouncing in my mind were only serving to distract me from the one question I wouldn't ask. *Would he live?*

"*Ohhh.*" I moaned aloud with a gasping of air as I reached the break in the trees that led to the pier. *Don't say it. Don't say it.* I cursed myself as my feet slapped against the sand. *Go. Go.*

The bird had set down at the base of the pier. Its rotor winding down, the wind settling, the noise slowly turning to the familiar breeze of the island once again.

I stopped suddenly. Fifty feet from the large aircraft. I stood still, my chest heaving, my hands clenched in fists, my heart seized in a tight knot in my chest. The door on the side of the helicopter slid open, and a woman jumped down to the uneven surface of the old pier. She began walking toward me.

I waited.

I stood in the morning sunlight, registering that behind her, two other people disembarked from the large helicopter, but my eyes remained on her. Her dark slacks, white shirt, olive skin. Black hair. Kind eyes. The details of her soothed me. Her red lips formed a questioning half smile, her neat brows furrowed with concern. She reached me in moments, but by the time she reached out to take my hand, I felt I loved her, this stranger. This pretty lady who had come, who was here and we would be OK.

Please, please, please, please, please. She took another step forward, still looking at me, a question in her eyes that I could clearly read; *Are you OK?*

No. My answer was no. I am not. *But we will be.*

She took my hand in hers, my fist unclenching, my grasp reasserting itself on her. I held her soft, golden, hand, tightly, and as she opened her mouth to ask her question, the one with the answer that was 'No'. I pulled her. Toward me. And *I* moved toward Lucas.

I was running again, pulling the pretty lady behind me, her feet as agile as mine as we leapt the fallen logs, following the now familiar path. To the village. To the church. To Lucas.

Chapter 29

They took him.

The two men who had chased after us, who had landed with the pretty lady.

One had gone back for a stretcher, and they had loaded him into the large metal bird.

They strapped me in beside him, sitting against the wall on a hard seat with shoulder straps and a lap belt. I held his hand and noticed nothing. Not lifting off from the pier, not leaving the island. Not the man who worked on Lucas on the other side, or the pretty lady who was talking, asking me something. I heard only the blood in my ears, and the constant prayer I had begun to chant in my mind. *Please let him live. Please let him live. Please let him live.*

The island released us without ceremony or tears, no goodbyes, no see you laters. We simply were there, and now we were gone. Going. Home.

I felt a pinch in my arm and looked down to see the pretty lady was inserting a needle. The needle led to a line, the line to a bag that hung above my head to the left. *Fluids. She must have been telling me she was going to give me fluids. That's fine. The baby needs fluids. Let them fix you.* I lectured the Sophia whose first impulse was to resist. But the lady didn't make me let go of Lucas' hand, so I let her tend me.

I wondered how long it would take to get there. *Get where?* And I realized I didn't know where we were going. I hadn't asked. I had actually only said one thing that I could remember now.

Save him.

Lady Sun

Standing in the church, clinging to pretty ladies hand, the men bursting in behind us. Lucas at our feet on the soiled woven mats, looking like he was beyond saving.

I turned to pretty lady now, to ask where to, and how long. She was bent over my IV, administering something into the line.

"What is that?" I began to panic, I reached to pull the needle from my vein.

"You need rest." Pretty lady grasped my hand, the one that wasn't grasping Lucas'. "It will help you sleep."

She was stronger than me. *Everyone is stronger than you. She's right, you need to heal, to rest, let her help you.* I recognized the wiser Sophia as my mother's voice. *I* was a mother now. Or would be if I went against my instincts to fight, to panic, and helped my baby to live. Helped me to health, which would help my baby.

I stopped fighting toward the needle, and the pretty lady placed my hand in my lap. She kept her hand in mine though, not as a restraint but as a comfort, and I held on to her. I held onto Lucas and pretty lady, and felt the drug enter my vein, slowly seep through what was left of me. What the island had released, and I sighed.

Let sleep come. When I wake everything will be better.

Chapter 30

I awoke in a bed. I registered sheets. Clean sheets that felt smooth and cool against my skin.

Somewhere in the back of my mind I worried about getting them dirty, I had sand in my hair still, and my skin felt rough and weathered compared to the lovely silk sensation of the sheets.

Then I opened my eyes and there were four walls.

Four walls. They were painted white. A clean, cool, smooth white. There was a door, firmly on its hinges, and a window that held glass. Past the glass, a view boasted blue sky that didn't herald a sunburn to come, for the air around me felt cool. *Air conditioning.*

I had known, the moment I saw the helicopter that I would return home to where these things were in abundance. But the feel of them, the sight, were luxuries, and I let them sink in slowly.

"How are you feeling?"

I knew that voice, not the pretty lady from the helicopter, *then who...?* I turned toward it, and stared in shock.

Clara. My older sister. The solid one. The responsible sibling who always did the right thing, who never partied too much, or wrote a bad check. Clara was here. *Where am I?*

"Clara?" I tried to sit up and a wave of dizziness washed over me.

"Lie still Sophia." Clara was at my side, a hand on my shoulder restraining me gently, but in a no nonsense way. It has always been useless to fight Clara.

Lady Sun

"Where am I?" My voice sounded raspy in my ears, and I cleared my throat. "Where is Lucas?"

"You're in Malé. You were flown in yesterday." Clara pulled a chair up to the side of the bed. She must have been sitting, waiting for me to wake. "Lucas, that's the man who you were found with?"

"Yes." I started to sit up again but stopped, not wanting the answers to stop, to be distracted by arguing about lying down. "Lucas, he was On the *Lady Sun* with me, we landed on the island together. Where is he?" A thousand questions were champing at the bit to get out, but I pushed them all aside, nothing mattered until this one was answered.

"He's not here. I'm sorry Sophie."

"Sorry?" I did sit up now. Lecture be damned. Clara rose again to try to convince me back down, but I held up a hand. "Don't touch me, I understand you're trying to help Clara and I love you for it, but you need to help me by answering my question. Where is Lucas?" Her apology had me spiraling. *Please, please, please, please, please. He had to make it. He was here, in the next room, Clara is confused.* I needed to find the doctor.

"He was here. He came in with you, he was in bad shape." Clara sat back in her chair but reached out and took my hand. "His parents arrived early this morning and had him transferred. I don't know where to Sophie, just to a hospital that could help him."

"Back to the states?"

"I don't know."

"To the mainland? To Sri Lanka?" I was pretty sure they were the closest big city, but had no idea about their medical care or insurance requirements for foreigners, or even if they would take someone with whatever he had. "Did you find out why he was sick? Have you talked to the doctor, to his parents?" I was crying, the tears trickling down my cheeks, my helplessness overwhelming. *He was gone. Not in the next room, not even nearby.* Lucas was gone, and I knew nothing.

"No, Sophie, I'm sorry, I've been focused on you, calling home, talking to the authorities.

I'm sorry." She said again.

I could tell she really was, she always hated it when people cried.

I wiped at my tears. Sniffling and trying to calm down. I needed a plan. A plan to find him, make sure he was OK. "I want to go home, I need to go home. Clara, can we leave?" I began throwing back the thin blanket that covered me and she rose to her feet again.

"Yes, we can go, but not yet. Sophie, this is a big deal. You've been missing for a month, it was all over the news for weeks back home. The police will need a statement, the hospital won't release you until you have a clean bill of health. The Maldivian government doesn't want to be held responsible for you leaving without being in perfect health." Clara smoothed the hair off my brow and gave me a gentle smile. "Calm down and we'll take this a step at a time."

A step at a time. I didn't care about the police, or the damn Maldivian government or the damn hospital that wasn't good enough to cure Lucas that he was taken from me.

"And Sophie," Clara was still talking, "about your health, I need to tell you something."

Oh God. That got my attention, *had I contracted whatever Lucas had? Would it hurt the baby? Oh please let the baby be OK.* "What?"

"I don't know how to say this, so I will just out with it." Clara squared up to me, reaching for my other hand. "You're pregnant."

I was confused. *Of course I'm pregnant, I already knew that, but how is the baby? Is it OK? Am I sick?* I was about to let fly the barrage of questions when Clara spoke again.

"We know about the pirates. We found out weeks ago. We all thought you were dead." Her voice had dropped to a whisper. And I realized she was holding back tears. Clara, my big sister who never cried, never got a traffic ticket, paid her bills before they were due and gave birth in three pushes, was choking up over me.

Dead? Wow, that had to of been awful. I hadn't actually thought about my family mourning me. I felt guilty all over again for having loved the island for a brief time, for wanting to stay even for a moment. And now here my sister assumed I was pregnant by rape of pirates. A fierce protectiveness rose up in me. A need to protect Lucas and his child against the claim of this life being formed out of anything but love. I prayed Clara hadn't told the family.

"Clara," I squeezed her hands, looking her in the eye. "I know I'm pregnant. This baby is Lucas', not the pirates." The word was like filth in my mouth and I had a sudden urge to spit. Gone were the days of romancing buccaneers, comparing pirates to Johnny Depp's portrayal was silly and thoughtless, for all those who suffered at the hands of real ones. Lucas had saved me from that suffering. *Oh god, where are you?*

"Clara, I have a lot to tell you, but I need some answers, I need to find Lucas, he saved my life, more than once, you owe it to him to help me find him." I knew guilt and obligation would work far better than pleading with Clara. She would repay a debt come hell or high water, and the debt of her sister's life would motivate her to help me.

"Oh thank god, I am so glad you knew" She reached out and hugged me to her. "I've been wringing my hands over how to tell you, I almost feared you would have a meltdown and I just couldn't handle that, not after a month of mourning you." She hugged me again. And then sat on the side of the bed. "You love this Lucas."

"With all that I have."

She was quiet and sat looking at me. I could see she was sorting through trying to put herself in my shoes. Escaping from pirates, floating at sea together, landing on an island, struggling together to survive, becoming pregnant and having no way home. In only took her moments to calculate the bond, the debt, the love.

"We will find him. What do you need me to do?"

Chapter 31

As it turned out, I needed an embassy.

Clara explained that the Maldivian police wanted a report on the capture of the *Lady Sun* by the pirates. What had occurred, how we escaped, when we escaped.

Everyone had assumed that we had perished at the hands of the pirates. Jok had been found a week ago after a long search and pressure on his family. He had told the police nothing, only that Lucas and I were alive, that we had escaped, and that we had not been killed.

The police believed he had only been saying that to keep from facing murder charges, but began a search at the insistence of mine and Lucas' families. As well as quite a lot of media coverage from the States.

That explained why the copter responded to my smoke signal. A search plane had spotted the smoke but was unable to land on the islands, the copter was sent as a quicker response than a boat. They hadn't known if medical treatment would be needed, or even if it was us on the island.

Clara had flown in two days after Jok was taken into custody to help keep pressure on the search. No one expected to find us alive. Lucas' parents had gotten on a plane the moment the call came in that we had been found.

I was grateful Jok hadn't mentioned the dead pirate. I didn't know what to do about that. I wasn't sure what Lucas would be held accountable for. Would it be self-defense? Would there be a trial? Was there a body? Who would even press charges? I decided to say nothing, not to Clara or the police. I wanted a lawyer. For that I needed an embassy.

Clara obtained a list of local American attorneys who resided in the Maldives from a helpful man at the American embassy in Sri Lanka.

After making a few phone calls, I had a meeting set up only hours after awaking in the hospital.

With the help of Clara, I had all visitors refused.

Journalists and even news casters had called and come visiting, hoping for an interview on the miraculous survival of Sophia Canon. *And Lucas Lael.* I had come to the quick conclusion that Clara was right. I needed to wrap up these loose ends so I could go home, begin my hunt for Lucas.

I was surrounded now by luxury, the availability of food and water. Soap. A shower, clean clothes. The rescue team had grabbed our suitcases from the church as well as my purse. What hadn't been used as bandages, or sail, was now a pile of salty, sandy rags. Every item suffered at least one tear or burn, and all of them were soiled, sweat stained, rumpled and filthy.

Clara set a stack of clean clothes in the bathroom connected to my hospital room, along with a new toothbrush, toothpaste and shampoo. "I'm sorry, I couldn't find conditioner at the little store down the street. Or deodorant, but they had a razor." She handed this to me and helped me from the hospital bed.

"Take your time, get cleaned up, and sort out what you need to say to the attorney. I'll be right here if you need me." She released my hand as I stepped across the threshold of the bathroom and I turned to her.

"Clara, I am so sorry." I paused, my mind still fuzzy, my heart still clenched and aching, and my panic still coursing quietly through me. I knew I had to compartmentalize, I knew I could do that. *I'm stronger now, I can take on anything. Except losing him...*

"I know you and the family must have been through hell, and this is just awful, this whole thing. Thank you." I reached out and pulled her to me, hugging her close, smelling my childhood on her. Growing up, fighting, playing, and learning. Now grown, sisters. *Family.*

"Thank you for coming. For being here."

"This is not awful Sophia." Clara released me and pulled back to look in my eyes. "This is wonderful. Awful would have been finding your body. Or never finding you at all." She smiled sadly, and I realized that was what they had all expected to find. A month. Yes, after a month you begin the funeral plans. "Go on now, you smell ripe and your teeth could use a vigorous scrubbing." She gave me a little push and a genuine grin. *Sisters.*

I laughed but immediately put my hand to my mouth in shame. Oh yeah. To be clean, the first step. After that I would tackle the chore of appeasing everyone and getting home.

I stood in the shower, the water set as hot as I could stand it. At first I just let it run over me. Reveling in the sensation, the feel of the tile under my feet, the white tiled walls around me that captured the steam and enclosed me in a cloud of hot mist. Then I opened the bottle of passion fruit shampoo and the perfume hit me. "Ohhhh..." I moaned aloud before I could stop myself and quickly squeezed a huge palmful of the soap into my hand. I lathered my hair, scrubbing my scalp furiously, then rinsed the long tresses until they were free of suds, and then lathered again. I used half the bottle of shampoo before I deemed my scalp free of sand, my hair free of any trace of the island.

The shower provided a little tile bench, and I sat down to attack shaving. I was dizzy, and knew I should prioritize eating, but strangely enough, felt no desire for food. My stomach was clenched in knots and my attention was still wholly focused on finding Lucas. Everything else was detail steps guiding to that end. Even shaving.

Once the hot water ran out I conceded I was pretty close to normal and turned off the tap. I wrapped a white towel around me and stepped out to tackle my teeth, take assessment and see if Clara's clothes would fit me.

I had lost weight. A lot of weight. I was dark with a tan and a few spots that showed burns where my skin simply didn't want to turn gold, insisting red was its color of choice. I suffered a few rashes, mostly from wet clothing rubbing me raw, or from sand gnat bites. Most of my burns were healed, the major change aside from weight loss, was the long ugly scar on my thigh. The scrapes along hip and waist had healed really well, but my thigh would forever be the mark of the island.

Looking at it now, I felt branded, like a slave or a prisoner.

I averted my eyes and finished the task at hand. Clara had provided a slip of a dress. White with a blue hem that hung to my knees. It was a size or two too big for me now, but I knew a month ago it would have fit perfectly. Clara and I had grown up stealing each other's clothes. The loose fit was comfortable though, and after twisting my hair into a bun to keep the wet mass off of my neck and back of my dress, I deemed myself ready for the next step. Food.

Although hunger had yet to rear up and control me, I knew the baby needed me to eat, and I knew my strength would be important in what lie ahead. Lawyers. Police. Reporters. Hospitals. *Lucas. Where are you?*

Clara vetoed my suggestion of cheeseburger and fries, and instead requested mashed potatoes, with gravy, peas and turkey. It felt like Thanksgiving and not a tropical meal at all. I loved it. As soon as it was delivered my primal instincts took over. The scent wafting up from under the lid of the dish had my mouth watering. I sat up straight in the bed preparing to attack the plate with gusto.

"Slowly. Sophia, you don't want to throw it up as soon as you're done." Clara was playing nurse, and I feared she would take the plate and spoon feed me if I didn't obey.

"Yes mom." I raised the forkful of mashed potatoes slowly. Grinning from ear to ear.

Every. Single. Bite, was heaven. Every single bite. Clara ordered a large glass of ice cold milk to go with the meal and I finished in seconds. She ordered another and sat quietly while I ate. Slowly.

I closed my eyes and let the textures thrill me. The salt and butter, the peas exploding with earthiness as I chewed them. It was an all American meal, and it transported me home, it seeped into me and healed the little spaces that had emptied out. That first meal brought me more than strength of nourishment, but of will and spirit.

I was ready. Next step.

I napped a bit while the hours passed. The sun rose high in the sky outside but didn't touch me even once as I nodded off in my air conditioned room, waiting for the attorney to come and tell me what to do. Finally, Clara shook my shoulder, rising me from dreams of storms, and pain, and the bland taste of fish. I wondered if I would ever eat seafood again.

"Mr. Kason is here." She gave me an encouraging smile as she left the room, allowing in a friendly, slightly portly man, who strode to my bedside and shook my hand.

The meeting with the lawyer was spent over a snack consisting of strawberries, melon, yogurt and ice water. I took each bite slowly. Chewing with my eyes closed to enable each flavor to be worshiped properly. I had made the decision to spoil myself and the baby, and eat as much as the hospital, and nurse Clara, would allow. The attorney smiled patiently, pausing between questions to allow me to worship my food, and would then continue gathering information.

After an hour of talking, and eating, reliving, and explaining, my friendly and helpful attorney, advised me to go home.

"Go home?"

"Yes, I will help you make a statement to the police. You do not know what happened to the pirate, no one is accusing you of anything. If it is not asked, then say nothing. Also, Lucas will not be questioned on it, I know that no one has come forward asking for anyone to be brought to justice for a certain pirate's death. We have no name, no body, no witness, and no proof. For all you know that man was napping on the hallway floor. Aside from the vagueness of it all, you and Lucas are survivors of a tragic circumstance that the Maldivian government wishes to put behind them. Quickly and quietly."

Mr. Kason leaned back in his chair and folded his hands over his belly. "Tourism is bread and butter here. Pirates are a very bad draw for tourism. The last thing they want is for you to give interviews. I am willing to bet that not only will you be expedited on your way home, but compensation for your tragic experience will be offered. Take the offer and go home"

I was relieved and grateful. The stress and worry began to recede, perhaps things would be simpler than I had feared. I begged my new best friend attorney to find Lucas for me. Help me find out the hospital he was taken to. But medical records are impenetrable and without representing Lucas he couldn't ask for the personals on him from the police.

Mr. Kason assured me he would poke around, see if anyone knew where he had been taken, and try to dig up his contact information. I made him promise to contact me as soon as he knew anything.

"Anything at all. I can't believe I don't have his phone number, his address." I confessed.

I had been wracking my brain since awaking, trying to remember every detail of every conversation, and I couldn't recall either of us exchanging personal contact info. So strange in this day and age when you friend each other on *Facebook* the moment you meet, or text each other, call, tweet... so many ways to talk. Yet we had never once said where we lived, had never needed to rattle off the seven digits it would take to pick up the phone and get some answers. I didn't know where to begin my search. *Montana. Somewhere outside of Billings.*

With my attorney at my side I gave a very brief statement to a police officer who seemed very sorry for my tragic circumstances indeed. He asked a few perfunctory questions, took notes in a small tablet, offered his apologies and went on his way. I couldn't believe it was that simple.

"There are no charges?" I asked my attorney

"What charges would they bring Sophia? You did nothing wrong. They have no *Lady Sun*, no pirates, only Jok, they are dealing with him, believe me."

I shook my head and gave a shrug. "It's taken longer to issue me a traffic ticket in the States. Just seems like they're missing something."

"They will continue contact with me, and I with you, but as I said, their main concern is keeping this quiet, and wrapping it up. They assume you will file charges against the company you were traveling to...the *Tropic Escape*, is that the name?"

"Yes." I wasn't sure how I wanted to handle that and left the comment hanging.

"Well, I will put together a summery for you that you can look at when you are settled at home and have things straightened out. The best thing for everyone right now is for you to get back, get healthy, and see your family."

"And find Lucas."

"Yes." He gave me a gentle smile and patted my hand. "You have been through a great deal. No one wants to cause you to suffer anymore."

Mr. Kason informed me he would send notice to all concerning parties that any future contact or questions were to be diverted through him. "Let me handle what I can, take some things off your plate so you can focus on you."

Chapter 32

Focus on me.

The next two days drug by.

The Hospital ran tests, the doctor informing me that I appeared surprisingly healthy given everything I had been through. He drew blood, took scans, and inspected my leg, assuring me that a plastic surgeon would be able to do wonders with the scar. And then he took me to a little room to do an ultrasound.

I knew I wouldn't see anything, he warned me not to expect much, he just wanted to be sure of the embryo's relative health, and mine. The scan showed me my uterus, my ovaries and a dot he said was the baby that I couldn't really see, but when the doctor pointed to it, I cried. It was there. The little seed of a baby, it was really there. Growing despite the struggles, and the stress, and the hunger, and thirst.

"You're strong, like your daddy." I whispered to it aloud. To make Lucas alive and beside me. To solidify all this as real and hopeful.

The doctor advised me that once back home I should schedule an appointment with my regular physician. In a few weeks I would be able to hear a heartbeat. *I'll wait until Lucas can be there, he deserves to hear it with me.*

While the doctors poked and prodded, and I napped, and ate, and stared at the walls, Clara had been busy. She contacted the airlines who graciously booked a return flight, free of charge, due to the publicity they would gain. First class no less. She then began replacing my lost items. My tablet had been completely destroyed, and no data was recoverable. But she contacted the manufacturer, and after hearing my lost on an island and kidnapped by pirates story, they jumped on the publicity bandwagon and replaced it free of charge along with a lifetime warranty. Next she pulled the same heartstrings on the makers of my smart-phone and returned with packages from the local shops in Malé.

Clara replaced my suitcase, my purse, and purchased bags of new clothing, bras, underwear, and makeup. She thought of everything. I spent the remainder of my hospital stay programming my phone, with the help of Clara's contact list, sorting through my belongings, tossing the unsalvageable, and storing the barely salvageable in my new purse and luggage. I downloaded apps and books onto my tablet and more apps and music onto my phone. It all seemed so petty, it didn't help me at all in my search and only served to pass the time, but I was grateful to Clara who was trying her best to get me back to normal.

I called my mother the first night as soon as the time difference allowed it was morning in Washington. We spent the first few minutes sobbing and trying to talk over each other before it all sorted out and she assured me the farm was fine, to just come home and she loved me so, so much. I hung up and dried my eyes, wiped my nose, and began to call Anna, but stopped.

I couldn't do it. I knew I wouldn't be able to talk and my throat hurt from closing up just thinking about her, about the princes, Audrey and Lily. I decided it could wait until I saw them. Then we would have a big cry fest and hug it out.

Once my tablet was online I spent hours Googling for Lucas. There was no Lucas Lael listed in Billings. There were no Laels listed at all. I didn't know the name of his ranch or if he *had* named it. I didn't have a clue what high school he graduated from, or college. I couldn't find him on *Facebook* or *Twitter*. He was a ghost, which I knew was typical for the Cowboy type. He had never made references to technology, even with all my pop culture jokes, he would laugh, but hadn't joined in with rebuttals. I began to realize that this search was going to be much harder than I thought.

Lady Sun

First class seats made me realize I wanted to grow up to be rich. There was no struggle for the aisle, no sitting on a strangers lap. I could lay my seat all the way back and the food was plentiful and actually really tasty. Any other day, in another universe, I would have enjoyed it to its fullest and been an annoying, new money, kind of traveler that made all the other first class travelers roll their eyes.

But this flight took me further and further from where I had last seen Lucas and closer and closer to where I hoped I would see him again. I felt confused, and stressed, and exhausted.

Clara chatted and filled me in on the happenings at home. How everyone had handled my disappearance. How it all unfolded.

"On January third mom got a call from the Maldivian police. They explained that the boat that you booked for your transport to the island you were to stay on had disappeared."

"It was a yacht." I could still see the *Lady Sun* glistening and shiny in slip number twelve. How impressed I had been, how excited. I closed my eyes and sighed, letting Clara continue with her tale.

"Yes, well we did discover that tidbit further along, but at the time the police informed mom that they had searched the island for you and another passenger, later we learned his name was Lucas, and the island was empty." Clara waved her hand vaguely. "Mom called everyone, and we all met at her house. No one left for almost a week."

I imagined that. I knew just what had happened. When our brother died we had all converged at mom's. We sat in shock, made calls, cried, drank coffee and slowly began piecing together the next steps. The funeral, the viewing, the obituary, flowers, notices, all the details you don't ever want to have to know how to do. The losing of someone dear.

I saw them in my mind's eye, the questions, the search, the tears. Mom thinking she had lost another child. I felt my chest tighten and looked out the plane window onto the cloud cover below.

"I'm sorry." I knew it wasn't my fault, but I had such a weight of guilt for that brief time when I had considered staying, escaping, not thinking of anyone but myself. I was ashamed that the temptation of a seeming paradise at the time, had clouded my reasoning. It took Lucas setting me straight, and the island revealing its not so paradise side, before I had conceded to reality. Now I steeled myself to hear the suffering of those most dear to me, as they searched for someone they thought was lost.

"We all started making calls, to governments and search parties, but no one was sent to look. The yacht, as it turned out, had a homing device, but its last known location was the Maldives, just beyond the island you were to stay on. The authorities assumed it had been disabled by the pirates. They told us they didn't know where to look. They didn't know where the pirates originated from, where they were going. This apparently happens often enough they quoted figures stating there were few to no recoveries of ships in these circumstances." Clara paused in her story and took a sip of water.

"After two weeks we all began to accept that you were dead."

I let that sink in. I had no reply, no way to take away a hurt that deep. Even my survival and return home wouldn't fix those weeks of loss felt. We were quiet for a while and then Clara finished her story.

"Last week mom got a call from the lead investigator. He said that they found Jok, the last known person to see you, and he was in custody. He told mom that Jok claimed you and Lucas were alive, that you had gone overboard but he didn't know where. The officer claimed it was a lie that Jok was trying to save himself from a sentence of murder. Everyone convened again, but we didn't know what to do. There had been a lot of publicity about your disappearance, and so I contacted the paper, the news. I called the Maldivian government and threatened to go national with my story if they didn't send out a search party. At least try."

I realized then what my lawyer had been referring to. The Maldivian yahoos had been afraid of my sister. My family. I knew it wasn't an empty threat. Clara would have done it. She would have brought hell and rain-fire down, and every camera in America to sensationalize the lack of effort made for an American woman taken by pirates in Maldives waters. I smiled now. *Way to go Clara*! But didn't interrupt.

"I booked a flight and took all my vacation days and flew in. They searched the Maldives islands by plane, some by boat, I could tell they weren't throwing everything at it, but all I could do was watch the small effort and hope. They were going to expand the search until they finally got Jok to confess where the pirates had taken the yacht."

This I was curious about and turned to face her in my seat.

"The Seychelles."

"Oh that's perfect. The notorious pirate coves and hideout?" I shook my head but didn't laugh. Pirates held no humor for me any longer.

"Yep, he claims they were running guns, and that he had been helping for a few months, but for some reason he didn't explain why they decided this time to take the boat too. Or why they had been so far afield from said hideout. Anyways, when they realized that you could have gone over at any point in the ocean, they were reluctant to expand the search claiming you would have never survived deep ocean with no land for hundreds of miles."

"Why would they assume that?" I asked. It didn't make sense. That's what life rafts are made for after all. To float and wait for rescue.

"Jok confessed that he stripped the *Lady Sun* of anything he could sell to fund the first run of guns months ago. The life raft was one of them. They sell for upwards of tens of thousands of dollars, not to mention a list of other items he pilfered off the yacht. He had come out with a tidy sum, but had to replace a few items with dummy items to fool an inspection."

"Ah... so if someone looked, they would see a raft but not know it was a piece of crap."

"Exactly. Inspections are rare, and lax but he couldn't take the chance. He couldn't remember the details of your raft, but the authorities hunted down the purchase. They confirmed there was no way, without food, water, cover from the sun, and with any heavy weather at all, that you could survive in the open ocean. They concluded you had been lost."

"You mean dead."

"Yes."

"Again."

"Yes. Again."

How horrible, to cling to a scrap of hope and then again, be told you had to return to mourning. I refused to correlate the situation with my hope for Lucas. My heart couldn't take any shadow of doubt. *He's alive* my stubborn inner voice insisted.

"What did you do?"

"I delivered on my threat." At this Clara smirked proudly. "I called every reporter who wanted to fly to Malé to interview me, investigate the lax search, and bring down a spotlight on the dangers of vacationing in the Maldives. I was actually surprised at the response. I was answering my phone every hour to talk to some reporter, and then I would give them the number to the lead investigator, the American embassy in Sri Lanka, and the mayor's office in Malé city. They quickly changed their tune and expanded the search. The next day a plume of smoke was spotted in the Chagos island chain, and a copter was sent to investigate"

"*What timing.*" I whispered. It seemed strange how it all fell together as it had. If I had started a fire when we had first washed ashore, it would have been futile. And we most likely wouldn't have tried again. But after Lucas fell ill and insisted I try as a last resort, it was, in the end what saved us.

I mulled over everything Clara told me and sorted through my internal questions. Turning back to face her I reached out and took her hand. "Thank you. For not giving up, for doing all you could even when they *told* you to give up." I leaned over and hugged her, truly thankful my older, bossy, sister had been the one the officials had to deal with. No one else would have persevered so ruthlessly.

"Thank you." She whispered. Still holding on to me. "For not being dead."

I grilled Clara about her contacts with the Maldivian government, her contacts in the media. Did she know any way to get a hold of Lucas or is family. She had no answers that would

help. The police confiscated all contact information from *Tropic Escape*. The contact in case of

emergency list. I had put my mother, her phone number, her relationship to me.

I had already called the office hoping to glean the same information, but it went to voice-

mail again and again. *Closed while under investigation, perhaps never to reopen.*

In the end I let the hours go by. I napped, and nibbled at the airline food, and drank a ton

of water, and fought off the constant niggling of nausea. I didn't know if the rolling stomach was

brought on by the flight, the stress, or the baby, but I held down each bite. Stubbornly refusing to

relinquish any nourishment that was intended for the life inside me, and maybe as a side benefit,

for me to gain back some weight and not look like a well-tanned zombie.

At four twenty five pm Pacific time, our plane landed in Spokane.

Chapter 33

My mother's house was full. So many cars lined the streets we had a hard time parking close enough to not have to walk far in the snow.

Snow. The second week into February and snow covered everything. I loved it. I stared at the dirty piles along the street as we drove from the airport and wondered at the sweeping blanket of it on all the yards and homes in my mother's neighborhood. It was lovely, and refreshing, and I reveled in loving the snow. Something I hadn't felt for this season since my school days.

When we walked through the front door I got the feeling everyone was going to yell *surprise*! But that felt completely wrong. Instead, they all stood and stared. No one moved, no one spoke. I heard the door close quietly behind me as Clara came in, and then I just looked around.

I stared back at all the faces, the pale, white, winter, faces of my mom, and sister, and Anna. My eyes locked on hers and I broke out in tears. Then we were across the room, hugging and crying and Anthony and Evan were hugging me, my legs wrapped in Evens strong little arms. Audrey quietly approached and joined the hug, and soon every one came forward, all at once, as if the spell were broken and it was my birthday, not a return from the dead.

My cousin clapped me on the back and said. "You look tan."

My brother-in-law pulled my braid and said, "You look skinny."

And then my mom was there, hugging me, whispering, "You look beautiful." and we all

Lady Sun

cried again.

What followed was food, more food, coffee, tea, sweet treats the women had brought, and questions, questions, so many questions. I answered as many as I could make sense of, but overlooked the ones about pirates, and Evan asking me if I could drive a boat now. There must have been some confusion in his little mind at the explaining of my disappearance.

After hours and hours of catching up, more tears, a lot of touching, and some hugs that lasted longer than a slow dance, people began to trickle out. First the friends, then the cousins, then the in-laws. What was left was my mother, it was her home after all, Lily, Audrey, Clara and Anna. The princes had left with their father to go be tucked into bed.

With these women I could be honest. We settled into the living room and slowly, I began to tell them my story. From the beginning. I shared with them my meeting Lucas, his rescue on the boat. The storm, the sex, (not in detail) the island and the reef. I showed them the scar, and told them of our days, the boiling of water, catching fish, the storm Fury, the village, the church, the baby. At the last I could barely speak. I was weeping openly and my heart was twisting, my breath coming in hiccups and gasps.

"I love him. I have to find him. How do I find him?" And then I cried while Anna softly stroked my back. I felt someone lay a blanket over me, and soon I felt sleep come.

*   *   *

I woke with the dawn. Coffee was brewing, I could smell the heavenly aroma drawing me to it like a siren. My mother was sitting at the kitchen table, but rose when she saw me in the doorway. She said nothing, she simply poured me a cup of coffee and handed me a set of keys. The spare set I had given her before I left.

"Your truck is out front. I had your cousin fetch it yesterday and bring it here for you."

Marni MacRae

"Oh, thank you." I hugged my mother and then sat at the table with her to enjoy my coffee.

"I know you're anxious to get back to the farm, check on things there. Frank from next door has done a great job in maintaining it for you. I don't know why you didn't just ask him instead of me when you left."

"Because Frank would have wanted payment I didn't want to give. But I'm glad you handed him the reigns, he's a good farmer."

The idea of going home, *my* home, was drawing me to the door. "Do you mind mom? I promise I'll come by tomorrow, but I would like to get home and settle in. Make some calls."

"Of course honey," she waved her hand in a shooing motion, "you go, feed your animals, change your clothes, and settle in." Her smile was sincere and encouraging. "Go find your man."

I paused at that and crossed the room to lean down and kiss her cheek. "I love you mom."

She smiled up at me, her eyes soft, and full of the love I knew was there, had always been there my whole life. "I love you too Sophia."

*   *   *

My driveway had been plowed. Again I was grateful my mother had called Frank. He would plow and feed the animals and call the vet if needed. He would even order hay if it ran low. He was a good neighbor, I made a mental note to get him a proper thank you gift.

As my truck wound around the last bend in the drive, my home came into view. A two story farm house with a wrap-around porch. Quaint and idyllic. Country chic. I have always been proud of my home, my farm, but no more so than in this moment when the view of it hit me full force.

I slowly came to a stop and shut off the engine. Sitting behind the steering wheel I took in the farmhouse, the fields, the barn, the garden, all of it covered in snow, waiting for spring, waiting for me. But now, although it still held my heart, my home seemed empty. Without Lucas, each moment went by with something missing, a conversation unspoken. A touch not felt. I had truly lost a part of me.

After so long together in every moment, with the intimacy we had shared, and the connection built, everything seemed *less* now. I caught myself turning to ask him questions this last week. Forgetting he was not there. He had *always* been there, right beside me, available to hear any little thought, laugh at all my stupid jokes. Now I held back on experiencing the world for he wasn't there to marvel in it with me. No one would understand the thrill of coffee the way he would. The appreciation of ice, or convenience of a drive through.

Now I stared at my front door and wished he was beside me to turn the key. Let me take him on a tour, show him my history, share *this* Sophia with him, away from the island. Begin planning, sharing our dreams for the future.

I heard the horses whinny and turned to look toward the corral. A truck was pulled up alongside the barn and I realized Frank must already be feeding the livestock. *Well best to get back to it I suppose.* I opened the truck door and stepped out into the cold February air.

I was bundled up in one of my mother's snow parkas, topped off with a pair of her gloves, worn from years of use. My light jacket had made it back with me, but was not sufficient enough to combat the winter air. I breathed in the scent of home and began my walk to the barn.

Gypsy trotted up to the corral fence and gave a nicker, most likely recognizing my truck and the scent of me on the cold air. I didn't have a treat, but made a note to get some from the barn and reward her for putting up with my mom and Frank in my absence. I reached the fence and leaned over the rail to give her nose a pat.

"Did you miss me girl? I sure missed you." I scratched under her chin and inhaled her horse smell. It reminded me of Lucas. The Cowboy. I wondered how his Gelding Boomer was doing. Who was feeding him, did he miss his master? I shook my head. Determined to wrap up the chores and begin my search in earnest. I turned toward the barn in search of Frank and saw him striding toward me.

Shoving my gloved hands into my pockets I approached slowly, hoping he wouldn't assume a hug was in order. Frank had been doggedly pursuing me for a date for a year now and I couldn't think of a nice way to turn him down that wouldn't hurt his feelings. I just wasn't in the mood to deal with that right now, so I kicked at the snow and averted my gaze as he drew closer.

"Thanks for plowing the drive while I was gone." I turned toward the house, giving him a side view in hopes of further deterring a welcome home hug.

"I didn't plow it."

Franks voice sounded different, familiar, but deeper, *perhaps he has a cold.* But if he didn't plow it, who did? I turned to look under the brim of his cowboy hat, his face in shadow in the early morning light.

"Then who..." He raised his head and the sun over the hill caught his face, lighting him up, making him glow, like an angel, a Cowboy angel. Not Frank. *Lucas.*

Chapter 34

My mouth still hung open with the question.

He stood only a foot or two in front of me, but my mind couldn't compute it. Like the moment with the orange on the island, reality was taking it's time catching up to me. *How can he be here? How did he find me when I couldn't find him?* And then, *He's alive. He's alive and here*!

And I launched myself at him. Two feet disappeared in the blink of an eye and I was in his arms, holding him to me, fiercely squeezing him into my chest, making sure he was solid, he was real. And then he lost his footing, and we were in the snow. I was on top of him, still wrapped around him, and his mouth caught mine and the world was gone.

No snow, no horses. We were on the island, in the sand, under the warm sun. His mouth tasted like honey, and coffee, and his familiar scent, that hint of leather, of home, it was all around me. I was crying, and laughing, and kissing, and the island melted away slowly, leaving me laying on top of a tan, skinny, Lucas in a snowbank.

"*You found me.*" I whispered in amazement.

"Your attorney assured me you wouldn't mind seeing me."

"How are you?" I looked at his face, it was gaunt, and tan, but I could see the strength in his eyes, determination.

"I'm better. Almost perfect. And you... how are you? How is the... baby?" This last he said almost as if it was a secret.

"I'm perfect, now. And our baby is fine. I saw it on a scan at the hospital in Malé."

"So you're both OK?" He sounded scared, or as if he needed badly to hear it again.

"Yes, Lucas we are both OK."

Lucas reached up and cupped my face in his hands. The hands that have touched every part of me, the hands that rescued me, healed me, fed me. Loved me.

"I missed you. Pumpkin."

Chapter 35

Sixteen months later

June is the perfect month for weddings. Cliché, yes. But clichés get a bad rap. Just because everyone is doing it, doesn't mean I should be different.

June is perfect, and so I chose the thirteenth for my wedding.

More than two hundred guests are packed onto the green, mown, field behind my home. Lucas and I come from big families. Loving families, and every invite had been returned with an RSVP. Of course I believe a little bit of that response is due to our minor celebrity status. Everyone still questions us incessantly about our deserted island adventure.

But today I am not thinking of the island. Today I am not thinking of the flowers, or the caterers, or is Lucas' mother OK with the baby.

I have found my Zen and stand now at the end of the aisle.

Music is playing, but I don't hear it. All the guests turn to see the bride as I move forward, but their faces are a blur.

I only see him. Standing there, waiting. Tall, and handsome, and mine.

I almost lost him. The island came close to claiming my one true love. It had been Malaria. A simple mosquito bite. Had it been me, I would have died. I was already too thin, too weak and malnourished. Lucas had the stamina, and the body mass, and the strength. It took months for him to finally get back to normal. He had left the hospital in Sri Lanka, transferring to

Seattle. After two days there, he had checked himself out, against the doctors advise, and come here. To me.

We healed together that winter. We hired help to take care of our farm and ranch, and we curled up and let the winter thaw. Our love flourish.

Now I walk toward him, forcing myself to not run. And all I can see is him.

I learned many things during our adventure. How to spear a fish, how to cut bamboo, how to laugh even when there is sand in your shorts and you haven't eaten for two days.

But the most valuable lesson I took from my time on the island, is that paradise is overrated. Chaining up, and getting through the frigid months, compares to sand flies and sunburns.

When you are happy in your heart, everywhere is paradise.

∞ The End ∞